Thomas Berger

MEETING EVIL

A NOVEL

RIVERHEAD BOOKS, NEW YORK

RIVERHEAD BOOKS
Published by the Penguin Group
Penguin Group (USA) Inc.
375 Hudson Street, New York, New York 10014, USA

Penguin Group (Canada), 90 Eglinton Avenue East, Suite 700, Toronto, Ontario M4P 2Y3, Canada (a division of Pearson Penguin Canada Inc.) • Penguin Books Ltd., 80 Strand, London WC2R 0RL, England • Penguin Group Ireland, 25 St. Stephen's Green, Dublin 2, Ireland (a division of Penguin Books Ltd.) • Penguin Group (Australia), 250 Camberwell Road, Camberwell, Victoria 3124, Australia (a division of Pearson Australia Group Pty. Ltd.) • Penguin Books India Pvt. Ltd., 11 Community Centre, Panchsheel Park, New Delhi—110 017, India • Penguin Group (NZ), 67 Apollo Drive, Rosedale, Auckland 0632, New Zealand (a division of Pearson New Zealand Ltd.) • Penguin Books (South Africa) (Pty.) Ltd., 24 Sturdee Avenue, Rosebank, Johannesburg 2196, South Africa

Penguin Books Ltd., Registered Offices: 80 Strand, London WC2R 0RL, England

This is a work of fiction. Names, characters, places, and incidents either are the product of the author's imagination or are used fictitiously, and any resemblance to actual persons, living or dead, business establishments, events, or locales is entirely coincidental. The publisher does not have any control over and does not assume any responsibility for author or third-party websites or their content.

Simon & Schuster trade paperback edition: 2003
First Riverhead trade paperback movie tie-in edition: June 2012
Riverhead trade paperback ISBN: 978-1-59448-644-9

PRINTED IN THE UNITED STATES OF AMERICA

10 9 8 7 6 5 4 3 2 1

To William G. Richards

Berger's Ambivalent Usurpations
by Jonathan Lethem

IS there any stronger evidence of the anhedonia of our reading culture than that Thomas Berger's novels don't flood airport bookstalls? There is simply no better way to destroy an hour or three. Before anything else let me say that here, reader, you are in for a treat. I envy you your first encounter, if that is what it is, with *Meeting Evil,* or with Berger's oeuvre per se (and, yes, this is a fine place to start). This book is one of Berger's most relentless and ingenious fictional "contraptions," as a praiseful reviewer once dubbed it, and now that it is in your hands—turn to chapter one and be shanghaied—it truly needs, as they say, no further introduction.

I'll give it one anyway. I'm grateful for the chance to shout that Thomas Berger is one of America's three or four greatest living novelists. I emphasize *novelist,* for Berger's greatness resides in the depth and extensiveness of his commitment to and exploration of his chosen form. I can think of no other American writer more invested in and trusting of the means and materials of *fiction qua fiction:* scenes and sentences, chapters and paragraphs, and, above all, characters—their voices and introspections, their predicaments in fictional worlds. He's cultivated this investment to the exclusion of all forms of topicality or sociology, autobiographical appeals to readerly interest, superficial "innovations," or controversialism. Berger's too interested in the mysteries of narrative to bother with metafiction, yet his world does possess a certain rubbery pleasure in its own artifice. He doesn't bother to disguise fiction's proscenium arch—his "realism," such as it is, resides in his assiduous scrutiny of daily existence, at levels both psychological and ontological. Berger adores novels too much to play at their destruction or to be embarrassed at his participation in a tradition.

Berger's commitment has another aspect: apart from a scattering of short plays and stories, he's devoted himself entirely to the novel and eschewed side work like journalism, screenwriting, or teaching. Nor has he spent his capital pontificating, issuing manifestos, attending conferences, or granting more than a small handful of interviews. What this may have cost him in terms of journalistic ink, who knows? I won't speak glibly of "neglect," though he certainly sells fewer books than do those writers I regard as his only peers, and, though not obscure, is less widely known. A few years ago I made the mistake, in writing an entry on Berger for a literary encyclopedia, of claiming that he'd fallen from a "critical and popular heyday" in the 1960s. Berger wrote me to gently correct my error, explaining that he'd never had a "heyday," dragging out the sales figures to prove it. No, Berger's hovered for fifty years in a middle distance, proof neither of the proposition that genius is always rewarded nor that it is universally overlooked. The paradoxical fate of a writer impossible to revive because he's never been sufficiently neglected is somehow quite suitably Bergerian.

That said, it's impossible for others not to rage on Berger's behalf for a larger share of attention and rewards. Take the words of the Pakistani-Texan novelist Zulfikar Ghose: "Novels whose subject matter is their greatest appeal are invariably vastly popular. . . . Novels which stand on their style alone win readers slowly, in little bands here and there, until the work becomes one of the layers which compose human consciousness. [This] explains why, among American novelists, Saul Bellow, who knows what to write about, is preferred to Thomas Berger, who knows how to write. . . . Berger is a novelist and nothing else. . . . Twenty or thirty years from now Bellow will be one of those obscure funny names one sees who were mistakenly awarded the Nobel Prize, like Pearl Buck, and Berger will be read seriously, like Henry James."

In material terms, Berger's been unflinching in his dedication: twenty-two novels since his 1958 debut, *Crazy in Berlin*. His shelf of work, while unified both by his unmistakable gentle irony and his uncanny ear for musical collisions of high and low diction, effloresces in wild diversity: a quasi-Updikean quartet of novels following the life stages of a lumpen, angelic alter ego named Reinhart; a pair of shambolic historical-legendary epics, *Little Big Man* and *Arthur Rex* (the former, his best-known novel, now followed by a sequel); and a handful of loving demolitions of genre—the private-eye novel in *Who Is Teddy Villanova?*, utopian and dystopian fiction in *Nowhere* and *Regiment of Women*, and fables of wish fulfillment in *Being Invisible* and *Changing the Past*.

The virtuosic novelty of those enterprises may sometimes distract readers and commentators from the core concerns of the majority of Berger's novels. The remainder of his books are harder to pigeonhole or typify—though all of them develop motifs of power, victimization, and guilt in human affairs, and all exhibit the curious capacity of his fictional situations to shift like a weathervane between farcical misunderstanding and ominous, sadomasochistic abuse. Many, including *Meeting Evil*, impinge on the material of the crime novel, or policier, though they never reproduce the tone typical of those genres. (Meanwhile, the audience that savors crime in fiction has overlooked Berger, much as the tropical explorers, in the famous

Mad magazine cover illustration, are unaware, as they scrutinize the trees, that they are huddled in the concavity of an enormous footprint.)

These less categorizeable novels, with their nominally realist settings, and full of human blundering ranging from adultery and murder to badly cooked meals, comprise the strongest argument for Berger's lasting importance, especially cumulatively. The sequence I have in mind begins with the monumental *Killing Time,* Berger's fourth novel, which I've described elsewhere as "Jim Thomson rewritten by an American Flaubert." That book, an inquiry into a beatific, existentially profound sociopath who regards himself as the enemy of time, contains as well the first of a series of portraits of faintly malicious, hugely pragmatic cops. Berger's fascination with policemen—the guilt they inspire in introspective souls, the morbidity they indulge as a by-product of their mission, the mental ambiguity filters they necessarily adopt—is matched only by Alfred Hitchcock's.

Next come *Sneaky People, Neighbors,* and *The Feud. Sneaky People* and *The Feud* are a pair of large-ensemble Midwestern urban novels, full of fond reproductions of American vernacular speech in its vanished splendor, full of unsentimental cross sections of turf mostly abdicated by American novelists after Booth Tarkington. *Neighbors* (Berger's favorite among his own books, partly for what he describes as the effortlessness of its composition) inaugurates a masterful triumvirate of novels of menace—its companions are *The Houseguest* and the book you now hold in your hands. Each of these three books is theatrical, tightly unified in time (and in the case of the two novels before *Meeting Evil,* in place as well). Each make a study of what I'd call *ambivalent usurpation*—uncanny scenarios wherein a terrifying struggle for power emerges from within a banal milieu. Each features a principal provocateur and a principal victim—but Berger is fascinated by the ways in which innocence and reserve are complicit with chaos and impulsivity. He makes a study of the malignancy of charisma but of the torpor of reflection as well. In the words of Reinhart: "People use us as we ask them to: this is life's fundamental, and often the only, justice." This theme of ambivalent usurpation—exchanges of unspecified guilt and obligation between pairs of human "doubles"—resonates with motifs in works by artists as apparently disparate as Dostoyevsky, Harold Pinter, Patricia Highsmith, Orson Welles and, yes, again, Hitchcock. It is typical of Berger that once his theme of doubleness has been established, rather than emphasize similarity between characters to a fatuous degree, he instead exercises his fascination with the fact that differing types *do* exist: however we might become ensnared by another, the lonely fact of self persists.

Beyond any other literary influence or comradeship, the paradoxical logic by which Berger unfolds his scenes connects him above all to Franz Kafka. Too many contemporary writers kowtow to Kafka in blackface: ostentatiously dreamlike settings, *Shadows and Fog*-ian Eastern European atmosphere or diction. Berger engages with Kafka's influence at a more native and universal level, by grasping the way Kafka reconstructed fictional time and causality to align it with his emotional and philosophical reservations about human life. Berger's tone, like Kafka's, never oversells paranoia or despair. Instead, Berger explores the fallibility of the human effort to feel justified or consoled in the gaze of any other being, with meticulous, even affectionate, gestures of reserve and regret. As in the elder writer, there is nothing so absurd or heartbreaking as the disparity between intention and act, or speech. The result of Berger's patient domestication of Kafka's method is, actually, never dreamlike. Instead, Berger locates that part of our *waking* life which unfolds in the manner of Zeno's paradox, where it is possible only to fall agonizingly short in any effort to be understood, or to do good. In doing so, he illuminates what it was that necessitated Kafka's exaggerations. And by splitting the difference halfway back to daylight—and setting his daylit persecutions amid strip malls and suburban developments—he unnerves us even more deeply.

Patricia Highsmith is the only other American writer I can think of who has attained this profound incorporation of Kafka, particularly in her *A Dog's Ransom* and *The Cry of the Owl*. The irony is that the justly acclaimed Highsmith does little else that is more than competent, while Berger offers this and so many other pleasures: paradox, wit, slyness, and the diction and vocabulary of a Henry James meets H. L. Mencken. Berger's as brilliant a student of American talk as Nabokov or DeLillo, and his favorite sentences, especially in dialogue, pivot on fragments of tabloid squawk elevated to odd majesty by their surrounding syntax. Indeed, to believe Berger's own (suspect) testimony, language is his *only* subject. Among his countless eloquent demurrals of discussion of the moral, philosophical, or psychological implications of his work, my favorite is one given to Brooks Landon, Berger's most important critic and explicator: "I have never believed that I work in the service of secular rationalism (the man of good will, the sensible fellow, the social meliorist who believes the novel holds up a mirror to society, etc.). I am essentially a voyeur of copulating words."

Those demurrals reflect Berger's distrust of the shifting ground of language, and his horror of abstractions and false certainties, which preclude nearly any human gesture less immediate than the cooking by one person of a delicious meal for another. All else is laden with presumption at best, grim manipulation at worst: every person is surely full of purposes, and Berger suspects his own as direly as anyone else's ("Remember that you will understand my work best when you are at your most selfish," he has also told Landon). The letters that I am so fortunate as to receive from Berger are full of enthusiasms: for character actors like Elisha Cook Jr. and Laird Cregar; for Superman comics; for Anthony Powell's *A Dance to the Music of Time*; for the novels of Barbara Pym, Marcel Proust, and Frank Norris; and as well for some but not all of the writers and filmmakers to whom I've presumed to compare him. Perhaps the feast of culture is another port in the storm of existence, though Berger's main characters are never artists or writers, and those few creative types that do appear are usually buffoons or ogres if not both.

Brooks Landon has explored Berger's sustaining relationship to Nietzsche, whose delineation of "slave" and "master" personalities certainly presages Berger's interdependent victims and victimizers. Another astute Berger critic, John Carlos Rowe, has discerned an engagement with existentialism of the type which was fashionable in postwar culture, when Berger began writing (and which can be seen to lay the ground for those rebellions of the 1960s, literary and otherwise, that Berger conspicuously resisted). I'm not qualified in philosophical commentary, but it seems unmistakable that the murderers in *Killing Time* and *Meeting Evil,* so unalike in other ways, nevertheless both reflect a fascination with existentialist rationales for motiveless murder, à la *Crime and Punishment* and Camus' *The Stranger* and Hitchcock's *Rope*. What's clear, too, is that in his novels of menace Berger is compelled by and attracted to his provocateur villains for their dynamism, and for their talent for testing the certainties of everyday life, the rote morals of policemen, etc. And yet, unlike the typical novelists of Berger's own generation, the Keseys and Kerouacs, and even the Updikes and Roths, the dissident against social complacency is *never* Berger's hero. In the case of *Meeting Evil,* Berger has confessed to me that while he had to consult a copy to even recall John Felton's name, Richie is one of his favorite among his own characters—yet elsewhere Berger has enthusiastically endorsed the verdict of the title: Richie is evil, and must be destroyed. What Berger resists in social rebellion is its resemblance to what it attacks: its self-validating smugness, its readiness to manipulate in its own cause, its cobbled-together moral jargon, its bottom-line disinterest in the mystery of daily existence, its poor listening skills.

Berger isn't an experimental writer in any of the usual senses of the word. But in his ferocious devotion to paradox and irony as investigatory tools, his fiction consists of an endless, irresolvable experiment into what can be translated out of the morass of lived human days into useful and entertaining stories—though Berger would likely argue that no story can be useful, and then jibe that no one was intended to be entertained beyond himself. Berger's uncertainty is his being, and his implement. The uniquely vertiginous nature of a page of his fiction is testament to the daily experiment of his art.

In the Bergerian world, masks are often peeled away to reveal further masks, yet just as often what was mistaken for a mask turns out to be a face. No irony is conclusive enough not to give way to a deeper irony, and the deepest of all is the realization that first impressions are sometimes adequate, or that it is the rare quandary that is actually improved by sustained pondering. Fate is for the embracing. As a Berger policeman once wisely remarked, "Death can happen to anyone." No one, however grotesque or ill-mannered, is so remote from the human predicament that he is ineligible for the occasional epiphanic insight, yet no one, however saintly or patient, is likely to be able to make use of the insights at hand in the flurry of a practical transaction involving another person. Just when Bergerian loneliness seems ubiquitous, contact is unexpectedly made, and though Berger's sex scenes are often barren and harsh his tender evocations of romantic hope and yearning may be the least appreciated aspect of his books. No grace can ever be earned, in Berger's world, but it does fall like precious rain here and there.

Meeting Evil is on the unmerciful side of his shelf, but odd, sunny moments break through even so—it wouldn't be Berger otherwise. It is also relatively spare, in the manner of all his later books apart from the *Little Big Man* sequel. The structure, hard to discern on the first roller-coaster plunge through, is elegant and ironclad: In the first section John Felton is persecuted and harassed by the police, by bystanders, and by his wife; in the third section, he is abandoned by all of them. Richie's incursion is the only consistent note in his reality, and it is one of purest mayhem; the only person responsive to John is a madman. Between, in the book's second section, Berger delves into Richie's self-justifying viewpoint, in pages as lean and shocking as an X ray of the brain of a shark. In those, we learn that the madman listens to John for the simplest reason: he likes him.

Berger is now seventy-eight years old. It's a rare privilege to witness a great novelist's arc beyond such an age, but Berger is still unflagging, and it may not be too much to wish for several more novels. The most recent books are gentler, more forgiving, and often serve as overt or covert consolidations of earlier sequences in his work. In this manner, *Orrie's Story* returned to the midwestern panoramas of *Sneaky People* and *The Feud,* while the almost completely overlooked *Suspects* (has it even had a paperback edition?) revisits the sincere and troubled (though, in inquisitory method, malicious) policemen of *Killing Time* while excusing them the duty of confronting an existential superman. And, just as the fourth Reinhart novel, *Reinhart's Women,* sheltered that beset character from the historical strife of the first three books, his newest, *Best Friends,* may be seen partly as a gentle capstone to the three novels of menace that include *Meeting Evil.* In it, the twinned characters, usurper and usurpee (can you tell them apart?), meet not as strangers but as lifelong friends who uncover the strangeness hidden inside familiarity. But it is also a pining love story, another Kafkaesque parable of shifting perspective, and much more: Berger has insisted, in his letters to me, that *Best Friends* felt to him, in the writing, like nothing he'd ever done before. As a fellow novelist this nearly brings tears to my eyes. I can only pray that at such an age I'll be not only working at all but working in Berger's manner, without presumptions, without a safety net constructed of all the good reviews he's gathered over a lifetime. Each time Berger writes he ventures out with only his style for courage.

As a favor to my friend I have avoided the word which has dogged his years on this planet: I have not called him *comic*. But I would fail here if I didn't report that his books have made me laugh harder, over *my* years on the planet, than any others on my shelves. I predict that you will laugh too, and that you will find, as I have, that this laughter sustains itself even after the contemplation, inevitable after absorbing more than one or two of Berger's books, of the vast distress at the universal human plight (though it is an even-keeled, contemplative distress, as in the way of the Buddha) which necessitated their writing. Berger isn't comic. He, like life, is merely, and hugely, fucking funny.

Meeting Evil

I

PERHAPS John Felton had got married too young, but he really did love Joanie and, besides, she was pregnant and came from a family which, though believing abortion was wrong, would have been disgraced by an illegitimate birth, with several of its members active in local church affairs and one in the politics of the county. So he became a father the first time almost simultaneously with becoming a husband.

Then before Melanie was quite three years of age she was joined by a newborn brother they prudently named for her mother's uncle Philip, a small businessman who had retired on the tidy sum paid for his prime-location premises (where he had sold floor coverings) by the firm that intended to demolish them along with neighboring structures and build a medium-sized mall on the property. But Uncle Phil was conspicuously healthy and still not nearly old enough to be considered a prompt source of financial relief for his presumed heirs. They were paying too much for a house though John was himself a real-estate salesman—at the moment in a buyer's market.

John worked weekends, showing houses to potential buyers when there were such, and took Mondays off, which permitted Joanie to catch up on her sleep in the morning, and in the afternoon shop or visit the hairdresser. Even so—and whenever he was home he shared in the chores, including wee-hour calls from baby Phil—having to care for two small children was leaving its mark on his young wife, who, he had to admit to himself, already looked as if she had been married twice as long as was actually the case.

It was on such a late Monday morning when, with the two-tone sound of the front-door chimes, the worst day of John's life began, though he had already been up for hours, feeding the children and running the first of two loads of laundry through the washer/dryer and folding the garments while they were still warm. Joanie, in rumpled pajamas, was breakfasting on sugar-coated cereal at the kitchen table. She wore no makeup, in which state her eyes looked very small, and her hair was tousled. There had been a time, not long before, when in a similar condition she would still have looked like a schoolgirl.

"Why don't you try one of those blueberry muffins?" John asked her now.

"Aren't they stale?"

"I just bought them yesterday, at Liebman's."

"I don't know," Joan said, pushing away at least half a bowlful of sodden cereal. "I'm just not that hungry." She drank some black coffee from her favorite mug of brown ceramic, with the yellow chipped place at the rim to avoid which she held the vessel in her left hand. "I always thought you were supposed to acquire a tremendous appetite when you quit smoking. It's just the opposite with me. I always looked forward to eating when I knew I had a cigarette coming."

John had never smoked his life long, the odor of burning

4

tobacco having always been nauseating to him. It was not because of him, however, that Joanie had lately given up the habit: she had at last been scared off by a series of antismoking exhortations on television. She really did take seriously her responsibilities as a mother.

"Spaghetti okay for dinner?" He made it every Monday evening. It was one of his specialties. He boiled it up and added the canned white clam sauce.

"Why not?" rhetorically asked his wife, supporting her head with her right hand, between sips of coffee from the mug in her left.

Melanie wandered in and said something her father did not hear distinctly, for it was at this point that the door chimes sounded.

"Be right back," he told his daughter, touching her button nose ever so lightly with his index finger, but she was not mollified by the gesture and began to complain.

John had inherited his mother's anxiety with respect to electric summonses: the sound of bell or buzzer was perforce an emergency to which one must give precedence over hemorrhages, flash fires, and all human importunities. Being way back in the kitchen, he now headed for the front entrance at the run, lest the unseen applicant have to undergo the horror of ringing again.

Owing to the same anxiety, he never took time to peer through the little gauze curtain that covered the rectangle of glass set high in the door for that purpose, but, as now, hurled open the portal without regard for the cautions about strangers that one heard so frequently these days. His father-in-law, for example, made all comers state their business to the tiny microphone installed above the bell-push, while they stood for inspection through a closed-circuit TV camera mounted near the ceiling of the porch.

The present caller was a man of about John's own age, a tall fellow somewhere between thin and sinewy. On the back of his head was the kind of billed cap worn nowadays by more people than just ballplayers. John himself had two: one purchased for the golf course, the other a promotional gift on the opening of the local branch of a hardware chain.

"My car stalled out, right in front of your house." A clump of dingy fair curls filled the space between the forehead and the bill of the cap.

"You want me to call the auto club?"

The man's smile displayed only his upper teeth, so that it took an instant to identify it as a smile. "You could just give me a push." He gestured with his shoulder. "Just to where it starts down."

The descent so signified began in front of the third house from John's. Once over the crest of the hill, you could probably coast without power for more than a quarter mile.

John accompanied the stranger to the curb, where he asked him, "You think that will do it?"

The man seemed not to understand the question. "Hey," he said, "in this baby I can smoke anything on the road."

John had never been fascinated with cars, but he recognized this one as being powerful, with its air scoop on the hood and its long red snout. "Yeah," he said. "It's hot-looking. Where do you want me to go, side or back?"

The man opened the door and got into the driver's seat. "Right here by the window." He slammed the door, and John braced himself against the frame and pushed.

The car rolled more easily than he had anticipated. He had the natural strength associated with a stocky build. But he had done little in the way of recreational exercise (playing golf maybe three times a season) since leaving high school, and he noticed nowadays that physical effort caused him to breathe harder than he had once had to.

Just as John was feeling a certain satisfaction with his current effort, the man behind the wheel complained. "Can't you give it a little more steam? We're hardly moving."

John was chastened. Could that be true? Maybe he should look at the ground. He lowered his head, staring at the asphalt under them, and put all his strength against the doorjamb. The vehicle certainly moved: there could be no doubt of that. But the driver was apparently one of those people who go public only with negative observations.

Now he shouted, "Hey! Will you stop!"

John looked up. It was quite true that they had gained the crest and there was no further need for exterior force. But the implication of emergency was unwarranted. This was the man who had lately chided him for doing too little.

"Just step on the brake."

The man snarled, "I don't have any brakes, jerk."

There was no call for nastiness, and though usually an amiable sort, John would have stepped back and replied in kind—had he not now discovered that the tail of his old work shirt, which, casually, as befitted his day off, he was wearing outside his old paint-stained chinos, had been caught in the door of the car when the other man slammed it shut at the outset.

Luckily the car was moving slowly as yet. Trotting, John seized the door handle. It was locked. He reached inside to pull up the button, but there was only an empty hole. He shouted through the open window, right into the driver's ear, but the man was preoccupied. John reached farther inside and tried to find and work the mechanism by touch, but he was unfamiliar with it, and now the car had begun to roll faster. He had to pick up the pace. Near panic, tethered to the mass of steel as it gathered momentum for the long downward slope, he gave up on the lock and struck the driver on the shoulder cap, and then, when the man made no response whatever—John was running now—he put both hands around the driver's skinny neck and would have throttled him had the car not quickly come to a shuddering stop.

Relieved of fear but even angrier than before, John took the hand from the man's throat but kept in place the one at the nape.

"Open the goddamn door!"

The driver obeyed the order, twisting away from the grasp.

John should simply have turned and walked away at this point, but he stayed, incredulous. "This was a joke? You had brakes all the while? What's wrong with you?"

The driver frowned. "I *don't* have any brakes. I stopped by putting it in gear."

"You didn't know my shirt was caught in the door?"

"I was busy! Wasn't that *your* business?"

Now that he had calmed down somewhat, John could see a certain justice in the other's argument, but he had invested too much of himself to admit it.

"Look," the other man said, "I can coast down from here. But where's the nearest gas station?"

"Turn at Randolph," John said. "That'll be at the bottom of the hill. Take a right on Walton, to Church. There's a station on the northeast corner. But how are you going to stop if you have to? Keep putting it in gear? That can't be good for your car. For that matter, it's level ground down there. Once you're stopped, you won't be able to get going again."

"Well, it's my problem, isn't it," the man said genially. "Thanks for this. Sorry about your shirt."

John reflected that only a moment earlier he had been trying to choke this fellow. The memory was embarrassing to him, though his victim seemed not to bear a grudge. On a guilty impulse, he said, "I better come along, just in case."

"If you want." The man worked the gear selector, and the car began to move. "Hop in. I can't stop again."

This seemed rude, in view of the charitable offer. By the time John got around to the other side, the vehicle was rolling at such speed that it was all he could do to reach the passenger door, open it, and hurl himself within, painfully bruising his knee on some projection.

Despite the speed, however, the driver was in no hurry to engage the gears. Which failure, by the time they were half-way down the slope, was inexplicable to John.

"Why don't you kick it in?"

The young man in the cap was steering now with one hand on a loose wrist—the left one, at that. He did not seem at all concerned about the state of the car. At last he lazily turned his head.

"You want some juice, is that it?" Still looking at John, he worked the shifter with his free fist. The car came to life with a thunderous noise. They had already reached a fast roll; with the new thrust the car plunged downhill like a rocket. Inertia held John against the back of the seat, though there was not much he could have done anyway but what he did: shout in indignation.

He fell silent when he saw, not half a block beyond them, the rear end of a commercial van, backing into the street from a private driveway. He was not wearing a seat belt, and his fantasies of instinctively knowing the right thing to do in an emergency proved useless. He was sure only that the imminent collision would be lethal for himself, and that certainty was paralyzing.

In fact, no crash occurred. Still steering only with a casual left hand and disdaining the use of the horn, the driver effortlessly swung wide, so wide his wheels must have been in the far gutter, and continued to blast downhill at an ever greater velocity.

John recovered his anger. "Are you crazy? If there had been any oncoming traffic—"

"But there wasn't any," the man crowed, slapping the wheel and hee-hawing.

John intended to get out when they gained level ground, where the car could be brought to a stop by using the gears. If the fool ignored the order, the use of physical force would again be justified.

But on reaching the bottom of the hill, the other man performed a conservative turn, at a speed that had somehow subtly been brought to a moderate rate, and drove the block to the gas station before there was a reasonable opportunity to demand that the vehicle be stopped en route.

On stepping from the car, faced with a substantial walk back home, most of which was uphill, John discovered that his knee still ached from the blow it had sustained in his leap into the rolling vehicle.

"Wait a minute," said the driver, hopping out. "I'll give you a lift soon as I get the tank filled."

John turned his back on the man. He had limped to the edge of the concrete apron before he was struck by the implication of what the guy had said. He stopped and turned around.

The driver, who had been watching his departure, smiled and said, "Can't you take a joke?"

"You mean the brakes?" John asked angrily. "Your brakes are okay. You just used them now to stop, didn't you?" The car, furthermore, was at the pumps, not positioned for entrance to the garage, where it would have had to go for work on the supposedly ailing engine and the allegedly missing brakes. "And nothing's wrong with the motor."

"You're wrong there," said the man, tugging at the bill of his cap. "It really needs a tune-up, and the brakes tend to fade." The attendant had arrived. She was a gaunt young woman, hair tucked up in her cap, no makeup. "Premium. Fill it." He walked toward John, a bony hand extended. "Come on, I haven't killed anybody, have I?"

John had always found it difficult to maintain a negative attitude toward any human being in the flesh. It was a kind of fear. He was anything but a coward in the routine sense of the word. He had once plunged into a flood-swollen stream to rescue a child, though never having been an outstanding swimmer. But he had no reason to think kindly of this idiot, and he ignored the outstretched hand. "Tell me this: why did you ring my doorbell?"

The man lowered his arm at last and said reproachfully, "I was just about out of gas. The needle was on Empty."

"Why couldn't you just say so?"

"I was afraid you'd think I'd want to siphon some out of *your* car." The man put his thin jaw forward, but in a display of earnestness, not aggression. "Nobody trusts anybody nowadays."

True enough, and in another situation John might very well have been the first to agree, but in the present case the sentiment was being voiced by the wrong man. "You're still lying!" he said, with a sense of outrage. "You had enough gas to speed downhill."

The other shook his head. "If you decide to think the worst of somebody, then there's absolutely nothing that will change your mind. But there's always some gas left in an empty tank, and going downhill at an angle, it sloshes forward and can be burned. But don't believe me—just ask that guy." He pointed over his shoulder at the attendant. "Look, I didn't handle the whole thing right, I guess. I might not know how to deal with people, but I'm not a bad person. I'm willing to apologize." He raised his hand again. "How about it?"

This was the sort of appeal that John could not have rejected without being an altogether different kind of person from what he was. "All right," he said, and even added the lie (for his knee was sore), "No harm done, I guess." He did not like the feel of the other's fingers, which, though appearing bony, were somewhat soft and yielding to the touch, as if the bones were gelatinous. "She's female."

"Huh?"

"The attendant."

The man looked back. Then he smirked and said, loudly enough for the woman to hear, "She's a dog."

A needlessly nasty thing to say, but at least the attendant did not show that she had heard it, and it was quickly followed by what seemed a sincere concern for John's welfare. "Let me run you back up the hill after I take care of this." He went toward the attendant, who was hanging up the hose. After exchanging a word or two, they both walked to the station office and went inside.

John had a moment in which to debate with himself as to whether he should accept the lift. He still did not like this stranger and did not really trust him. There were people, Joanie's brother among them, whose routine technique was to act badly and then beg for forgiveness. After a series of such episodes, the victim grew wiser, unless of course his judgment was corrupted by blood ties.

Later on, looking back, John would identify this moment as being one of the many early opportunities he had to avert

12

the catastrophe toward which he was unwittingly headed, but he failed to take it and instead waited for the man to return. He did not yet enter the car. He stood with his back to the office. He did not buy his gas here, a full-service station facility, but saved money by pumping his own at a station a mile east. Nor were there properties in this neighborhood of small shops with apartments over them (so near and yet so far from his own) of the kind likely to be listed with his agency, which specialized in the nicer kind of homes, on up to those priced at a million and beyond, which naturally were handled by one or another of the two fortyish partners who owned the agency, Miriam and Tess, and not by himself, whose specialty was considered to be, appropriately enough, houses within the reach of young couples, or rather what they could be convinced were within their reach, for a reasonably priced property was a thing of the past even during the periods called slumps. How often had John been told by prospects that they grew up in the finest house on the block, four lavatories, in-ground pool, gym-sized garage, for all of which their parents had paid fifty, and now there was nothing cheaper than *this*, two bedrooms, one and a half baths, roof that needed reshingling, for two twenty-five?

The man in the cap appeared at the hood of the red car. He wore a pair of expensive-looking running shoes, so large and dazzlingly white, with lightning stripes of royal blue, that John did not understand why he had not previously taken note of them.

The other angrily asked whether John remembered his telling "that ugly bitch" to check the oil.

"I didn't hear you say that. Anyway, why are you so mad at her? She's just somebody who pumps gas."

"She didn't want to take my credit card!" He jerked his head in annoyance and gestured. "Come on, let's get out of here before I really lose my temper." He went around to the driver's side and got into the car. When John reluctantly took his own place (his knee was throbbing; he needed the ride), the young man said, without trying again to shake hands, "My name's Richie." He started the engine.

"John Felton."

"Okay, Johnnie, here goes nothing." Richie slowly pulled out of the station.

"No," John said, "not Johnnie or John Boy or Jack."

Richie grinned. "You want things your own way, don't you? I respect that. I know I let people push me around too much, and then I get mad. I wish I could be more like you, lay it on the line right away, it's a free country. Instead I do a lot of weaseling, I admit. I got to get over that. Who am I trying to impress?"

John found these remarks so meaningless that in an effort to disregard them he also briefly ignored the fact that Richie had turned in the wrong direction on leaving the gas station. When he came to, however, he spoke sharply.

"Take this next right and then another right at the next block, and get back to Maple. I want to go straight home."

"Isn't that what I said I would do?" Richie asked in exaggerated dismay. "Jesus, what a touchy guy you can be, *John*. I don't care. I like you, *John*. You're my kind of person. What I'd really like to do is buy you a nice breakfast someplace, to pay back the favor you did me."

"I've had breakfast," John said decisively. "And you owe me nothing, because it wasn't much of a favor."

Richie pulled the cap lower on his forehead, concealing the dirty curls in front but revealing more in back. "You're not gonna deny me a cup of coffee, I hope. I haven't eaten anything since I got up." He pointed a long, skinny, gnarled finger at something out John's window, which proved to be

14

a doughnut shop, and steering with the free hand, swooped the car up to the curb just in front of the establishment, though the space was posted with prominent loading-area signs and gaudily striped in no-parking yellow.

John had had enough. As soon as the car stopped, he threw the door open. But when he put his weight onto his feet, he found he could hardly use the leg with the bad knee, which had stiffened since being at rest. What a damnable predicament to find yourself in as the result of giving someone a hand: it was not fair.

Though he had been exclusively self-regarding up to this point, Richie now noticed him, asking, "What's with the limp?"

"Forget about it."

"Come on."

"Bumped my knee. It's nothing, it'll go away."

Richie frowned. "Gonna sue me?"

"For what?"

"You're always taking a chance when you pick somebody up." Richie showed his teeth. "He might just be looking for an excuse to claim injury and hit you with a lawsuit."

"You *didn't* pick me up. But don't worry, I'm not going to sue you, for God's sake. It didn't have anything to do with you." Of course it did, but John spoke so from motives of pride.

The other stared at him for a moment, through pale-blue, watery eyes that gave an impression of moral triviality and perhaps a touch of physical ill health. Though John was aware that judgments of this sort were notoriously unreliable, he could not refrain from making them. When he first met his father-in-law, he assumed from the round, fleshy face that the man was of another sort than he in fact proved to be. For that matter, when John had first seen Joan herself, as a fellow college student, he had found her not his type, with her rather awkward gait and his least favorite hairstyle, but in her case it was the eyes that grew on him, as well as her lively personality, which had become somewhat subdued by motherhood.

Richie terminated the stare with what he obviously considered to be his trademark grin. He did not, however, have the requisite freckles to make it assertively cute, for which John was grateful.

"Ought to have it looked at," Richie said. "I'll run you to the nearest clinic. Just let me pour some coffee down me."

"Sure," John replied, impatient now to escape. "Go on in. I don't want anything." He was prepared to resist some argument, but Richie nodded docilely and went toward the decal-laden glass doors of the doughnut shop.

John had decided to walk from here on, but the pain of the first few steps caused him to look away in distress, and in so doing he by chance noticed, just across the street, the narrow office of a local taxi service. Suddenly the traffic was too heavy to permit him to cross in the middle of the block. It was while he limped uncomfortably to the intersection that he heard the ominous screech of skidding tires and turned his head to see the little white compact car strike Richie's automobile at an angle, carom away, and spin through the intersection, miraculously evading all the other vehicles at hand, including one big truck against the brutal-looking steel grille of which it might well have crushed itself had fate not determined otherwise.

John went first to inspect the damage to Richie's car because he was closer to it than to the other, which anyway had come to rest without further collision and the driver of which seemed okay as she hopped out, with amazing energy for someone in such a situation. She was small but had a great head of orange curls. She was wearing a miniskirt and high heels. Even at that distance he could see her heavy makeup.

On the driver's side of Richie's car was a long smear of damage. The young woman was heading John's way.

When she reached him she asked, with apparently genuine concern, "Anybody hurt?"

"No. How about you?"

"I don't think my car even got damaged much," she said, making her eyes, with their artificial lashes, even larger. She brought her purse up and began to rummage in it. "I'll cover everything." She produced and waved some little documents that could be a driver's license and a registration.

"I think," said John, "what you also need is the insurance card. It's probably in the glove compartment." That was the law. "But I don't own this car."

"Hey," she shouted, scowling, "if it's not your car, what's your stake in it?" She had a strong voice though being small of body and reminded him of one of those talented children who sometimes turn up and belt out a song in public performance, with the volume and delivery of a Broadway veteran.

But he was irked. "I'm a witness."

Obviously she had not thought of that. She did so now and sulked, her plumped lower lip oozing forward. "If you've already decided it was my fault, what can I do?"

"I haven't decided anything at all," said John. "But it's not the kind of thing anybody would do on purpose, I'm sure of that." He smiled. "I'm just a passerby. The guy who owns this car is in there." He indicated the doughnut shop.

"Oh-oh," said the young woman, staring across at her car, "the cops are here." She came close to John and seized his arm. "Do me this favor, say you were with me." He recoiled, but she hung desperately on. "You don't have to say you were driving. I'll take the heat for that. But I've got a learner's permit, the kind you have to be accompanied by a regular driver with, you know." She was shaking his arm with both hands. The crowd that had formed because of the accident would soon notice them. She had been identified by someone near her car, and a policeman was strolling their way. *"Please,"* said the woman. "We can have a date if you want."

The fact was that John did find her sexually attractive, in the abstract fashion of women seen from a distance, or in show-biz illustrations, not by personal experience. She was not someone with whom he would ordinarily have, or want, contact. He looked forward to making a joke of it with Joanie: how he had had his chance with this bimbo, with her flaming head and too-bright eyes. But, more seriously, he could not approve of someone's driving without being fully and properly licensed: no joke in this day and age, especially if you were the parent of children who might be run down by such a delinquent citizen. Yet it went against his grain to reject the appeal of anybody, let alone a female. It was just unfair that he found himself in this situation.

But it was *not* his business. By rights, he should not have been here at all. It was that goddamned Richie's fault—and where was he, anyway?

"Look," he said to the red-haired woman, disregarding her sluttish proposal, "I'll find the guy who owns this car. That's the best I can do."

He marched to the doughnut shop and pushed the door in against a cluster of people who had come there to stare at the street scene. Richie was not among them, nor could he be seen amid those gawking out the windows. John was exasperated, but then he wondered why he was bothering about this matter. He returned outside.

The policeman was in conversation with the young

woman. John assumed that if the latter were in serious trouble, she would have no hesitation in offering herself to the cop. He turned his back on them and started in a homeward direction. In the excitement of the accident he had momentarily forgotten his sore knee, but remembered it unpleasantly now. He had taken only two painful steps, however, when he was halted by a command at his back.

"Hey, you!" It was the policeman, ruder than they were supposed to be nowadays.

John limped back at the summons of a crooked finger. "I had nothing to do with this," he said coldly.

"Nobody said you did," the cop replied, making it a slightly threatening rebuke. "Let's have your license, please, sir." This was more polite, to be sure, but John had never heard of such a demand to passersby.

He reached for his wallet before remembering it was at home. He had left the house intending to go no farther than the curb in front of his house.

"I don't have it with me. I wasn't driving a car."

"You were a passenger in a vehicle being driven by a person with a learner's permit only." The officer was if anything younger than John, with the rosy cheeks of a boy, but his stubborn policeman's sense of representing the exclusive truth had been fixed in place with his shield.

"No, he wasn't," Richie said from behind John, appearing from thin air. "This man was not in that car. *I* was."

"You were a passenger in the car?" The young cop's voice was professionally noncommittal.

Richie stepped around John. He was no longer wearing the billed cap, and his hair was wet, the curls combed flat and looking almost black. Just that little alteration changed his appearance considerably, so that John might not have recognized him for a moment had he not heard the voice.

"Passenger?" Richie asked incredulously. "I was *driving*. The young lady was the passenger."

"Not according to this young lady," the cop said stubbornly, his chin stiffening.

Richie had produced a wallet from his back pocket, and now he plucked from it what looked like a driver's license. "Officer, my fiancée is one in a million, but I'm not going to let her take the rap for me." He handed the license over. "Truth is, I dropped a lighted cigarette on the floor. When I reached down to get it, I lost control of the car."

"Lady says," the solemn policeman insisted, "something happened to the steering and she—"

"Sir," said Richie, "excuse me for interrupting, but just ask her again." He turned to the woman. "Honey, you just tell him the truth."

The redhead shrugged and said, "Okay. Yeah, it's like he says."

"He was driving?"

"Right."

The policeman nodded heavily, reluctantly, annoyed at having first been lied to. He took a slight revenge on Richie by asking him to come to the patrol car and wait while a radio check was run on the driver's license. And added, peering at the document, "You oughta complain to the DMV: they took a lousy picture."

When they were out of earshot, the young woman discreetly asked John, "What's he up to?"

"Richie?" John asked disdainfully. "How do I know?"

"He's your friend."

"Not on your life! He was only giving me a ride—it's a long story."

"I realize he's doing me a favor . . . "

20

"Don't ask me," said John. "All I can say is you better go over there with them. You ought to know what he's saying."

"Okay," she said with fervor. "Only, listen: will you come along?"

"Me? I really am just a bystander." He looked down on her for having offered in effect to go to bed with him, not to mention that none of this affair was even remotely his business, but when she said "Come on" and seized the crook of his elbow and tugged, and added, "You're the only one I can trust," he let himself be drawn further into a situation he was apprehensive of but certainly did not yet recognize as a growing calamity. He had never been able to reject the plea of an importunate woman.

The cop sat in the police car, holding the microphone in one hand and Richie's license in the other.

John started to ask the latter a question, but Richie rolled his eyes significantly and turned away. He did not want to talk at the moment, apparently concerned that the truth might be revealed, though actually John's intention was merely to remind him that his car had not been locked, an imprudent omission in this day and age. Even in the suburbs there were plenty of people abroad on the sidewalks who would not hesitate to drive it off while its owner was conferring with the police.

The young woman was not so easily evaded. She successfully drew Richie away from the door of the cop car and said, quietly but including John, at whose elbow they stood, "Thanks, but what's the deal here?"

Richie carefully eyed the officer and then said, smirking, "I expected more gratitude."

"Sure," she said. "But right now I can't figure it out. We never saw each other personally before, am I right?"

He murmured, "Who says chivalry is dead?"

The cop hung up. He spoke out his window. "Okay: you check out."

Richie seized John's wrist. "And this gentleman agrees to work this thing out with our insurance companies."

The policeman stared at John. "You're the owner of the other vehicle?"

It was a mistake not to end his involvement right here, but John could not bring himself to lie outright. Therefore he said nothing at all in answer to the question, hoping the young cop would repeat it and insist on a response. Instead, Richie quickly broke in.

"The Triple-A wrecker is on its way. That's where I was, right after it happened: on the phone."

The cop called the woman to his window and returned her papers. Then he bent his capped head to write on a pad held against the steering wheel. Subsequently he presented Richie with a summons, saying, "I'm doing it by the book: reckless driving. You'll have to explain it to the judge. That's not my job. My job is to protect the safety of the public."

"Sure," Richie said, accepting the ticket without looking at it. "I understand. You've been very nice, Officer."

"Now just pull your vehicle over to the curb there while you wait for the wrecker, if you can," said the policeman. "Does it run, or do you need a push?"

"No problem here," Richie said.

The cop looked across toward the car that had been in front of the doughnut shop—that which he thought belonged to John!—and said to its supposed owner, "I see you already moved yours. Where is it, around the corner?" But he did not wait for an answer, putting the cruiser into a slow roll as he spoke. "Okay, now try to keep out of harm's way for a while."

22

Whether the last was said ironically John could not tell as he turned and saw that, as he had wanted to predict, person or persons unknown had driven Richie's car away. It might be a routine matter nowadays for the Samaritan to be punished, but it did not usually happen so quickly after the commission of the good deed. For helping the red-haired woman Richie had received an even more negative reward than John had got for coming to *his* aid.

John ran to the compact. Richie had just climbed in behind the wheel.

"Somebody stole your car!"

Richie smiled and said, "Relax."

"He can't have gotten far—"

The redhead was in the passenger's seat. She stared at the back of Richie's head in an apparent mixture of emotions, of which apprehension would seem to be one. Now she asked, "Does it run? If it does, I can take it from here."

Richie ignored her. To John he said, "Then somebody did me a favor. You saw the trouble I had with that piece of crap. Now I can claim the insurance." He winked. "Come on, climb in."

"Yeah," said the young woman, straining to be seen. "Come on along. *Please?*"

"I can't," John told them. "I have to get home. I don't have any business being here in the first place." It seemed like hours since he had answered the knock on the door. While at home on his day off, he never wore a watch, so he now did not know the precise time, but he had been away long enough for Joanie to wonder what had become of him, perhaps even to worry.

"See," said Richie, jerking his head in reference to the woman, "everybody wants you."

It occurred to John that the redhead might have made

Richie the same proffer she had presented to himself. In truth, it would only be fair: he had certainly saved her bacon with the cop. But perhaps she now had second thoughts. Richie irritated him, but being the more physically powerful, John hardly felt threatened. A woman, however, might have another point of view.

"Do you live near here?" he asked her. "Or are you going someplace nearby? If it's close, I'll ride along. But then I definitely am going home."

Instead of answering him, the woman anxiously addressed the back of Richie's head. "Listen, give me that summons. I'm not going to let you pay for what I did."

Richie said to John, "You've *got* to let me give you that lift home. Your leg is getting worse."

He was quite right, and John was amazed, even flattered, that the man could notice such a matter in the midst of what had happened—when even John himself had been distracted from it. Nevertheless, he intended to part company without further compromises.

"On second thought," he said, "I think I'll just get a cab." But so as not to be too stark, he asked, with a smirk of incredulity, "Are you really just going to let your car be stolen like that?"

Richie made a speculative moue. "It's already been done. I wouldn't have any idea where to look by now."

Behind him the woman was gesturing forcefully at John, but John did not know what she wanted except perhaps to inveigle him into an uncomfortable situation. His conscience was clear: she had not bothered to answer his question.

To Richie he said, "I meant, at least report it to the police?"

"The *police?*" Richie asked derisively. "They are probably the ones who stole it! That little skunk talking to me, it was probably his partner who sneaked over there and drove it

24

away." He slapped the steering wheel with his elongated fingers, which gave the impression of having more knuckles than most. "John, you and I both know it's the police who commit most of the crime these days."

There was no reason to respond in any way to such a ridiculous statement. "Okay," John said, and without thinking added one of the meaningless departure-clichés he had used all his life. "Take care." He turned.

"John!" the woman cried. "Can I talk to you, please?" She was out of the car, on the far side.

"Hey!" Richie's tone was threatening. "Get back in here."

John did not like this. He told Richie, "If she wants to talk to me, she can. Also, it's *her* car."

Richie lifted his hands from the wheel in a submissive gesture. "Okay, okay. What a touchy guy you are."

The woman met him halfway, at the back bumper. She spoke in a tone designed to be too low for Richie to overhear, but in a moment he had rendered that measure needless by putting the radio on at high volume and also closing his window, providing them with so much more privacy than was needed that it seemed derisory.

"I want you to come along," the woman said. "I don't trust this guy. I know he helped me out just now, unasked, but there's something wrong with him. Believe me." Her eyes now looked sore within the heavy liner and blue-green shadow.

"Just throw him out of your car," John said. "I'll back you up on that, if you want. But I'm not going anywhere else."

"He doesn't care if his car was stolen." The woman checked on Richie through the back window: he was tossing his skinny head about to the music. "You can figure that out: he stole it first himself."

John sighed. Hearing such an alarmist view, he was inclined to think the man even more harmless than he had earlier believed. John was by nature skeptical of exaggeration; he had always been that way. Things were rarely as bad or as good as assessed by the overexcitable.

"Look," he said, "do you want *me* to throw him out?"

The car was still angled into and blocking one lane of the street, and the traffic had to swing around it. Some drivers sounded their horns in annoyance. Now Richie suddenly gunned the engine and accelerated away.

"Hey," the woman shouted, "he's stealing *my* car!" She ran in pursuit, red hair flying.

John actually felt relief. She could notify the police, and he would be well out of it. She undoubtedly had insurance against theft.

But as it happened, Richie had belatedly done only what the cop had instructed him to do: pull into the nearest space at the curb, twenty yards up the street.

Before either of them could involve him again, John limped to the office of the taxi service. Within, an enormously fat woman sat at a desk filled with gadgetry: PC, fax machine, telephone console with a selection of buttons, and a CB radio, all of which hardware looked to be well maintained. But the rest of the place was squalid: stained walls, filthy floor with conspicuously sticky patches, wastebasket overflowing with discarded fast-food containers and ex-soda cups.

"Where to?" the fat woman asked, or rather grunted, disagreeably. John gave the address, and she squinted at him through little eyes that glinted from deep within her cheeks. "Let's see your money."

He wondered how she suspected he carried none, and then remembered he had caught a glimpse of his own reflection in the plate-glass windows of the doughnut shop and for a

26

moment thought it was someone else, unshaven and dressed in shabby clothes. A far cry from the workaday John Felton, in green blazer with the yellow breast-patch logo of the national real-estate association to which his employers belonged, and gray-and-white striped tie.

He quickly explained all that might justifiably puzzle the taxi woman, and added, "I live at the address I gave: I can just run inside and get the fare."

The woman snorted porcinely. "Take a hike." The phone rang, and she seized the handpiece in the pudgy fist at the end of a pneumatic forearm. "Twelve-oh-eight Fillmore. You got it. . . . Eight-ten minutes." She pressed something on the radio and spoke into the little standing microphone. A crackling response was heard from the appropriate driver. When the exchange was completed, she glanced up malevolently at John. "I thought I told you to get outa here."

"If you could just call my wife," John pleaded. "It's a good neighborhood, right up the hill. It's right next to De-Forest." By which designation, taken from the name of a park, one of the most affluent sections of town was popularly known (nouveau-riche types used it as part of their addresses, though without official post-office authority).

The fat woman won the stare. "The only call I'll make is to the cops. Unless"—she reached under the desk, making the grunting noises elicited by the effort, and brought to view an aluminum baseball bat—"you'd rather take a damned good beating from me."

There was nothing John could do at the moment, but he planned to drop in when he was back in his blazer and embarrass her for shaming a fellow local businessperson. After all, he was in a position to throw some trade her way. New homeowners often asked for a list of reliable electricians, plumbers, lawn-maintenance services, and there were times when anybody might need a cab—e.g., when leaving a lone family car for a change of oil.

On emerging from the taxi office he was in the rare state of mind in which he could see with relief that Richie was still at hand—or at any rate, the little compact car was yet at the curb where it had been parked earlier. He limped up to the passenger's side and saw the by now familiar red hair. He bent and said wryly, "Hi. I'm back."

Her head turned quickly, birdlike, to the open window. Nevertheless, her nonphysical responses seemed to have lost their previous edge. For an instant it did not look as though she recognized him.

He chuckled mirthlessly. "I got thrown out of the cab office, believe it or not. I don't have any money with me." He bent more extremely, to look beyond her. Nobody was behind the steering wheel. "I guess I can use that ride after all. Where'd Richie go?"

"He's getting breakfast." She nodded toward the dough-nut shop across the street.

That had been Richie's mission before the accident. John asked, "Do you mind if I get in?" While saying nothing, she made a movement of the head that was hard to interpret, but John took it as permission. It seemed most sensible not to disturb her but rather to enter by way of the driver's door, lowering the seat-back and climbing into the constricted rear compartment, where there was space for his legs only if he angled them, for lanky Richie had moved the front seat back as far as possible.

Suddenly the red-haired woman came to life, swiveling her head. "I thought you were going to drive! Let's get out of here while the getting's good."

In all decency, John pointed out, "The guy's own car was stolen, for God's sake. I'm not going to strand him here while he's buying doughnuts. I wouldn't worry so much about him if I were you. He might be eccentric, but he's harmless. I've known plenty of people like that." Because his motives in saying such were of the highest virtue, he was not consciously aware that this was not at all true.

"He stole that car. I'm begging you to drive. I'm not in any condition myself. I was stupid: I took something."

Obviously some sort of tranquilizer. Joanie occasionally took a pill when under certain strains, and he never failed to warn her against driving at such times.

He leaned forward. "All right. When Richie gets back, I'll do the driving, if that's what you want."

"That will be too late." She returned to her earlier state of torpor.

John went ahead and climbed out and into the front seat, sliding it forward somewhat to accommodate his legs, which were shorter than Richie's. At five-ten he was certainly no midget, but he really did regret not having reached six feet, for most of his forebears had been taller, though he was among the thicker-set. He had been husky enough to play fullback on his high-school team, but at 185 he was too small for the college squad, not to mention that his speed was not sufficient to compensate. Today he was in the neighborhood of 210, despite trying to watch what he ate. But it was rare that he exercised.

When he looked at the ignition, he saw that the keys were missing: he could not have stranded Richie if he had wanted to.

A moment later Richie was back, paper bag in hand and a smile on his face. He professed delight at John's return.

Not wishing to leave the impression that he had come back for any reason but necessity, John explained about the woman in the taxi office.

Richie scowled. "Scum. They're everywhere these days." He handed the bag to John. "Help yourself. I got extra doughnuts and coffee, just in case. I'll be right back." He walked rapidly away.

"Hey," John shouted, but Richie vanished around the back of the car. John could not see where he went from there. "Goddamn him," John said to the woman. "He's been doing that to me all morning, and as usual I'm trapped. . . . Look, I hate to ask, but I assure you I'm good for the money. Could you possibly lend me the taxi fare to get home? It couldn't be more than five bucks. I live just up the hill. I swear to you I'm a respectable person. I sell real estate, have a wife and two little kids, one just a baby. I look like this because it's my day off and I didn't expect to be out of the house." He handed the bag to her.

In a hollow voice she said, "I don't have any money. He took it all."

"Richie? Are you saying Richie took your money away from you? He just *took* it?"

She acquired more energy. "He asked me for money. He didn't have any."

"Well, that's different, isn't it?" John said reproachfully. "I'm asking for a loan right now. If you had any to give me, and you gave it, would you say I stole it?"

She looked at him. There was no life in her eyes. "I told you I'm afraid of that guy. He's dangerous. I didn't have the nerve not to give him everything I had."

John began privately to fume. Richie was taking forever, leaving him with this woman, who seemed quite as nutty a person as Richie himself. After all, she had begun their acquaintance by offering to have sex with him, a perfect stranger. He still did not know her name.

"Look," he said, "I'm John Felton."

Her response was mumbled.

"Sharon?" he asked. "Is that your name? . . . Okay, Sharon, I'll get your money back from him—less, of course, what he paid for the doughnuts—and everything will be all right again, you'll see. Then I'll drive you home. Maybe at that point you'll lend me the cab fare. Meanwhile, maybe you have a quarter left, somewhere way down in your purse? I know my wife sometimes finds change down there." He had spotted a public telephone set into the outside corner of a savings-and-loan building a few doors down. Unfortunately the S&L was not one of those which he recommended to home-buyers when they asked for places to go for mortgages. The ladies who owned Tesmir Realty had several other preferred institutions. Else he could have gone inside and borrowed a bill or two from one of the loan officers who would have known him.

But before Sharon could react, Richie had returned, coming to the driver's window and giving John the keys, his manner that of an obedient boy surrendering the family car to his father. Before he reached the passenger's door, Sharon desperately scrambled out and jumped into the rear. She was short, so presumably would be more suited to the little backseat than Richie, but still it did not seem altogether right to John for her to give way in her own car to a stranger, though perhaps it was otherwise if Richie could be called a guest.

But he himself was under no such restraints, and when Richie was in place beside him, John turned and said, "Let's have Sharon's money."

"Let me get settled first," Richie gently complained. With some difficulty, given his tight jeans, he dug into the left-hand pocket and extracted a sheaf of paper money and then some coins. He offered the handful to John, who gestured toward Sharon.

"Better count it," Richie said, pushing it between the seat-backs. "I don't trust anybody these days."

"It's okay," she said quickly.

It seemed probable enough to John that Richie had not extorted money from her but instead had taken only enough to pay for the food, which furthermore was intended to serve as refreshment not exclusively for himself but for the whole group. In fact, he now asked Sharon, who was still clutching the bag, to help herself to the contents and pass the remainder up front.

John had impatiently started the engine and was waiting for a break in the bumper-to-bumper traffic that inevitably appears from nowhere when you want to pull away from any curb anywhere in the world though all had been clear a moment earlier. He waved the bag away when, from the corner of his eye, he saw Richie offer it.

"Where to, sir?" Richie asked his shoulder.

"I'm driving myself home," John said firmly. "Where I'm getting out and staying." He felt like adding *And you won't be invited in,* but he really found it difficult to be rude, so settled for, "Where you two go from there is *your* business." But then he regretted saying that, which maybe would seem callous with respect to Sharon, whose fears might be unwarranted but were no less psychologically real. "No, I've changed my mind. I want to drop *you* off first." He had turned to address Richie.

Richie narrowed his eyes, but from the tone of his voice it seemed he might be joking. "So what have you two cooked up behind my back?" he asked. "If you want a little privacy, I can always look the other way."

"All right," John said sourly.

Richie was grinning. "I'm an understanding guy."

Sharon had moved forward until her anxious, pale, red-framed face was near their respective shoulders. "We're not doing anything behind your back," she said fearfully.

Richie did not acknowledge her. He continued to grin at John. "You're not as straitlaced as you want me to believe. You won't turn down a piece of free tail. Hell, why should you?"

John refused to participate in this banter. He was back to watching for a chance to pull the car out.

Sharon tried again. "We're not—"

Richie said, "Shut your mouth."

John swung around. "Don't talk to her that way. This is her car, remember?"

"Yeah," Richie said wryly. "They stole mine."

"It's not *her* fault."

As usual Richie was quick to placate. "Anything you say, boss!" By now John was becoming accustomed to the deference habitually paid him by the man, who appeared to be the cowardly sort who would readily defer to other males but would bully women when they could get away with it.

"I don't have any designs on Sharon," John said. He had a hunch that behind his back the traffic had now opened up, but he wanted to make this clear once and for all, lest Richie continue to make tasteless and embarrassing remarks. "She should have nothing to fear from either of us. That's why I want to drop you off first." He stared at Richie, who as always backed down.

"You're the doctor!"

"Well, where to? Where do you live?"

"I don't want to put you to any bother like that. Just let me off at the nearest movie."

There was something basically feckless about the man and hence, to John, who was himself of the absolutely opposite character, something at least a bit likable—in spite of all. "There aren't any movies open at this time of day in the suburbs. It won't be any bother to run you home."

"Hillsdale?" Richie asked skeptically.

Hillsdale was fifteen miles away, making for a round trip of thirty, which in the morning traffic meant the better part of an hour. John regretted extending the offer, but he had done so and was a man of his word.

"Why, sure," he answered, concealing his disappointment under a rising tone. "Hillsdale it is! But first I really do have to call my wife." He turned to Sharon. "I still need to borrow a quarter."

Coin in hand, he left the car and went to the telephone niche in the outer wall of the bank. His knee no longer hurt as much as it had earlier.

Joanie was seething, and he in turn was annoyed that she did not want to hear an explanation. "I know it sounds crazy, but take my word for it. I guarantee I'll be back before you're due at Elaine's: that's the important thing, isn't it?"

But she hung up abruptly. He only hoped that no one who could recognize him had seen him in the company of Sharon. She did not much resemble the kind of people who were his normal clients. Nor did Richie, to be sure.

When John got back to the car, he asked Richie what time it was.

"Damn if I know," Richie said indifferently.

"My wife's going to be really mad if I don't come home soon. She's got an appointment." He suppressed the information that where she had to go was the hairdresser's, because it might sound trivial to someone like Richie, whom he looked down on but nevertheless did not want to give an occasion to sneer.

"Swing around by your house and pick her up," Richie said. "I don't have to be anyplace soon."

John said frostily, "That won't be necessary." He looked back at Sharon, who managed to look small even when in such a compartment. "You're wearing a watch."

"Huh?"

"What time is it?"

She took an extra moment to find her wrist. "Eleven-ten."

"God Almighty," John cried. "No wonder Joanie's mad. I can't believe it! I've been at this two hours?" He started the car again. Joanie's appointment was at one. There was just enough time to make the round trip to Hillsdale if nothing happened that was untoward.

Richie held a container of coffee. John, who had breakfasted lightly almost four hours earlier, found the aroma seductive, but when Richie offered him the bag again, he again refused it: he wanted nothing from this guy.

"Joanie?" Richie asked now. "That's your wife's name? Cute. She about your age? What color hair?" He put the bag between his feet. "Must be nice being married to the right person. How many kids?"

John simply ignored the questions about his wife, for any answer at all would have compromised him with Richie— though he could not have explained why he felt that way— but decided to mention his kids, for suddenly they seemed a strength. "Two."

Richie nodded enthusiastically. "You don't say? That's fantastic. You made 'em, eh, John? You're all right."

Immediately John began to regret having admitted that much. He could finally see a break in the traffic, and he gave his attention to it.

Richie meanwhile asked, "Boys? Girls?"

John pulled away from the curb and was rolling cautiously toward a traffic signal that he suspected was on the verge of changing.

Richie continued. "Do you want some more? But I hope you're planning these things. We don't need more kids coming into the world by mistake."

As it happened, John agreed with the principle, but it went against his grain to discuss the subject with this man. The traffic light, too, was trying his patience, staying red interminably. He eventually had to come to a full stop.

"It's stuck," Richie said. "Run it."

In fact John felt like doing so, he who rarely suffered unduly from impatience. Perhaps some of Richie's anarchistic tendencies were rubbing off on him. Just as the car came totally to rest, the light turned green. Had he taken Richie's advice, he would probably have gotten away with it. As it was, he did not put the vehicle in motion again quickly enough to forestall a chorus of horns behind him, led by the belligerent tuba of a colossal tractor trailer, the enormous chromed radiator-grille of which was too large and too close to fit within the rearview mirror.

Richie's reaction to the episode was focused in anger on the truckdriver, whose cab was too elevated for him to be seen at so short a range. "When we get out of this squeeze," he told John, "pull him over. I don't take shit from his kind."

John regarded this as empty bluster. "Sure," he said derisively. "I'll run him off the road with this tank. That'll show him."

Without transition Richie returned to his former topic. "Know what I approve of? Your wife is home with the kids, not out of the house all day at some job like some bitches think they ought to be."

If the truth be known, John was in a certain agreement with this sentiment, though he would never have expressed it openly to his wife. At the moment no trustworthy child-care facilities were available for Melanie, at least in Joanie's opinion, in these days when all one heard of were those in which the children were abused. And little Phil was still too young to be deprived of his mother for long. Even so, John disliked Richie's idiom and did not want to encourage him in the further expression of his ideas on this or any other subject. But it would make for an oppressive atmosphere if he tried to get him to shut up until they reached Hillsdale. Including Sharon in the conversation might be an answer to the problem.

He looked for her in the mirror. "How about you, Sharon? Are you married?" She was not wearing a ring on the relevant finger, but then some married persons did not, especially women of a pronounced feminist bent, along with the usual men who assumed they were thereby duping potential pickups. To John this kind of deceit was almost as deplorable as adulterous sex. He had always told himself that if he were attracted to another woman than his wife, he would at least be honest enough to define himself, taking the consequences.

"Not any more," she answered.

Richie sent some air derisively through his lips and kicked his feet in the assertive running shoes. "Don't tell us your troubles. So your old man found a boy who was better-looking."

John admonished him. "Will you stop being so insulting?" He addressed Sharon again. "You just go ahead, say anything you want."

He saw her silently shake her head and wondered what kind of medication she was on, if that could explain the state into which she had fallen. But then he was distracted again. The street had become a three-lane county highway, on which it was possible for him to increase speed, the traffic ahead having suddenly melted away. But though he went to the posted limit, forty-five, and then to fifty, the tractor trailer stayed virtually against his rear bumper, an ominous situation to be in, for the middle lane at the moment was monopolized by a series of cars traveling in the opposite direction, and he was as far to the right as he could be, almost onto the narrow shoulder, beyond which was a drainage ditch.

Again Richie was quickly aware. "Don't speed up. Gradually slow down, drive him nuts. He won't hit you unless you stop without warning."

This took a lot of nerve, for as soon as John began subtly to decelerate, the truckdriver sounded shattering blasts of his horn. The only way to persist in the tactic was to avoid looking in the mirror, grit your teeth, and put your being on automatic pilot. He had once successfully employed the technique as a passenger on a light aircraft in stormy skies. Whether it would have worked again he was not to determine now, for after another mile, by which point he was still going better than forty, the highway became positively spacious, with two full lanes separated by a grassy median strip from the two that went the other way.

His sigh of relief, however, proved premature: the truck stayed directly behind him even when both vehicles had gained the wider road. Furthermore, the deafening sound of the horn had become constant.

When he quickly changed lanes, so did the truck.

"Okay," Richie cried in elation. "We got him now!"

What scared John about this sort of dueling was the irrationality of it. He put the accelerator to the floor. The car responded more vigorously than he had anticipated and sprang out to a substantial lead on the truck. But the driver of the larger vehicle was quick to answer what he took as a challenge. It was unfortunate that, as John could see only now that the highway began an ascent, the powerful tractor had no trailer in tow, which undoubtedly meant that Sharon's little car would be no match for its brute power even when going uphill.

"Christ, why doesn't a cop come along *now?*" He regretted the need to express fear in Richie's presence. Though he was going flat out, the truck was overtaking him, its windshield reflecting the sun in an impenetrable glare. He still could not see the driver.

"We're in luck," Richie shouted, over the noise of an engine at maximum power. "A cop would only take the bastard's side. Don't worry. We've got him now!"

An empty boast if there ever was one! John had reached the crest of the rise and looked down a long slope of highway on which its weight would give the truck an even greater advantage in speed. Furthermore, several cars were in sight ahead, in each lane, so that he might be trapped behind them in either. To be sure, were they driven by good citizens, perhaps by some effort of them all in concert the truck would be the one so confined or captured. Then, too, car phones and emergency CB sets were commonplace. An observant and law-loving driver might well alert the state police to such conspicuous and illegal slipstreaming.

Yet while entertaining such fantasies, John was aware that no help would be forthcoming. Though accompanied by, and in fact responsible for the well-being of, two other souls (both of them strangers, so that while providing little effective company, they denied him privacy), he stood alone.

But Richie suddenly helped. "Let him get right up against you in the right lane, then suddenly switch to the left. You can maneuver a lot quicker than him. He can't turn that fast at speed without being in danger of losing it. Soon as you get over, slow down some. He'll have to go on by. Once we get behind him, we'll own his ass."

But who wanted it? John looked forward only to seeing

the last of the menace. To him the driver was a potential homicide, without a motive: he yearned for no revenge on such a depraved human being. Naturally, if he saw a cop he would report the incident, but that was another thing entirely. As to "letting" the truck ride his back bumper, it had arrived there once more without his permission and would stay there. What Richie had suggested was better than that.

He gave a warning to his passengers, and Richie heeded it, seizing the handhold above the upper left corner of his door, but Sharon apparently did not, and when he made his abrupt lane-switch, he heard the sound of her body being flung across the backseat by centrifugal force.

Richie's tactic worked! The truck thundered by in the right lane, its rushing bulk and giant brutal wheels even more frightening than its seemingly static and one-dimensional image had been in the mirror. By such a simple device, the thing that could have flattened them was now rendered harmless. Perhaps the madman behind its wheel would roar on to threaten other defenseless motorists. If so, who cared? Quite a natural feeling at this instant. In the next, he would continue to look for a policeman.

Now he was able to ask Sharon, "Are you okay back there?"

She mumbled an affirmative. At such a time there was surely an advantage in being tranquilized.

"Okay," Richie said eagerly. "Now let's nail him."

The truck was already fifty yards ahead, John having diminished his speed so as to fall far behind and thus recede from the immediate memory of the driver, who might just be crazy enough to retain a grudge. Nowadays you were always hearing about people who on the occasion of traffic squabbles produced the guns they carried in their cars for just such a purpose, and shot adversary motorists or even others who were faultless.

"Forget about the bastard," John said. "Good riddance." He was relieved to see Richie accept this with a stoical shrug and fall back into the seat, slumping so low that he could barely see over the dashboard. John had feared that a need for revenge might be the man's dominant emotion. What was his own? He was conscious of a lifetime urge to do right. This put him at a frequent disadvantage, as in the case of the tailgating truck. It was true that he had now escaped from the situation, but it was unfair that he had been in it in the first place. He had given no rational offense. How could one do so by driving in an orderly manner at the speed limit? To behave otherwise would endanger the lives of human beings: that was what had been at issue, not the narrow concerns of traffic law.

Richie grumbled, down in his slump, kicking the firewall. "Those kind of people make me mad: they don't have any respect."

All John wanted to do was get to Hillsdale, and back, without further incident. What Richie said might be true, but nothing could be done about it beyond complaining, and John hated to waste his time in negative lament.

"How big a town is Hillsdale?"

"I don't know."

"Have you lived there long?" John glanced at him. "Do you live there at all?"

Richie grinned. "I said I did, didn't I?"

"Well, that's where I'm taking you."

"Then that's where I'm going." Without emerging from his slump, Richie made a long reach for the knobs of the radio.

"Do you mind?" John asked. "I don't want to hear any music now." He did not quite understand why he had said that. Had he been alone he would have switched on the radio and listened to almost anything but elevator music, though what he preferred were the records popular when he was in the latter years of high school, which to younger people were already far out of date.

"Do you ever enjoy yourself?" It was Richie's sudden question and bore an implication John did not care for.

"I've done some things in my day. I wasn't always married, with little kids. I've been around."

"I'm talking of right now," Richie said. "You interested in some partying? We'll pick up a couple bottles." He jerked his thumb over his shoulder. "She's got everything else. Maybe go to a motel, do it right."

"Oh, come on," John complained. "Just let that—"

"Think I'm kidding? Should of seen what she had in her purse. That's why she was so worried about the cop back there. Junkie bitch."

John was hit hard by this information. He lacked the spirit to ask Sharon to confirm or deny, but assumed she would have protested had the charge been baseless. He did not even wish to know what sort of drugs were at issue.

"I'm dropping you off in Hillsdale and then going straight home. Since this is the only form of transportation available to me, I'm driving myself home in this car." He had made the latter statement for Sharon's benefit, should she herself be (despite her professed fear of Richie) inclined to acquiesce in the proposal, and looked for her in the mirror, but she was presumably lying on the seat and could not be seen.

"Just an idea," Richie said.

John saw something that brought him back to the moment. A quarter mile ahead, the truck that had tailgated him was parked on the shoulder, which had widened with the broadening of the highway. Instantly chilled, he would have turned and run if he could, but the road was one-way and at this point on the median the simple grass had given way to bushes, so it was not physically possible to perform an illegal U-turn and head back where they had come from— for such he might well have done, in a sudden and unprecedented access of mortal fear.

In another moment, however, he again was in command of himself. The truckdriver was surely not waiting for *him* but rather immobilized by mechanical trouble. John was in fact instantly ashamed of himself and grateful that he had said or done nothing that could have revealed his fright to Richie, whom he glanced at now.

Richie, too, had already seen the truck. "Hey, look!"

"I guess he's broken down," John said hopefully.

Richie eyed him. "Maybe we just ought to stop and ask. Maybe he's in real trouble."

John took refuge in a sardonic tone. "I doubt it's life or death." They were not far from the truck now, but he had yet to see the driver.

"Pull in," Richie said abruptly. "You can stay in the car if you want. I'll see what's what."

Insulted by the implied slur on his courage, John accelerated onto the shoulder and then had to brake hard, skidding on the loose dirt and gravel, to stop the car before it collided with the rear of the truck.

He jumped out, in a certain disorder. He disliked hearing the sound his old sneakers, normally quiet, made on the gritty shoulder. Before he reached the truck, the driver's door was hurled open. A burly figure emerged and did not jump but rather descended to the ground with the deliberation of the overweight.

So that his intentions could not be misinterpreted, John quickly said, "Hi. Anything we can help you out with?"

The driver wore a dirty plaid shirt but was clean-shaven and pinkly scrubbed of skin. He spoke in some kind of hick accent. "You mess around with me, and I'll make you cry." He was taller than John and wider, but much of his poundage consisted, visibly, of lard, and he looked to be about forty. He held a metal bar.

John had not been in a fight since childhood, and in fact had not been offered one since then. But now that he was out of the car and actually in this situation, he was not unduly apprehensive. He was a salesman, and knew how to talk to people.

"Hey, I just stopped to see if I could help out." He smiled. "Really. We thought you just might be in some trouble."

"I ain't," said the truckdriver. "*You* are." He lowered his heavy head, on which the thick hair looked freshly combed.

"Now take it easy," John said, suppressing his annoyance. "I mean it. If your radio's out, I'll be glad to make a call for you at the next phone. How about it?"

"I could of squashed you like a stinkbug," the trucker said, "in your little gook automobile." He tapped the iron bar against the palm of his left hand.

John decided it would be cowardly to disclaim ownership of the car at this point, though he had begun to take the weapon seriously. "I didn't do anything to you," he said firmly. "You tailgated me and wouldn't pass when you had the chance."

The truckdriver said, "And now I'm going to take you apart, smartmouth."

John did not give ground. "I'll say it again: I don't have anything against you. But if you threaten me with *that*, you're breaking the law."

The fat man laughed sourly, showing lots of pink mouth. His stomach hung over the waist of his pants, obscuring most of the oversized belt buckle, but that also could be said of the world's strongest men, the weightlifters of the superheavyweight class.

"This here's the law of the road, you skunk." The trucker continued to slap the bar against his other palm as he advanced. "Should of wrote your will before comin' out today."

Hands in the air, John began to backstep. "What have I done to you? Take it easy." He despised himself for the beseeching note that had entered his voice.

"You just think what I'm going to do to *you,*" the man cried with a rage so venomous that John could not stand against it: he broke and ran to the car.

Richie was at the wheel, and the engine was running. "He's got a tire iron!"

"Look out," Richie said, leering ahead. The door handle was torn from John's grasp as the car shot forward, striking the truckdriver, lifting his heavy body as though it were stuffed with straw. It struck the hood and bounced away.

Richie braked. For an instant John tried to believe it was a mishap of the sort that was common enough, though usually with older drivers: the car is accidentally in gear, the foot by chance comes down on the gas and stays there in momentary panic. But when the vehicle reached him in its reverse travel and he saw Richie's triumphant face, John recognized that the trucker had been intentionally run down.

Richie was shouting at him to jump in on the passenger's side. In confusion, he obeyed the order. He knew he was not acting well, but he had to collect himself. He needed a moment or two, but there was none to spare. Richie pulled onto the road and stepped on the gas.

"He was going to kill you, no doubt about it, but we

nailed him instead! The fat hog." Richie was crowing: it had been no accident.

John now hoped that this self-serving version was true, though even in his distress he thought it depraved to wish that someone killed in your interest had brought disaster on himself by trying first to be himself a killer. What kind of world had replaced the one he knew?

He finally had the strength to say, "We better go back and see about him. We can't just let him lay there."

"This is one-way. Anyway, go back to what? He's not gonna do us any good, dead or alive."

To his horror John found himself wanting to agree, but what kind of person had he become to accept such reasoning? "He didn't actually touch me. Maybe it just would have stayed a bluff."

"I saw him coming at you with murder in his eye and a tire iron in his fist. One swipe would have opened up your skull. I sure couldn't wait and see."

"Why did he do that?" John asked in anger and guilt.

"I say he was going to kill you. I'll stick to that."

"Why. *Why?*" John looked back at the road through the rear window, but they were already too far away to see more than a kind of blur that must be the truck. Richie was apparently traveling flat out, but John had no sensation of speed or even of movement.

"Some people," Richie said, "just go around looking for trouble. I don't even ask why. If they meet up with me, they get it: that's all I know." He gave John a quick wink. "That's all I need to know."

John had never seen anyone be struck head-on by an automobile. He had no idea what could be done for such victims, were they still alive. He prayed that the truck-driver, however evil, still was, and could be healed, though

46

of course if that proved to be the case, he himself might be in trouble, however guiltless. The victim had never seen Richie. John could hardly breathe. His heart was in more turmoil than when he had merely feared being brained by a tire iron.

"Take that exit there," he told Richie, and was desperate enough to have hurled himself at the man had his command been defied, but as always the other acquiesced. What was especially terrible about the running-down of the truckdriver was that Richie assumed he did it in John's interest. There was something very wrong with him.

Within three hundred yards of where the exit ramp joined a state road was a dirty-white little house with a screened-in porch.

"Pull in there!" said John, and Richie drove into the unpaved driveway that led to a garage out back.

John left the car. The screen door was latched. He pounded on the desiccated wood of its frame. There was no visible doorbell. Repeated blows of his fist on the flaking green paint brought no response. He came down from the step and half circled the house. It was hard to tell from the windows whether anyone might be home, but on a warm day all of them were closed.

He went to the car, where Richie, the source of all his troubles, had remained. "We've got to get to a phone."

With a genial shrug, Richie stepped from the car and walked jauntily to the house, punched a hole in the screen, and opened the door. He forthrightly broke the glass of the inner door with one kick of his formidable running shoes, reached within, and disengaged the bolt.

John had not meant to break in, but it was small damage compared to running a man down by car. He pushed Richie aside and shouted through the open doorway.

"We don't mean any harm! It's an emergency. A man's dying, and we need your phone."

There was no answer. He saw a telephone on a little table within a few feet of the entrance. He picked up the handpiece.

The line was in use. "Lock yourself in the room," said an authoritative voice. "We're on our way. . . . *Who picked up that extension?*"

"Excuse me," John said. "I have to get through. There's an emer—"

"*Who are you?*" The voice was threatening.

"A man might be dying on the highway!"

"*Did you kill him?*"

"No. He was hit by a car."

"*Your car?*"

"Will you get off the line?" John shouted. "He needs an ambulance."

"You just stay on the phone, sir," said the voice, less threatening and with a new note of sympathy, which was suspiciously fake because it took no account of what John had said. "Don't move from the phone. Are you by yourself in the house, or is somebody else with you?"

In the *house*. How did this man know where he was calling from? Suddenly he understood. Someone *was* at home, in another room, and from there had called the police!

"Are you a cop?" John asked, and though he received no answer, continued as if he had. "Then send an ambulance out to Forty-five A northbound, somewhere not too far south of Hillsdale: a man is lying on the shoulder, next to a tractor trailer."

"Listen," the policeman said, "you just keep talking to me. I want to get everything straight. Give me your name, if you don't mind, and—"

"You heard me," said John. "I'm not a criminal. I'm a passerby, and I had to get to a phone. I'm leaving money for new glass and screening." He was saying this as much for the resident of the house as for the cop. "I'm sorry the damage had to be done, but this guy's life might be saved."

A woman was on the line, moaning. "He's going to kill me."

"No, he is not, ma'am. He's got too much sense for that."

John hung up in desperation. He had not noticed what became of Richie, and now assumed the man returned to the car. But crossing the porch, he could see no one in the front seat of the automobile. He had a wild impulse to leap into the car and drive himself as far from this mess as he could get, leaving Richie to pay the piper—for was not that bastard single-handedly responsible for all of it?

But whether he would have proceeded further with his impracticable scheme, he had not quite reached the vehicle when he heard the screen door bang behind him. At least he regained the driver's seat.

Richie leaped into the passenger's side. He was carrying a pint bottle of vodka.

John pulled out to the road in high-speed reverse. No doubt the woman was watching from an upstairs window and would write down the license number and a description of the car. Perhaps she had even seen him and Richie. And only now did it occur to him that there must have been some drivers in the southbound lane of the highway who saw the running-down of the truckdriver. The police were probably already looking for them. By now it had become a virtual crime spree.

He decided that the cops would expect someone fleeing to use the fastest road at hand—namely, the highway from which they had recently exited. Therefore it made most sense to continue on the county road and, if possible, find an even more modest thoroughfare, and there to slow to a speed that would attract no undue attention. He was amazed, and given the situation, as pleased as he could be, with his ability to think clearly and effectively, he who had no experience of crime. He did not even care for the fictional cop shows on TV (to which for some reason Joanie was addicted), with their excessive discharge of ammunition that never found its mark if directed at the good guys but was unerring with the bad.

Richie was sucking at the mouth of the vodka bottle.

"Why'd you have to steal that?" John asked him angrily. "Can't you see it hurts our argument that we broke into the place only to call for an ambulance?"

"Who would begrudge us a drink?" Richie asked. "I'd of just had one there if you hadn't run out so fast. I'm all shaken up. I need something."

John might have welcomed this expression of human vulnerability had he believed it genuine. "You've really got me into something now. I should have stayed back there with the truckdriver and flagged down a car. I should have stayed at the house till the police came. But I panicked. I've never been in trouble before in my entire life. I'm panicking now, and I can't help it. I don't know why I'm driving away like this." Nevertheless, he saw a quiet road of the kind he was looking for and turned onto it. After a stretch of field on either side, woodland took over. Nobody else was on the road, but in the left-hand field a distant figure was riding a piece of farming equipment.

"I'll tell you why," said Richie. "It's self-preservation. We didn't do anything wrong, but you realize the cops would throw the book at us, for something we didn't do."

"Didn't *do?*"

"You know what I'm talking about. We didn't do anything wrong. That guy was going to beat your brains out with the tire iron: we only did what we had to do in self-defense."

"It wasn't *we*," John said vehemently. "It was *you*."

Richie lowered the bottle. "Tell me I'm in error, John," he asked quietly, "but what did I personally get out of it?"

"That's not the point."

"Then what *is*, for heaven's sake? You're not making any sense. I don't want to make a lot of myself, but some would say I saved your life back there on the road. Then going to that house: whose idea was that? Who had to get to a phone? Why you cared whether that big fat sack of shit was dead or dying, I don't understand: he was going to kill you. Think he would care if the situation was reversed?"

John realized he was trying to reason with someone whose principles were different from his own, and he understood why he himself was endeavoring to keep away from the police: because of an instinctive conviction (shocking in a member of a civilized society) that the cops would listen to him with no more comprehension than Richie displayed now. Whatever his own motives, he had served as an accomplice in an intentional hit and subsequent run, and then a breaking and entering of a private dwelling place, which was furthermore occupied at the time, and by a woman who sounded as though she might be aged or ill or both. But theft of a pint of vodka was hardly serious burglary. Perhaps foolishly, should the truckdriver die, John sought mitigation.

"Did you take anything else?"

But Richie had turned and was leering into the rear. "Hey, you! Want a drink?"

John had momentarily forgotten about Sharon. He tilted the mirror to see her. She rose slowly from the supine, looking the worse for wear. There seemed to be a question as to whether she was aware of what had happened during the last half hour.

Richie snorted. "You look like a pig."

"Cut that out," John said. "We're all in this together." He was immediately sorry he had put it that way, which served to confirm Richie's position. To Sharon he said, "Anything we can do for you?" The question was hypocritical, of course, for he would hardly have stopped the car at this point.

Sharon gave the impression of trying to smile. "God," she said. "I've felt better."

Richie sat back in his seat and drank more vodka. "We ought to get rid of her," he said.

What John found especially disturbing about this statement was that it did not appall him—as, in all decency, it should have. He would very much have liked to see the last of Sharon. He resented her: as if dealing with Richie were not already too much to handle.

Nevertheless, he again reminded Richie whose car it was, little as that fact might mean to someone who had responded to the theft of his own car with indifference.

The road had now reached the woods and taken a turn that would have concealed them from the sight of any pursuers on the main road, though frequent checks of the rearview mirror had revealed none thus far. There would be little reason to suppose they had taken this obscure route when wider thoroughfares, leading to municipalities into the traffic of which they could merge, were available—but even while making this argument to himself, John was aware of its possible weakness. With no precedent by which to judge, he might well be doing exactly what the police would expect, and could encounter a roadblock around the next bend.

He appealed to Richie. "You have any idea where we are?

I've lost all sense of direction. The sun was over there, wasn't it?" It had disappeared behind the clouds some time earlier, and the nearby trees were very tall. "Are we anywhere near Hillsdale?"

"Damned if I know." Richie had almost emptied the bottle by now.

John exploded. "Have you ever even *seen* Hillsdale? You don't live there, do you? This whole trip has been a wild-goose chase! Goddamn you, what's your game?"

"Is this the time to fight with *me?*"

John gave in to an impulse. He slammed the brake pedal down, causing the car to skid to a stop, diagonaled across the roadway. Richie was hurled toward the dashboard. But his manual reflexes were quick, and he caught himself without damage.

"I should have done this much, much earlier," John shouted, continuing to indulge himself in the excitement of selfish irresponsibility. He threw the door open and stepped out of the car. "You're on your own, it's not my affair!"

Instantaneously he conceived a plan: he would hike back, find the police, and patiently explain what had happened. He was prepared to be initially misinterpreted, but being a respectable man with an honest job and a wife and family, he could not be disbelieved forever. He turned his back on the car and began to walk in the direction whence they had come. He expected Richie to pursue him but was not disappointed when this had not happened by the time he reached the point where the woods gave way to the fields. He had not wished to look back, feeling nothing but a gratifying relief that he was at last free of those people, both of whom had been so basically alien to him. He could not blame himself for responding originally to Richie's call for simple assistance, nor for later on doing what seemed a far from extravagant favor for Sharon. He still was not ready to say it was inevitably, necessarily, foolish, let alone hazardous, to be kind to strangers. What a rotten world it would have to be for a fellow like him, who had always thought of himself as normal in every respect, to arrive at such a cynical conclusion!

The man on the tractor was closer to the road now. It looked as though he was doing nothing but taking a ride on it, with no earth-altering equipment in tow. He appeared to be fortyish and had a well-groomed face. He wore Walkman headphones; the home unit was in an upper pocket of his shirt of moss-green linen.

John waved at and advanced toward him, in an unfenced field covered with stubble. The tractor continued to roll. It was on the small side and moved slowly, but John anyway politely stepped out of its direct path long before it reached him.

He lifted a hand and said hello.

The man on the tractor stopped the vehicle and disengaged his headphones, hanging them around his neck.

"I've got to get to a phone," John said. "I'm sorry to bother you."

"Yeah," the man said. "Phone." He shook his head. "I don't see your car."

"I walked here. I lost my transportation."

The man frowned. He had a nose with a square tip. "Funny way you put it. Your car broke down—is that what you mean?"

"You could say that," John agreed, for convenience' sake. "I have to get to a phone."

"I'll bet you do."

Speaking of odd ways to put things, what did *that* mean? But John was in no position to get into another unpleasant encounter. He added some self-pity. "I'm lost. I'm not that far from where I live, ten-fifteen miles, but I'm not at all familiar with this area."

"Where do you live?"

John told him, but the information did not change the man's skeptical expression. "If I take a right on the main road"—which was now in sight, and John pointed that way—"how long till I come to a village?"

"Too long." Now the man finally smiled and so immediately transformed himself into a regular sort of guy. "But there's a house in less than half a mile."

Could he be referring to his own home? John did not want to ask. He thanked the man and started down the road. Behind him he heard the tractor engine rev up. It appeared to be the kind of machine that was designed more for the recreational use of the gentleman farmer than for serious labor.

Reaching the highway gave him a sense of accomplishment. The temperature was moderate, with the sun still masked by clouds, but walking warmed him to a sweat. He could probably be smelled. He wiped his face on a shirttail, having no handkerchief. Through the fabric he could feel his whiskers, which had been growing for what by now must be thirty hours. What a sight he must be. He had to get his message across quickly to whoever occupied the house he would presumably soon reach.

To his relief the road made a gentle descent and was often in the shade of big old oaks. His knee no longer bothered him. His spirit was showing its resilience. He felt sure he was at last on his way out of the mess. He was able to reflect on the terrain. Next time it was appropriate, he could tell someone, "I'm a town guy myself, but you know where's some nice country? Out Hillsdale way." Joanie might even be placated by such an observation: she had begun direly to predict that by the time the kids had gone far in school, their neighborhood, already showing the signs, would degenerate beyond the point of no return (realtorlike, he had exaggerated somewhat when telling the woman in the taxi office that his home was practically in the posh DeForest area), and she kept asking, why wait, why not move someplace where you could stretch a little and grow vegetables? What he, the practical one, had wondered instead was how far would the children live from schools, friends, activities, and how much extra hauling would be needed? Not to mention the distance from his own work, such as it would be, plus the matter of isolation, for he enjoyed having proximate neighbors, having had them all his life.

He reached the restored farmhouse: thirty yards back, full porch, new roof, professionally landscaped shrubs and lawn, surely four bedrooms with at least two full baths, lavatory on the ground floor, chimneys for two fireplaces, probably a big kitchen with the proportions of yore but brought up to contemporary speed with rewiring, new cabinetry and lighting, and high-tech appliances. The graveled side driveway lined with young poplars led to a red barn behind the house, but not so big a one as the standard working farmer's model and obviously not old but recently erected to serve as an outsized garage, and high enough for a little studio apartment upstairs: from the roof protruded stovepipe and toilet vents.

As John was about to take the flagstoned walk to the front door, he saw the little green tractor pull up before the garage and the man hastily jump from its seat.

So the vehicle had proved pretty slow after all, for John had beaten it on foot, taking the right-angled route while it traveled the supposedly shorter hypotenuse. He crunched up the driveway. As usual when on such a surface he pitied the guy who had to mow the adjoining grass, but there was no question gravel was more fashionable than blacktop.

The man looked startled to see him—though having directed him here.

"If I could just use your phone."

"Oh, sure." The man was a size larger than John but did not seem all that substantial. He pointed to the barn. "Right here, in the office."

Inside, they walked past the upscale white utility vehicle a guy like this would have, and there was room for other cars though none was present at the moment. On the far right was a railed flight of steps. John headed that way at the movement of the man's hand.

"You lucky enough to work at home?"

"My wife's. She's a designer."

John opened the door at the top of the stairs and stepped into a broad, bright room, fitted out for professional use with a large desk and a wallful of modular cabinets. At the other end, before an array of windows, was a tilt-top drawing table flanked by other wide and flat surfaces. There was a lavatory cubicle in one corner. Unless the man's wife was in there, the place was empty, though all the batteries of overhead fluorescents were lighted.

"All right," the man said with a certain impatience. "There's the phone."

John went to the desk. Weary, he sat down on the chair and only when in place asked, "Do you mind? . . . Can you tell me just where this *is?* I'll explain the whole thing as soon as I can, but right now I just want to give my wife instructions on how to get here to pick me up." His plan to go straight to the police had been replaced when he realized that the man was going to stand by and listen to what he said.

Inevitably, when the cops arrived there would be a transitional period in which the man believed him a criminal. John could not have endured that. Better anyway to get Joanie's collaboration: no one who saw her at his side could doubt him.

"You're just outside Meredith."

"I must seem rude," John said, putting out his hand. "My name is—"

"Go ahead and make that call," the man said. "I'll be back." He left, closing the door behind him.

John had to accept the fact that strangers might well be wary of him, in this day and age. Look at what he himself had got into by not keeping remote from Richie.

The many electronic sounds he heard before the ringing-signal finally came suggested that this was an extra-local call, not covered by allotted message units, and he must not forget to reimburse his host—though of course he carried no money. He would mail him a check.

"Joan," he began as soon as the instrument was picked up at the other end, "I got myself embroiled in quite a mess. I can't take the time to explain now, but can you come and pick me up? I'm at a house in the country near Meredith." He still could not give usable directions but nevertheless persisted. "It must be near Hillsdale, out Route Forty-five A. There should be a map in the glove compartment. . . . Joanie? I'm in trouble. I haven't got any money, and I look like a tramp. I hurt my knee and had to walk for miles." This was not the moment to mention the fallen truckdriver or the possible pursuit by the cops.

"You walked out of here early this morning," Joan said. "I've lost the entire day by now. One day a week for myself! And now I don't even get that. And you ask me to drive to

58

some godforsaken place? What do I do with the children? Bring them along? Are you drunk?"

"I wish I were. Please listen to me. Through no fault of my own, I've got into a sticky situation. It's hard to explain just like this, but it all began when I tried to do a simple favor. You remember, the doorbell rang, and—"

"I'm mad, John! I want you to know that."

"I need help," he said. "I don't have anyone to turn to."

"You son of a bitch, you bastard, get down on the floor, face down, you piece of filth, or I'll blow your dirty head off." It was the man, who had returned with a long gun and was pointing the muzzle of it at him.

John dropped the telephone and fell to the carpet as ordered, for the man had been trembling so violently that he feared the gun might go off from the vibration.

The man marched to stand over him. "I'd be perfectly within my rights to shoot you down: you're on my property and you're a known felon. Just give me the excuse, you garbage, you. Go on, *please*."

John was frightened, but he could not let the charge go unanswered. "Felon?" he asked, face against the floor. "I'm a respectable person, with a wife and two little children. I'm with a real-estate agency in—" He felt cold metal against the back of his skull.

"Keep it up, scum," his captor shouted, "and you won't have a head." Having made the point, he pulled the gun away. "You guys are all the same: big tough characters when you're alone in a house with some sick old lady, but"—here John was poked again, this time in the small of his back— "Stretch those arms over your head!" He struck John again: it was beginning to hurt.

John considered his plight so outrageous that he persisted

in speaking despite the threats. "My wife might still be on the phone: just talk to her. Or call her back. Then call my firm and talk to anybody there. Call—"

"I made all the calls I'm going to, filth," the man said. "I called the cops from the house."

To hear this was now a relief: John had begun to think him a crazy vigilante. "Good," he said, and carefully rolled over to the supine position.

"I swear to you, if you make another movement I'll kill you."

John realized he still might get shot by accident. "Just take it easy. Wait for the police. You don't want to do something you'll be sorry for."

The man produced a weird chuckle. "I'm throwing a scare into you, tough guy! Now you know what it feels like to beg for mercy—only people like you never grant any to anybody."

"May I just inquire," John said, staring up at one of the fluorescent fixtures, "why you think I'm a criminal? All I did was ask if I could use your phone. I never lifted a hand against you."

"Because I'm a *man!* You're not going to take me on except if my back is turned. I know that."

"But what did I do to *anybody?*" John cried.

"I just hope the police don't come too soon," the man said. "I just hope you try to make a break for it, so I can shoot you down."

John understood that this was the bluster of a frightened person. He had mixed feelings about the arrival of the cops. This overwrought character, a local property owner and obviously a respectable figure, a man of means, would undoubtedly have greater weight with the law than he, and surely at first he could expect to be greeted, badly dressed and ill-shaven as he was, with skepticism at best. At worst he might

60

be detained, at least until his bona fides could be established. He had never had a difference with the police except in the matter of some Halloween mischief back in high-school days, and he would be appalled to be thought of, even temporarily, as a suspect. But he had to steel himself against such an experience, for it might well come about before he was able to extricate himself.

He tried to bring reason to bear on the situation. "I guess that when I thought you were listening to a cassette on those headphones, you actually were tuned in to a radio. You probably heard a report of the break-in at a house over near Hillsdale, with the perpetrators at large. Then I came along, a stranger and pretty disreputable-looking by your standards." It was ineffective to address the light fixture on the ceiling: he turned his head to look for his host, a movement that also involved a shoulder.

The man fired the gun, producing a terrifyingly loud sound. John did not know where the bullet went—perhaps it was in some part of his body—but nothing could be worse than that noise. He clasped his ears and squeezed his body into the form it had last had when carried inside his mother. His captor was speaking, but John's ears were ringing and he could not distinguish a word. He now began to fear that the man had gone beyond empty posturing and might well murder him before the police came. He moaned and begged. "Oh, God, please don't kill me, I'm no criminal, I don't mean any harm, I've got a wife and kids, don't kill me, please . . . "

The man's response was to bend over him and press the muzzle of the gun against that bone behind the ear. John's hearing returned, to the degree that he could hear the man say, as if calling to him from a great distance, "The next one takes your head off."

John was desperate. He did not know what he was expected to do to keep his life. He would have complied with any order, but he got none, only one threat after another. The fear was unbearable. He could take no more of it! He lashed out with one of the hands with which he had been clasping his ears. He knocked the gun aside and though expecting to hear it fire at any instant, he rolled over and grasped the barrel, used it to pull himself to his feet, then with a violent effort made it his own.

The larger man proceeded, strangely, to fade away. He seemed intangible. Not that John wanted to touch him, let alone do him harm of any kind, but the man appeared to think otherwise and shrank behind crossed arms while growing shorter owing to a joining of knees, schoolgirl-fashion: he was undergoing a process of physical degeneration through fear.

John might have been more compassionate had their relative situations not been exchanged so recently. "I'm not a criminal," he repeated, for now he could support his claim. He held the gun muzzle to the floor. "If I were, I'd point this at you, wouldn't I? In fact, I'll unload it if you tell me how." John had never owned a gun and did not know one from another, did not like them, and was uneasy near any. "I'm turning the other cheek," he said. "You could have killed me!" His late fright had become anger.

The man was still distracted. He was whimpering incoherently. He had not heard a word John uttered.

"Oh, for Christ's sake!" John shouted. "I'm getting out of here. I'm not going to stay and have you frame me with the local small-town cops. I'm going to get back to my own territory, call my lawyer, and tell my own police department the whole story. I advise you to settle down. I haven't hurt you or damaged anything of yours. If I knew how to unload this gun, I'd leave it here. As it is, for my own safety, I'll take it along and hide it someplace outside. I'll even call back later and tell you where."

He waited a moment for any kind of response from the quivering man, but received none. He went down the stairs as quickly as he could, the firearm held firmly in both hands. When he reached the yard he had to decide quickly which way to flee, for surely the police would be coming by the road, which therefore was out of the question for his use— he could not know from which direction they would arrive. That left the field full of stubble, which could provide no cover, or the woods across the road.

To reach the trees he had to climb a slope that proved steeper than it looked. Despite the possible danger in so doing, he used the gun as a staff. He was weary after half a day of more exercise than he had taken in years. The crest of this ridge could not have been more than twenty feet above the road, yet on gaining it he was so exhausted that had he not heard the distant wail of a siren he might have lost all strength to go farther before resting. As it was, he kept going. This was a place with as much undergrowth—clutching, clinging, tearing—as trees. It scratched his skin, and so as not to tear his clothes, he halted frequently to pluck himself free. In an effort to avoid the densest thickets, he soon lost all sense of direction. After what probably seemed longer than it actually was, he suspected he was wandering in circles. As he might well emerge into the hands of his pursuers, he had nothing to lose and perhaps something to gain by taking the rest he needed so badly.

Also, once he stopped fighting the bushes, perhaps he could hear some orienting sounds from the outside world. He found a clear patch at the base of one of the larger trees and sat down on the earth. It proved to be, just under the thinnest of dry surfaces, a damp seat. For all he cared! He was in terrible trouble. He had nearly been killed by a man to whom he had done nothing but ask for the brief use of a telephone. All right, so he had been erroneously thought a criminal: even so, should such a person be shot point blank when offering no resistance? Then, what might have happened, when he grappled with the man, if the gun had discharged and killed its owner? Could he ever have proved his innocence?

Could he prove it *now,* though he had not touched the man even in the struggle, nor pointed the gun at him? He had been scrupulous in that regard. But the man had demonstrated the characteristics of a bully and a coward, and might find it necessary to misrepresent the situation in the interests of pride.

John felt so alone, so defenseless, that he would have welcomed the company of Richie at the moment, even though Richie was the source of all his troubles—but being so, was uniquely capable of clearing his name, at least in everything up to the moment they had parted ways. John would still be on his own as to the matter of the country gentleman, but he would be much more believable if it could be established that he bore no personal responsibility for being in this area in the first place.

He knew a sudden access of hope, as if lifted on a rising wave: it was by no means too late to set everything right, if he could only manage to get someone in authority not to jump to conclusions but rather listen to his voice of reason. He realized this might be unlikely were he to appear before such an authority looking as he did now. He *must* get home somehow. He had no money or credit cards, and given his appearance would certainly not have done well at hitchhiking—even if he had not been a wanted man for whom the police would be looking on every highway. He did have the gun.

That he could ever consider pointing a firearm at a human being, for any purpose whatever, would have been impossible throughout his life up to this moment. Of course he had played with toy weapons as a kid, shooting rubber-tipped darts at brothers and friends, but had had no difficulty, however young, in distinguishing a game from reality, even though that reality had been purely theoretical: he had never seen a real gun being fired, for in movies and TV though the firearms were genuine, the bullets were not, as everyone, even small children, had always recognized. He had not grown up to be one of those adults who suppose killers get their start by training on water pistols in childhood, or believe that owning a popgun at the age of six created a warmonger who in later life would be eager to nuke the world. Take him: he disliked guns, yet here he was, holding one that he had taken with force from its owner so as to save his own life. So far so good, but he had not discarded it. It was the one thing of value at hand. It looked expensive, like the rest of the gentleman farmer's possessions. Perhaps he could sell the weapon or use it as security for enough money to get home. No, that was wrongheaded: his only hope now was to get back in contact with Joanie and have her come to pick him up. Even if he found the fare, he could not risk using any form of public transportation.

He felt worse the longer he rested. Not only did certain delayed reactions to the struggle for the gun now make themselves known, but his sore knee had returned. The back of his left hand was deeply scratched: had adrenaline served to numb him to damages received in the struggle to control the gun? Or were the scratches due to the thicket through which he had lately plowed? He pulled himself to his feet.

Walking was painful, but he had been strengthened by a resolve to take no more abuse. Although he might have something to explain, he had nothing for which to apologize, and he was determined neither to forget the distinction nor to permit anyone else to do so. In future encounters he must deal with the probability that strangers would think the worst of him because of his appearance alone. If in addition they had heard the same broadcast as the gentleman farmer and would take him for the wanted man, no argument of his was likely to be listened to. And in a rural area like this, he had to face the possibility that other locals would routinely keep guns at hand.

He could not have said how far he walked, having anesthetized himself against time and distance, but eventually he cleared the woods, and there, at the edge of a meadow, on the far side of which some black-and-white cattle were grazing, was a plain clapboard structure that needed a new roof, and beyond it what would seem to be, from the rusty equipment nearby and the dusty, strawy dim reaches of the interior visible through the open and sagging doors, a working barn.

John liked a real barn. As a child he had once visited an upstate farm owned by a man who had been a pal of his father's in the army, and got to sit on the back of a real horse and in a barn had watched a cow being milked. The fresh milk, however, tasted from a dipper plunged into the pail, was disgustingly warm. But it gave him an affectionate feeling to remember that visit.

It was precisely such pretexts for softening that he must guard against now, when he had decided he had no choice, if he expected ever to get out of this morass: he must use not violence—he was no criminal—but force, by which he meant the threat or potential thereof.

When he knocked at the door, prepared to point the gun at whoever responded, his plan was ruined by the appearance of a bright-eyed young boy.

"Season's not open yet," said the boy, speaking through the screen door. He was full of energy and looked about twelve. "If you want to shoot clay pigeons, use the west field." He pointed. "Animals get spooked. Hope you look and see you haven't loaded any deer slugs by mistake. One guy did, last year. They carry further than you think. Came down and hit somebody's pickup driving by. Cracked the windshield."

"I just want to use your phone," John said.

The boy was suddenly more guarded. "Just give me the number. I'll call it for you and give them your message."

"It's not that kind of call."

"Afraid it'll have to be," the boy said levelly.

It occurred to John that the lad was exercising the caution urged by public authorities, TV advisers, et al., on persons who opened the door to strangers. He himself had certainly been unwise, as it turned out, to respond to Richie's knock that morning, though even in retrospect he could not think of an alternative.

"This is some business between me and my wife."

"Sorry," said the lad, starting to close the main door. "That's not good enough."

"Please wait," John cried to the diminishing sliver of boy. "All right, *you* call her."

The door stopped closing. Through the narrow gap that was left, he was asked for the number.

"Okay," said John. "We'll be glad to pay you when she gets here. Tell her I'm stranded—where *are* we, incidentally? Near Meredith? Wherever that is."

"Meredith?" the boy asked derisively. "This is Beckworth."

"Just tell her how to get here."

"By car? I'm not old enough to have my license yet. I don't know much about roads except just between here and the village."

"That's okay," John said, trying to keep the boy calm. "Fine. Just tell her how to get here from the village—that's Beckworth?"

"Naw, the village that's closest is Bolton."

"Bolton?" John asked. "Okay, just tell her that, and then what road to take to get here."

"Does she know where Bolton is? Where's she coming from, anyway?"

"She can find Bolton on a map." Desperation was gaining on him again. Joanie was an excellent driver, better than he in precision techniques such as parking parallel to a curb, but she was hopeless with a map and, uncharacteristically for her sex, had the aversion to asking directions from strangers for which males are traditionally noted. Her explanation was that men might get the wrong idea if so accosted by her.

"Where'd you leave your car?" the boy asked through the slit between door and jamb, which he prudently had not widened. "Want me to call the Triple-A?"

"I didn't come by car."

"No car and yet you've got a twelve-gauge pump gun?"

The non sequitur made John sigh. "Would you mind first making that call to my wife? I'll explain while I'm waiting for her. The gun doesn't belong to me. I don't even know how to unload it."

The boy spoke in a sneering tone. "Then what are you doing with it?"

"I really think I ought to talk to her," John said, turning the weapon to offer it butt-first. "I'll bet living out here you know how to use this. Take it and cover me, if you want, while I make the call. In fact, you keep the gun as a present from me. I'll repay the guy I borrowed it from."

"Know what one of these costs?" the boy asked skeptically. "You don't have that kind of money. You look like some kind of a bum."

It was amazing to John how much the comment hurt him, though it would seem to be the least of his complaints on this day. No doubt it was worse because a minor had made it. "I'm no bum," he said reproachfully. "I'm a respectable man with a wife and children and job, a good position with a fine firm. I have an excellent reputation in my town, which has many well-to-do residents, including some television personages who paid a million or more for their homes: that red-headed woman on the morning news, I don't know if you've seen her? And others. I've just had some bad breaks today, that's all. I'm a good person."

"You don't exactly look it."

John lost his temper. "God damn it, you let me use that telephone!"

The boy slammed the door and loudly latched it.

John tried unsuccessfully to open the screen door, but the hook was fastened. He pounded on its frame. There was no response. He had been stupid to boil over like that. The boy was probably home alone for some reason, maybe recuperating from an illness that kept him from school. So the sick child is threatened by an infamous-looking tramp with a stolen gun. There could now be a list of charges against John for a multitude of crimes he had not committed, some of which had never even occurred. The matter of the truckdriver, however, *was* serious: that could not be forgotten. But not only had he not run the man down, he had called an ambulance on the nearest phone he could reach. He was still utterly clean, if he could just find somebody who would listen to and believe him.

On an impulse, he ran down from the porch and located where the telephone line came in from the roadside pole.

Using the gunbarrel as a lever, he forced the wires to rip away from the porcelain connector. If he was not permitted to phone his wife, he would not suffer the boy to make an unwarranted call to the police. This unfairness simply had to stop. He did not deserve it.

He returned to the porch and propped the weapon against the wall of the house. Face against the door, he cried, "I'm leaving the gun out here. That should show you how you misjudged me. When I get to town, I'll call the phone company. Sorry I had to put yours out of commission. But you should have believed me!"

There was no answer, and John had no means of telling whether the boy had heard him. He could have tried to peer in through one of the windows that gave onto the porch, but refrained from doing so lest he frighten the lad even more. He was considerate even under conditions of extremity.

He had come out of the woods on the left side of the house. He began to leave now on the dirt driveway to its right, and had almost reached the road when an automobile turned in and stopped abruptly before him. For the briefest of instants he took it for some sort of official vehicle, and believed he had the choice of surrender or flight.

But it was Sharon's car, and Richie was behind its wheel. Sharon sat next to him. She looked more alert than when last seen.

Richie pointed at the house and asked, out of the window, "Who's in there?"

John had hoped never to see him again, but the events that had occurred since so changed his feelings that he could put up with the man if it meant getting home.

"Nobody."

Richie emerged from the car. He stretched in a self-indulgent way and smiled at John. "What are you doing here?"

"I might ask you the same, but the hell with it. Let's get out of here."

"We can't go anyplace right now by car. The cops have set up roadblocks down there."

John could not believe it. "Roadblocks? It's some kind of manhunt?" He sighed. "Then we've got no choice. Maybe they're looking for someone else, someone dangerous, and it's not for us at all. But even if it is us they're looking for, we have to turn ourselves in. That burglary, so called, was hardly major, and it must be on record that I phoned for an ambulance, which should help with the truckdriver thing. I'll support your claim that you were saving my life; the tire iron was right there beside him, after all. We can expect trouble, but I don't see why we can't beat the worst of it." To be speaking in this fashion was outlandish for him, and if someone from his old life, preeminently Joanie, had appeared at this moment and said, "You *got* to be kidding," he might have smirked and so conquered the nightmare, gone back inside his house, and, after cleaning up the breakfast dishes, put in the rest of a normal day off.

But he really was here, not there, and Richie had broken away from him before he finished, bounded up on the porch, and snatching up the gun, slid forward the wooden handpiece under the barrel. He deftly caught the red shell that flew out. "Hey," he cried with delight. He proceeded quickly to eject all the shells and then reload them into the weapon.

John reacted too late. Stepping onto the porch, he said, "That belongs to a guy down the hill. He was pointing it at me, and I had to take it away from him. We'll leave it here." He reached for the gun, but Richie swung it away. "Come on, hand it over."

"I'm sorry, John, but I got to keep it. I need the protection. Cops don't fight fair. They'll be all over the place, with machine guns and tear gas. But maybe they won't be able to find us. Let's get that car out of sight."

John could no longer regard Richie as being merely an oddball with whom he felt uncomfortable. Even after the running-down of the truckdriver he had tried to maintain that illusion, for what was the alternative? He now said aloud, but mostly to himself, "All this can't be just because of that hit-and-run."

Richie bounced down one step from the porch, shotgun across his left forearm. John looked around for the optimum route of escape. It would probably be that by which he had come, through the woods. But he had momentarily forgotten the boy inside the house, who would be defenseless if he left, he who had put the phone out of commission.

"Come on, John," Richie said. He shouted at Sharon to drive the car to the barn. They followed on foot as she drove slowly along the bumpy unpaved lane. "I was going to dump her," he said, "but she's got her uses."

"You can't keep this up forever," John said. "The longer you do, the worse it gets. You can't really be thinking of a standoff with the police?"

Sharon stopped at the open barn door. Richie yelled, "Go on in!" To John he said, "Besides, she's harmless. Her brain's like a rotten pear."

Sharon drove the car inside. When they reached it, Richie told her to put it in neutral and stay at the wheel. "Do you mind, John?" he asked. "You're stronger than me. Could you roll it over there?" He pointed to a far corner, the only area not obstructed by partitions or farm equipment in disrepair, including what had once probably been a tractor but was now a rusty relic with two wheels of bare iron.

With an effort, pushing against the frame of the driver's window, John was able to get the car moving. Its weight made the old floorboards groan, but once started, it was easy to keep moving.

John felt guilty about having deserted Sharon earlier. He spoke to her in an undertone. "Are you okay?" She showed no physical damage.

She kept her eyes on where she was steering. "I'm feeling better. He just drove around, looking for you."

"He's no friend of mine!"

"Tell *him* that," she said, tight-lipped. She stopped the car and watched Richie's approach in the rearview mirror. "We can beat him, but *you're* the answer."

John was taken aback by her new energy. He was not quite sure what she meant and could not ask for elucidation, for Richie was at hand, carrying an old tarpaulin he had found. He barked at Sharon as she left the car. "Cover up the automobile!"

John helped her with the heavy oil-soaked canvas. When they were done, it was obvious that a car was concealed underneath it, but Richie said it would be sufficient to delude the cops, if there was no other evidence that the fugitives had come to this farm.

"We'll get inside the house and keep it buttoned up," he said as they walked back. He brought up the rear with the shotgun. Sharon was in front.

John remembered he had to protect the boy. "That's really a dead end. Why not hike out through the woods? They're going to be looking for the car for a while, not for people on foot."

"Much as I like you, John, I realize that what you want to do is get caught. So all your plans are going to have that idea back of them."

This was so rational a statement as to give John at least a small hope that Richie could be talked to. "Okay," he said, "but they're going to find us sooner or later, you must know that, and the longer it takes, the worse it looks, the tougher it will be to make your case, and—"

"I don't have a case, John!" Richie cried, in what sounded like glee. "They have to take me as I come: this is it, like it or not."

They arrived at the back door of the house. John prayed that the boy would have escaped from one end or side of the building, by door or window, while they were at the other, but knew it was an unrealistic hope: like any normal human being, the lad would feel most safe in his own home, whatever the menace, with the possible exception of fire or flood. That's what a home is, beyond its provisions for eating and sleeping: all the fortress most of us will ever require, and John was in trouble only because he had been lured out of his own.

As ordered by Richie, Sharon mounted the one-step platform that constituted the back porch, swung the unlatched screen door aside, turned the unresistant knob, and opened the unlocked door.

John caught himself before blaming the kid. How could a boy be expected to have the mentality of a combat soldier? The young fellow was probably crouched in some closet, shaking with terror. Richie would have broken in anyway. Yet John was chagrined to see that Richie had been more successful than he in gaining entrance to the house. Perhaps it was an odd reflection to have at this moment. But had the boy let him use the phone, none of this would be happening.

The back door opened directly into the kitchen. Richie came in last. He shut the door and threw the bolt. "How about that for negligence? Living way out here on the hill, no near neighbors, and you don't even lock the door. Anybody can walk right in, at any hour of the day or night, take everything you own, and cut your throat while you're asleep." He stared at Sharon. "You think I'm kidding?"

John asked, "You've done that?"

Richie shook his lowered head. "I'd sure like to figure out, before we're done, just what horrible thing I did to you to give you such a low opinion of me. . . ." He raised his face. "I know I've got your gun. I explained it's for self-protection only. I don't go around looking for trouble. I just want to be ready if it comes. You got nothing to worry about, John. I'll get us out of this mess."

Sharon came to life, looking around with a certain enthusiasm. "A kitchen! I'll make coffee."

Neither man responded, but Richie did not attempt to restrain her as she went bustling about, opening cabinets and drawers. John watched her inconspicuously, so that he might see where the carving knives were kept. In his own home kitchen they were conveniently mounted in a slotted chunk of butcher block kept on the countertop: this set of quality German steel had been one of the usable wedding gifts presented to Joanie and himself on the occasion of their wedding, a time of hope not so long before as to be forgotten.

He could not imagine plunging an eight-inch chef's blade into Richie's person, but he might prove capable of presenting such a weapon as a threat. However, he was across the room from Sharon, and in her search she was soon blocking his line of vision.

"They're not going to break in unless they've got some reason to think we're in here," Richie said. "So we'll try laying low." He looked at John. "I want you to give me your word you won't try to signal the cops if they show up."

"What I wish you would do instead of asking for my word is just once listen to what I'm saying."

Richie shrugged. "It seems to me that's what I've been doing all day, John. You've got to admit, if you're being honest, that we wouldn't be where we are if you had let me do the driving back there. I don't like to throw that in your face, believe me. And then not leaving well enough alone, once I took care of that fat bastard for you, instead of busting into that house and getting the cops on our neck. It would really help if you could just stop this negative way of thinking and see that we're a team. If we can't work together, then we don't have a chance."

"I don't have anything in common with you! If you didn't have that gun, I'd—" But common sense put limits on John's anger. It might be dangerous to speak so freely to an armed person who was probably demented. He was not obliged to prove anything. He continued so to assure himself when Sharon suddenly displayed some petulance, stamping her foot and saying "I can't find the coffee!" and Richie, shifting the gun to his left hand, slapped her so hard with his right that she fell back against the sink. John did nothing. He did not even protest.

She should not have provoked the man. She would get herself killed, and even then, what could *he* do? But self-exculpation is like none at all. He found the energy to go help her stand erect, taking her hand. As he did so, she slipped him an object: a knife. A little paring knife, so dull he did not cut himself while identifying it by touch. Surreptitiously, he placed it on the countertop.

"Far be it from me to interrupt this romantic moment," said Richie, behind him, "but remember you're a married man, John. That's what I like about you. Now let's look around this place."

76

He herded them through the adjoining dining room and into the sitting room that looked onto the front yard, the driveway, and the road beyond through two standard-sash windows framed with inner gauze curtains and outer draperies. The couch and a flanking chair had matching slipcovers. A big oval rag rug lay before the fireplace. A staircase was at the far end, just beyond the front door. John could see no evidence of any recent renovation: e.g., cast-iron radiators were still in place.

After peering through the windows, Richie said, "Just keep back. I noticed when we were outside, you can't see much from the yard. If they come up on the porch, though, and look in, there's no place in here to hide. We could go upstairs, but then we couldn't see much ourselves, and I don't know about you, but it drives me crazy to operate blind. I say at the first sign of anybody, we go in the dining room. The windows there are up a little too high to look in from a standing position, and they could get something to stand on, but why do it if there's no other indication anyone's home?"

He addressed these remarks to John, as if they would be received sympathetically. John walked away. He wondered where the boy was hiding. He tried not to condemn himself too bitterly for putting the telephone out of order. Richie was right about one thing: a negative attitude did no good. Instead of incessantly deploring all the mistakes he had made, he should concentrate on not making any more, though of course if such a concern grew too obsessive, it could become still another negation.

Sharon showed no ill effects from Richie's blow. Though she had been silent since, her carriage was spirited, as was the look in her eye. When Richie went to check the lock on the front door, John looked at her. Her response was to pantomime what took him an instant to identify as stabbing. He winced and glanced away.

Richie returned. "Do me a favor, John. Look around and see if you can find a bottle of something."

"Did you drink all that vodka?"

"It was only a pint," Richie said. "I guess it's metabolism: I burn it up in a hurry, don't even feel it." He surveyed the room. "Nice here. Is this like your house, John?"

"Not really. This is a lot neater. We've got two little kids."

"Lucky you," said Richie.

John's basic difficulty was that after being at close quarters with Richie for hours now, he had acquired no sure sense of the man, how far he could be pushed, what were the weaknesses that might be used against him. He tried to speak normally. "I do consider myself fortunate. I love my family. Of course, I could always use a bit more income, but the downturn's sure to phase out, and business will pick up."

"Did you tell me what you do?"

"Real estate." John was trying to avoid exchanging glances with Sharon. Richie's back was to her.

Richie gestured with his index finger. "Listen, I might throw some action your way. I've been thinking of settling down one of these days. Why not now? In a locality where I've got a friend."

John realized uncomfortably that the reference was to himself, but he pretended otherwise. "Friends are nice, and I've got quite a few in my town. I grew up there. But my wife's ready to move away to maybe someplace like this, in the real country."

Richie frowned. "No good. Too isolated." He went into a smile. "Somebody like us might show up. Weren't you going to look for a bottle?"

"Look for yourself. I don't work for you."

78

Richie threw back his head, exposing the cords in his scrawny neck, and groaned. "You're right about that, and I beg your pardon. Here's a matter I've thought about sometimes, John: the things we hate the most when other people do them are faults that resemble our own. Do you agree? Me, I hate bad manners, people who don't show basic courtesy. And there I go, doing just that myself. Will you *please* look around for something to drink?"

John's bluff had effectively been called. He could not properly protest again in view of the apology, though the same objection remained: he was still being asked to serve. Of course, Richie held the gun.

"I'll help," Sharon said brightly and jumped up from the couch.

Richie whirled around as if in danger from an attack, though he had been presenting his back to her for some moments. John, just embarking on the quest for the bottle, was taken unaware and lost an opportunity to jump him, which Sharon had probably intentionally provided. She had so much more energy than he.

She now ignored Richie's menacing posture and went to open the little cabinet used as an end table at the extremity of the couch farther from the fireplace. There was nothing inside but a yellowed newspaper and an empty ceramic vase.

John opened the closet near the front door. On a high shelf stood a box of mothballs. Coats of several lengths hung from the rod, and on the floor below was a pair of green boots in rubber or plastic, in either a woman's or a boy's size. He closed the door.

Richie had taken a seat on the arm of an overstuffed chair from which he could keep an eye out the window. The butt of the gun was on the floor, the barrel between his knees.

Sharon headed for the adjacent dining room.

"Where are you going?" Richie shouted angrily.

"I'm looking for your liquor. I'll try that sideboard."

"Just don't get out of my sight." He asked John, "Do you think maybe when we get out of this you might invite me over sometime? You don't have to go to any trouble."

It now occurred to John that the most effective way of dealing with the man would be to pretend to be his friend and abandon the sporadic antagonism that had, after all, been unsuccessful all day. He had waited so long before coming to this conclusion because he was basically averse to hypocrisy in social relations. In real estate it was another matter. Naturally you presented a property in its best light and tried to divert a customer from asking about apparent flaws and, if questions were asked, gave answers that avoided candor.

He took in more air than he would normally have needed and said, "Well, why not?"

"You mean it?"

John could see that Richie was prepared to be gleeful, and though his intention had been to string him along with a simulation of friendship, he balked at affording him genuine satisfaction. "We're not out of this yet."

Richie's mouth went slack. "You *don't* mean it."

"Of course I do, but frankly I can't think of much of anything at the moment but—"

"All right," Richie cried warningly into the dining room. "Get back in here."

"Wait a minute," Sharon called back. "I think I found some."

She was squatting, in her short tight skirt, at one of the lower compartments of the big old sideboard, a period piece that covered most of its wall.

"Excuse me," Richie said to John. "You were talking about having me over to your house for a meal or something. I tell you, I want to meet your wife. I think I know you fairly well by now, and we've been through some rough times together—which is the only way to know anybody—and I'm just curious about what kind of woman you'd want to connect yourself to on a permanent basis."

For an instant of panic, John saw no means of sustaining his new strategy. Richie's view of their association was unacceptable; he could not permit it to stand. But in the next moment he was able to remember that his previous vocal rejections of alliance had had no effect whatever. Richie's reality was wholly self-created.

John almost bit his tongue, but he actually managed to say, with justice, "She's very sensible. She's better with money than me, for example. She'll look for the best price. I'm too impatient. She has good ideas. She's smart."

Richie was seemingly studying the rag rug. He nodded slowly. "Still, I imagine there are times when you'd like to kill her, right?"

John had not forgotten he was speaking to a special kind of man. "No," he said levelly. "No, I don't, ever. But I would kill anybody who tried to hurt her. But if you mean do we argue from time to time and sometimes get mad enough not to speak to one another for hours, then sure, that happens."

Richie considered the statement briefly, his head at a quizzical-dog angle, but when he spoke it was to call abusively to Sharon, "Get back in here, pig!"

"I thought you hated rudeness."

Richie smiled and said, "But the truth is the truth." Sharon had come back with a bottle in her hand. He gestured at it.

"Sherry," said she.

Richie took the bottle and twisted the cap off. He tilted his head back and drank. Then he leaned forward and spat the mouthful on the rug. He hurled the bottle at the fireplace.

It got only as far as the hearth and broke, releasing a flow of wine that spread to the wood floor.

Again John found it impossible not to protest. "Was that necessary? To damage this house? Nobody here did anything against us."

Richie squinted. "I know what you're thinking. 'Will he do something like that when he comes to my house, if my wife serves him something he doesn't like?' I know regardless of what I said about manners, you suspect I don't have any. Well, that's just something I'll have to prove." He had looked solemn, but now he resumed his smile. "But listen: I just came up with the idea we need to get out of here in one piece. It won't matter how much this place is messed up, spilled drinks or whatever. We're going to torch the dump!" He stared gleefully at John and spun the gun on its butt-end. "Simple as that, create a diversion. By the time the local volunteers get up here, it'll have taken real hold. They'll be occupied for hours, and the cops will have their hands full with traffic, firemen coming in their own cars, rubberneckers, and so on. We can slip out through the woods and down the hill and get out of the area before they're back to thinking about us."

A blackened poker leaned against the outer wall of the fireplace. John was wondering to what point they had to go before he could actually seize the poker and swing it at Richie's head—and this fantasy did not allow for any self-defense on Richie's part, by gun or any other means, being constructed purely for the purposes of judging what damage John was capable of doing to another human being—but he stuck to his resolve to keep calm.

He now even managed to produce a false laugh. "That'll only call attention to us. And bring in more people than ever to clog the roads. We'd hardly be inconspicuous, out here where you can bet everybody knows everyone else."

Richie winked at him. "One minute you're a regular guy, husband and father, and next you're thinking like a bandit, John. This stuff agrees with you!"

Uncomfortable with such praise, John added, "And they'll find the car soon enough."

"So?"

"It's registered in Sharon's name, isn't it?"

"It's not in either of *ours*. We don't have any connection with her."

It was true that discovering Sharon's identity could lead to nothing: they were three strangers who had been brought together by chance. John was momentarily in the grip of an awful conviction that, in Richie's context, he had no effective argument against burning down a house—any more than he had been able to make clear his objection to running a man down with a car. The best thing he could come up with now was, "Look, my business is selling houses, not burning them down!"

"All right, John, if you feel that way. All you ever have to do with me is state your wishes. You don't want to set a fire, you don't have to." Richie yawned, throwing his arms wide. The gun could have been snatched from between his knees at this point had John been close enough, but of course he wasn't, being instead near the poker, which he had already rejected as a weapon, for it could deliver too fearsome a wound. He would do anything he could to get the problem solved without any further hurt to anyone, including Richie. Nothing was more important than avoiding violence.

Richie stood erect, the gunbarrel over his left forearm, the butt in his armpit. "I'm willing to do all the dirty work and take responsibility for it, but it would just be nice if I got a word of commendation once in a while. Let's face it, I could have run off hours ago, leaving you in the lurch. What's keeping me around? Am I making any money?"

John could not help saying, "I really do appreciate what you're doing for me."

He had not gone too far. Richie seemed sheepish. "Well, okay. That's all right." He strolled to the couchside cabinet, bent, and removed the yellowed newspaper. He found a little box of matches on the mantelpiece. John could have kicked himself for overlooking them, for they might have been useful. Richie went to the staircase, where he set fire to the balled sheet of newsprint and threw it onto a step.

During most of this sequence, taking advantage of the distraction, John was looking at Sharon and trying to get across to her, through facial expression alone, that patience and caution were needed.

But looking past him, she now cried out.

He turned and saw the flames, which were only blackening the riser of the step that held the loose ball of blazing paper. The latter was already almost consumed. He felt a sudden triumph over Richie, who was too ignorant of the basic rules of reality to know that you could try all day in vain to burn a house down in that fashion: arsonists always use an inflammable liquid.

Richie suddenly peered up the staircase and raised his gun to the ready. "Come on down here!"

It was the boy. He descended the steps, displaying no fear even though the gun was pointed at him. When he came to the blackened ash, still glowing at points and in more or less the same balled shape in which it had been formed, he stamped it into fragments and asked straightforwardly, "Why are you trying to burn this house down?"

84

"Don't get fresh with me," Richie said. "If I was trying to burn a house down, it would look like that paper."

"Then what *are* you doing?" the boy asked. He had reached the living room, and he saw the smashed bottle and flood of wine.

He had addressed the question to John, who shrugged guiltily and said, "We're just resting here temporarily, if you don't mind, and—"

"Well, I *do* mind," the boy said. "You broke in. You burned the stairs. You're a gang of crooks."

"No," said John. "No, that's not true. If you had let me explain earlier—"

"You cut the phone off," said the boy. He now stared at Sharon.

"Hey, John," Richie said merrily. "You didn't tell me that!"

Sharon smiled at the boy. "Hi, what's your name?"

The boy retained his solemn expression. "Tim."

"Mine is Sharon, Tim. Don't worry about your house. We won't stay long, and I'll clean up that mess if you show me where the mop is."

"You're not going to do anything," Richie told her. "Are you alone here, kid? Don't lie, you'll regret it."

"I'm not lying. My father doesn't live here since last year. My mother works at the school cafeteria, and then she stays on for the accounting class in adult ed."

"Don't you go to school?"

"It's over for today. The bus just left me off before *he* got here." He nodded at John.

"Kid, you're in luck," said Richie. "If you hadn't come downstairs and I had to go look for you, you would have got hurt. Just do what you're told, with no smart-mouth, and you'll be all right."

"We don't have any money," said the boy. "If that's what

you're after. My father didn't leave any behind when he took off."

Richie grimaced. "We don't need to hear your troubles. We just want your house right now. We feel like burning it or throwing wine around, then we'll do it. We'll shoot your cows out there if we feel like it."

"They're not ours," said the boy. "We rent out that field."

"Tim," Sharon said, "come on over here and sit by me. You'll be okay."

Richie smirked at John. "Look who's talking." To the boy, who had not accepted Sharon's invitation, he said, "How'd you like a piece of that, huh? You old enough? You just play with yourself, right?"

"Let him alone," John said, trying to sound indifferent. "He won't cause any trouble. We have to think of how we're going to get out of here."

Richie nodded, but he seemed fascinated by Tim. "I can remember myself at that age. I lived with these foster parents. He caught me playing with myself—"

"Yeah," said John, repelled. "What do we do if the police don't come around? Or if they do, and then go away? Have you figured that out yet? What will we do in the long run? *I* can't keep running. I've got a family to take care of, a job, a life to live."

"Don't worry," said Richie. "I'm always several steps ahead of the situation." He patted the barrel of the gun, with what significance John could not, and should not have wanted to, understand, and then, without a transitional phrase, went back to his reminiscence. "I tried to stick it back in my pants, but he says, 'Hey, let me give you some help with that,' and comes over and—"

"Aw," John interrupted. "There's the boy and Sharon."

Richie barked with laughter. "That's what she does for a

living!" He swung the gun's muzzle toward the crotch of Tim's jeans. "Play your cards right with me, maybe I'll have her do it to you. Would you like that?" Maybe John could have successfully jumped him then, but the instant came and went.

Sharon had not replied to one of Richie's verbal assaults all day. Perhaps it was the boy's presence that caused her to do so now. "No," she said, "I'm not a prostitute. What you're saying is not true."

Richie turned to John as if seeking support. John looked at the rug. "She's a cocktail waitress. They're all for sale."

"That's a lie!" Sharon cried.

"How about it, kid?" Richie asked Tim, and now he poked him in the groin with the muzzle. The boy bent and backed away. Suddenly he uncoiled and made a dash for the dining room. There was an instant in which John could have made his move, hurling himself at the gun, diverting its aim to the floor so that, if the trigger was pressed, no one would have been hurt. But the next moment Richie was out of range.

The man had the reflexes of an animal, and such speed that he caught Tim before the lad got far, yoked him with the gun, marched him back.

Richie leered at John. "This little bastard needs to be taught a lesson. I had respect when I was his age. Somebody bigger and stronger than me, I listened to them." He pushed the boy onto the couch and put the gun to his face. "Get those pants down! I'm going to show you how they did it to me when I was younger than you." Using his left hand, gun in the right, he began to zip down his own fly.

Sharon's eyes appealed to John, but there was nothing he could do at this moment. He felt that anyone who would judge him must realize what a gun could do to human flesh. It would probably be necessary to let Richie begin the act before an effective move could be made against him. This might prove to be the diversion that was so sorely needed. Thus John made no protest now. Instead he turned, as if washing his hands of the matter, and gazed out the window . . . and saw a police car glide soundlessly to a stop on the road in front of the house.

Behind John, Sharon was screaming. He whirled around. She had moved on Richie, who was in the act of thrusting her small body away. John looked out again at the car. The cop was still inside it and had probably not heard the scream. This was the time to jump Richie, who would certainly ambush the policeman if he knew he was coming. But before John had taken the first step, the officer left the vehicle and slammed its door too loudly not to be heard inside the house.

Richie's reaction was instantaneous. "Get in the dining room!" The command applied to them all. Gathering John in, he herded them with gestures of the gun barrel. "Everybody sit down on the floor."

They were lined up between the sideboard and the dining table, in too narrow a space for any to sit next to another. Their captor knelt in the rear. He leaned forward and quietly asked John, who sat just ahead of him, "You looked out. Who is it?"

John decided to embellish the truth. "The police."

"How many? I just heard one door."

"I don't know. I only glanced. *You* look."

"That's the kind of mistake I don't make," Richie whispered. He raised his voice slightly so the others could hear. "I'll blow the back out of anybody who makes a sound."

They could hear the policeman on the wooden porch. He pounded at the same door John had knocked on earlier, and not long thereafter could be heard to walk, boards squeaking, along part of its length, probably peering through the windows into the living room. During this sequence, Richie leaned past John and poked Sharon, next in line, with the long gun, then did the same to Tim. Of course he thereby offered John another opportunity to disarm him, overextended as he had to be to reach the boy. Very little lateral force would have been needed to divert the long barrel. Had Richie pulled the trigger then, the shot would have alerted the officer outside without harming any of the captives.

John decided that what he should do henceforth, rather than brood about his past delinquencies, was to keep himself in a state of mind that made him ready for the next opportunity. But that was a difficult thing to manage, for he was neither an officer of law enforcement nor a combat-trained soldier. He had been thrust into an extreme condition through no fault of his own, and . . . He recognized that he was whining, and felt shame. He was supposed to be a man. How could he have defended his wife and children had this criminal gained entrance to his house? Tormented by the thought, he would now have wrested the gun from Richie, but, as things seem to go with those who live by excuses, he was not offered a second chance of the same kind.

The policeman could be heard to descend the porch steps, surely en route to the rear of the house and then the barn. Would he find the car? If so, the situation would change dramatically. He would radio for reinforcements, and an army would arrive to besiege the house. What Richie might do in such a predicament provided good reason for worry. Mass carnage was not out of the question.

But the next exterior sound was that of the car, starting up and driving away. John was enraged: the policeman had not even taken the trouble to walk around the house, let alone inspect the barn. What a lousy job the cops had done thus far today! They had not come close to catching anybody. He was aware of the irony in which "anybody" included himself, but he refused to surrender to the state of mind, well known to TV journalists, by which hostages begin to identify with their captors. While it was true that when not in Richie's company he had himself disarmed the man who held him for the arrival of the police, his intent had not been criminal. Obviously, his judgment had since been proved wrong. If only he had tolerated the gentleman farmer's threats and waited to be taken into custody, he would at worst have worn handcuffs for a while and endured an hour or so under arrest, perhaps not even behind bars, before Joanie brought a lawyer to spring him.

Richie now stole around the other side of the table and crept into the living room, there cautiously to peep out at the road. He soon rose from the crouch and motioned with his gun.

"Back to the party!"

John was determined not to accept any further molestation of either Tim or Sharon, to intervene regardless of mortal danger, but as it happened, Richie was in another mood now.

"I don't like this. He left too soon. He might be a hick cop, but even so, he'd look around more. He *saw* something." Richie asked John, "Don't you think?"

John shrugged.

"Sure. That's it." Richie gestured at the others. "Come on, we're going to look. If I'm right, he'll be back with World War Three. I can't waste time."

He ordered Sharon to unlock and open the front door, and she did so. John was relieved that the command had not been given to Tim, who wore a more rebellious expression than ever. The aborted rape had not broken his spirit. That was good for his own sense of self, no doubt, but a precipitate move might get him hurt as well as damage the general cause.

Outside, Richie said, "Look around, John. What could he have noticed?"

Could this be a sincere question? Did Richie actually trust him to do as asked and then report truthfully? "He didn't see anything. Everything looked completely normal, so he decided there wasn't any reason to hang around. I imagine they're searching a pretty wide area, if they got up here, and probably don't have that much time and men to spare on wild-goose chases."

Richie was smiling. "Always look on the bright side, don't you? That's why I like you. But that's also why you're at a disadvantage when it comes to the police. You forget they carry guns."

John could not resist saying, "I can't forget *you've* got one. Cops' guns don't worry me."

"That was before this," Richie said smugly. "See what happens next time. All they need is an excuse." He was surveying the facade of the house. "You're right: I can't see anything, either."

He led them on the tour around the building that the policeman had not made. When they were on the front lawn again, Richie stared at the road. "Still, I've got this instinct. I'm always right when it comes to people who want to do me harm: that's the only reason why I'm alive today. I'm a hard one to take by surprise. That's *my* game. I take care to see it's not used against me."

"Who in hell *are* you?" John asked suddenly, surprising himself.

The question seemed to startle Richie, too. He winced, as if having difficulty in finding an answer that would suffice. As he stared into the middle distance, Tim broke away.

Sprinting with the speed of an animal, the boy gained the corner of the house before Richie got the gun to his shoulder.

Richie too was fast, but he had really been taken off guard this time. He dashed to the corner but turned back quickly to shout at the others. "Come on! We'll get him."

So Tim had made a successful escape! John joined Richie, to say with satisfaction, "You'll never catch him now. Nobody can run like a kid!"

Richie snorted. "That might be true if he had headed for the woods. But he's not that smart. He went into the barn. Come on."

"*You're* the dumb one," Sharon said, wobbling along on her high heels. "What about the cop who's coming back with World War Three?"

The remark infuriated Richie but did not divert him from his purpose. "You're going to get yours once and for all, Missy. Just wait."

"Why not now?" asked Sharon. "You yellow-bellied sapsucker."

John held his breath. He knew what Sharon was trying to do, but believed it might be a mistake. Richie made an ugly laugh and said, "You silly whore, you: you actually think you can distract me? You're not going to save that little punk any more than you're going to save yourself. I promise you."

They had reached the barn doors, which looked to be as firmly closed as when they had left them so, but Richie had presumably seen Tim enter the building. He asked John to open the doors.

"What's the problem?"

"They're fastened from inside," John said, putting his weight against the big panels. But they were hinged to swing out, not in. He put his eye to the space between them, but could not see the latch. "Probably something simple, just to keep them from blowing open in bad weather if somebody's working inside." John stepped back. "If I had a piece of wire, I could probably slip it in and lift whatever's there." He did not ask himself why he was being so helpful, but he hoped that Sharon would understand. As long as he kept Richie occupied with details, nobody was being hurt.

But she did not. "Why are you helping him?" she cried. "Can't you see he's going to kill us when he's ready?"

"Okay," Richie said with glee, "then I won't wait!" He raised the gun. She ducked under it and kicked him in the crotch with her pointed toe. He howled in pain and outrage, but still hung on to the weapon.

Sharon was trying to wrap herself around the barrel while avoiding the muzzle. She and Richie wrestled each other to the ground. Though impaired, he remained the stronger.

John watched this in a state of paralysis. He had lost his nerve entirely but had not understood that until this moment. All of it was simply too foreign to his nature. He had been able to struggle with the gentleman farmer only because the man seemed ready to kill him. Apparently he had so exhausted his moral energy. That Richie was likely to murder Sharon after besting her in this fight did not move him. . . . And yet watching himself as though from the perspective of a neutral bystander, he felt a shame so intense it was almost pleasure.

Richie was prying her fingers from the gun barrel, perhaps breaking them one by one in the process. It was an ugly sight. John turned his back on it. He looked down the driveway to the road and saw that he might escape while Sharon kept Richie occupied. Enough of a head start, and it would not be worthwhile for Richie to chase him: he would be halfway down the hill to the roadblock. Meanwhile, Sharon and Tim could hide in the woods.

The fact was, Richie would surely kill her as soon as he regained control of the gun. . . . But he would not harm John in any way; he had made that clear again and again, and in return John had not really resisted him. A fair exchange—and as loathsome a transaction as John had ever made. But one that had thus far ensured his future as husband and father, which was necessarily always his fundamental concern, secure against the claims of personal pride, compassion for strangers, chivalry.

He decided to flee, no matter how it might look. He started to run . . . but could not move his feet. The connection between his will and his body was simply not available. He was not even able to struggle. He just stood there, looking wistfully at the road, and eventually he turned back. The sequence took forever, but once he had returned to reality he was aware that in elapsed time it had lasted no longer than a sigh.

He joined the fight on Sharon's side. In a moment it had become a personal contest between the men. Though conspicuously more robust than Richie, John was no more effectual than Sharon had been. Richie had a strength the source of which could not be rationally accounted for. John's forearms were half again as thick as Richie's. Nor did the wrestling tricks of boyhood, when John was champ of the sandlots and backyards, work against this wily adversary, whose leg you could hook with your own but whose balance could not be shaken despite his having no substantial center of gravity. In fact, it was John who was upset. But he held on as he went down, and pulled Richie with him.

Richie fell on top of him and leered into his face. John

94

believed that the man was enjoying this in a vile way. He averted his eyes and, with a strenuous effort, rolled Richie off him. The gun was still between them, its muzzle invariably directed, at any given time, at some part of his own body. Not only was he unable to wrest the weapon away, he could not even divert its menace.

Where was Sharon? Now *he* could use *her* help, but was too proud to cry out for it. . . . Nor could he believe that this man was beating him. But Richie was a criminal and knew no limits. It was unnatural for John to be in such a fight. How could he expect to win against a man who was ready to kill another human being in cold blood? Sharon suddenly appeared over them, clawing at Richie's eyes with her fingernails. Richie cursed and took evasive action. John rose to his knees and looked for the gun, which he had lost track of in the struggle. Richie was covering most of it. John seized the protruding stock and pulled, but Richie performed a maneuver by which he deftly twisted John's hands from the gun and regained its total control.

At this point John quit the battle. He had not lost absolutely: he had saved Sharon's life for another few moments. Of course, it was gone now, along with his own. He had made a widow and two orphans for nothing better than a sense of male honor that meant little to anyone else. No doubt this was true of many a hero. The events of his last day on earth had served only the cause of cynicism.

Richie's hand was extended, and without thinking John allowed his own to be shaken. "Good try," Richie said, with his trademark grin. His face seemed to have escaped damage. "You gave a good account of yourself. You have nothing to be ashamed of."

When John belatedly realized what he was doing, he retrieved his hand. He continued to gasp for breath.

Richie said, "You've got no stake in this. Go down the hill and find the cops if you want. I won't stop you. But I'll get her and the punk before they arrive. There's no way on earth to stop that. *I don't let anybody make a fool of me.* Maybe you don't understand that, John."

In his own fight John had once again forgotten Sharon. He was suddenly aware now that she had fled. His chest was still heaving: he was not accustomed to such contests. With difficulty he asked, "She got away?"

"Behind the barn. But she's not going to get up the hill without me seeing her."

He was right. Erosion had produced the sheer dirt face of a minor cliff back there. "I'm staying," John said. "You're not going to kill them."

"See? That's why I like you so much, John. You got principles."

"I only wish it were true," John said. He found himself speaking to Richie as if to himself. "Then we wouldn't be here at all. Trouble was, I couldn't make my mind up about you. At first I thought you were just some kind of joker, and then, well, I don't know what I thought after you ran down the truckdriver. I just tried to keep from thinking. Tell me this: how'd you know it would be me who answered when you came to my door this morning?"

Richie guffawed. "What a question! How could I know who lived there? I really was running out of gas."

"You were cruising the neighborhood, looking for victims?" It gave John a chill to think of Joanie and the babies.

"You've still got me wrong, after all this?" Richie asked reproachfully. "You think I'm a burglar or something?" As he spoke, he continued the surveillance he had been maintaining on the barn.

96

"What *are* you? *Who* are you?" John's respiration and heartbeat were not yet back to normal.

"A human being," Richie said. "Keep that in mind. You mean, how do I spend my time? I'm working on a number of ideas right now. I'm trying to get on a solid footing for once."

John pretended to himself, out of desperation, that this was a response on which he could build. "All right," he said. "That sounds good. Then why—"

"I got delayed for a while," Richie went on. "I made some mistakes when I was young, and I admit it. Nothing really bad, you understand, but it took me a while to find my bearings. I'm coming back strong now, though. You don't have to be ashamed of knowing me."

"Well, then, you don't want to jeopardize your future. You're still not in too deep to straighten things out. If you mean you've got some kind of record as a juvenile or young man but the slate has been clean in recent times, then you won't want to mess it up now. Give me the gun. You haven't shot anybody."

Richie cocked his head. "Damn, John, you don't give up, do you? You just shut your eyes and stick to your own version of what's what. I just wish I could oblige you, I really do. But I can't. I'm a marked man."

"What do you mean?"

"It doesn't matter what I do," Richie said. "I can't run forever. I might as well stay and go out fighting."

John's references in this area were all from TV. "You mean, something to do with the mob? Are you on the witness-protection plan or something?"

Richie stared at him. "Do you think *they'd* want to hear my side of it? I know some things I've done don't exactly qualify me for a medal, but not everything everybody does is *always perfect,* is it?"

John was lost. Therefore he returned to an earlier statement. "But you just said you were coming back strong . . . ?"

"I am, I am." Richie nodded vigorously. "I wouldn't kid you about that, because I know you care about me as a friend. *And I don't let friends down.* Remember that, John. I think you are aware by now that I would put my hand in the fire for you: you name it, you've got it. But *they* won't let me get clear."

"I don't understand this," said John. "Who are *they?* And what does 'get clear' mean?"

"The people in charge," said Richie, tossing the heavy gun back and forth between his hands, making John nervous when the muzzle was briefly pointed in his direction. "They're never going to let me get my point across."

"Well, *I* will," John said. "What point are you trying to make?"

Richie gave him an affectionate smirk. "I'm not going to put you in jeopardy, too. Better you don't have more than a vague idea. Then they can't beat it out of you."

"I don't even have that."

"Good!"

"I'll tell you, though," John said, "I can't conceive of any reason why you want to hurt either Sharon or Tim, a woman and a child who haven't done anything against you except try to save their lives. What kind of cause or philosophy would justify what you're doing?"

Richie pursed his thin lips, as if he were about to spit. "I wish I could always be a nice guy, I really do. But I just can't afford to put myself in a position where I can be destroyed."

"They're hardly going to destroy you. They're small and unarmed."

"Ha!" Richie exclaimed. "I beg your pardon. The bitch just tried to claw my eyes out. I don't care who does me dirty—man, woman, or child, they'll pay for it." He winked at John. "And the same guarantee covers my friends."

John thought this an ambiguous statement, which could just as well be menacing as generous, but pointed out, "Even though *you* started it?"

"Listen," said Richie. "Don't think I'm going to accept responsibility for everything that happens in the entire universe. This is a free country."

"I still don't understand."

Richie shrugged. "You know as well as I that lots of people died for our way of life, John. I'm not going to make a mockery of those sacrifices. I know, turn the other cheek. But to me that's a poor example to set for young people. Talk about kids, there you are. Look at this one. He's got no manners, no respect. Who knows how long he was sneaking around upstairs? If I hadn't burned that paper, just to kid you a little, he would have stayed up there, would have had to be dragged out and maybe got himself hurt."

Whenever John thought about Tim, he remembered breaking the telephone line and felt wretched. It was useless to talk of right and wrong with this man. John's purpose now was only to delay the hunting-down of Sharon and the boy, and he thought he might try to do that by agreeing with Richie. "Maybe there's something in what you say, but that's all the more reason for getting away from them. Who needs them? They're only slowing us down. You and I could hike out through the woods, the way I came. There's a guy in a house down there with a car."

Richie's smile was benign. "I know you consider yourself a close friend of mine and that what you do is supposedly with my welfare in mind, even though it might result in me getting hurt or going to jail. If you're honest, you'll admit that. So we go down to get this guy's car and if the cops aren't laying for us, then this guy is."

"By now the cops have surely left his place," John said, with the pretense of being reasonable. "And it's his gun you're holding now. That's the man I mean. He couldn't give us any trouble."

"No!" Richie cried sharply. "It's the principle that's at stake. I couldn't live with myself if I let them get away with this."

Richie went to the side of the barn and rummaged in the weeds there. John's freedom to leave continued to be useless. He stayed where he was and tried to think of what to do next.

Richie emerged with a handful of some kind of rubbish, which he proceeded to put against the base of the barn doors. He struck one of the matches from the book of such that he had taken from the house, and had ignited the material before John recognized that it contained inflammable paper and rags and Richie's purpose was to burn the barn.

John ran there and stamped at the rubbish, which, being damp, produced more smoke than flame. It stank and made his eyes smart. Richie stood by, laughing, and made no move against him. It was the incident of the stairs all over again, and perhaps again was only Richie's idea of a joke. Even so, in such a place fire could get out of control in no time.

It was while they were both so distracted that the policeman managed to steal into close range behind them and shout, at a volume that was probably exaggerated by the suddenness of it, "DROP THE SHOTGUN OR YOU'RE DEAD."

John reacted as though to a gunshot, but Richie remained

frozen in position, still smiling at the smoldering rags. John was sure a gunfight was imminent and he was in danger of being hit in the crossfire, but within the next moment Richie lowered the weapon, reversed it to point the muzzle his own way, and walked calmly toward the cop, in obvious surrender.

"HOLD IT," the officer shouted. "HOLD IT RIGHT THERE. . . . PUT THE WEAPON ON THE GROUND. . . . BACK UP. . . . LAY DOWN FLAT AND TOWARDS ME." He glared ferociously at John. "THAT MEANS YOU, TOO, YOU BASTARD. MOVE!"

"I don't have a gun," said John.

"YOU WON'T HAVE A LIFE, EITHER, IF YOU DON'T MOVE!"

John lowered himself to the prone position. Either his chin must rest in loose dirt and pebbles, or one or the other cheek must do the same. He would have liked to put a hand up as a cushion but was afraid to. He chose to lower the left side of his face. He saw the thick-soled shoes coming. They stopped for a moment while a hand picked up the shotgun. Then, judging from the sounds, the weapon was emptied of its ammunition and hurled aside. The shoes resumed their march toward him and went past. Immediately thereafter his wrists were seized and manacled together in the small of his back.

"ON YOUR FEET."

It could not be done without the use of his hands, roll and jerk and struggle as he might. The policeman cursed at and derided him.

"I'm sorry, Officer," he pleaded. "I can't get any leverage."

The disgusted cop ordered Richie to help. John was astounded to see that Richie wore no handcuffs, though he was the criminal and had been armed.

"All right," said the policeman, a stout young man whose face was purple with excitement. "I got only one set of cuffs, so I won't try to take you in myself. I'm going to radio for backup. Blink an eye while I'm waiting, all I need's an excuse to kill you." His scowl was directed principally at John. He motioned with the outsized pistol he held extended in both hands.

"Would you mind?" Richie asked, as they started the march. "Are you the same one who came by here earlier? How'd you know somebody was here after all?"

The cop was breathing heavily behind them. "I looked through the window and saw the bottle broke by the fireplace, liquor on the floor." He stopped talking to breathe awhile. "But it didn't hit me till I was down the road a ways: out of the ordinary in a house with nobody home. Could of been the cat, of course." He gulped some breath.

"Congratulations," said Richie. "Nice work."

"Shut your damn mouth," said the officer.

"There's a boy in the b—" John said as fast as he could, but before he could get it out he was kicked savagely just below his manacled hands and projected against the police car, which they had now reached.

"*You,*" the cop told Richie. "You stand where I can watch you. I shoot expert on the state range. I'll drop you if you run." To John he said, "I just wish you would resist, you piece of filth, I really do." He reached inside the car and brought out the handpiece of the police radio. Speaking into it, he called himself Swanson and announced his apprehension of both fugitives at the top of Rose Hill Road.

"Got more address?" was the audible though crackling response. "State guys will need it."

"Off County Two-forty A, about a mile north of the traffic circle," said the stout policeman, whose yellow-and-brown shoulder patch identified him as being with the PD of Smith-

102

town, which was probably a township comprising a number of villages.

From what the radio dispatcher said, the state police were involved as well: this was obviously more than the hit-and-run and breaking-and-entering. John had long since suspected that but had lacked the resolve to insist on getting Richie's version, which he would anyway have been disinclined to believe. Now, however, despite the officer's threat, he spoke again, tensing himself for the expected blow.

"Did he die? Is that what this is all about?"

Having lowered the radio mike into the car, the policeman addressed no one in particular. "It's what I said from the start: he'll act mental once he's caught." He was breathing more easily now, though his jaw and the hand that held the pistol looked as whitely tense as ever.

John found the response very cryptic, but he feared asking for an elucidation might further infuriate the officer. He instead made another attempt to speak of Sharon and Tim. "There's a boy in the barn and a young woman somewhere in back of it. They don't have anything to do—"

"*Sure* there is," said the cop.

"Is it okay if I yell to them to come out?"

"You're not going to make no noise at all. You're going to listen." The officer's left hand plucked open his top left pocket and removed a little card. He proceeded to read the statement of "rights" so familiar from crime movies and TV shows. But it had an altogether different resonance under these conditions. John had to accept the fact that he was being arrested unjustly. Having been Richie's victim all day, he was now being victimized by someone officially representing the interests of society. Was there no one to speak for him?

He shouted in the direction of the barn. *"Sharon! Come out! The police are here."*

Incredulously, Swanson asked, "You're yelling when I specifically told you not to?"

"Look," John pleaded. "I'm desperate. I want you to at least hear my side."

He was surprised when Richie spoke up. "He didn't do anything wrong, Officer. He just came along for the ride." It was an eccentric way to put it. Nevertheless, John was grateful.

Swanson's nose and mouth showed revulsion. "What else would *you* say?"

"Please," John said. "Will you please listen? You got completely the wrong idea here. I know you're just doing your job, but believe me . . . " He was well aware of the unlikelihood of Swanson's taking him seriously, and he even forgave the officer for being skeptical. After all, how could Swanson know the truth at this point, with the limited and distorted information available, evidence of which was the handcuffing of himself instead of Richie? But where was Sharon? She could set the policeman straight if only she would come out of hiding.

He shouted to her again, and now Swanson approached him in a hostile manner, holding the gun in an attitude that would suggest a pistol-whipping was imminent. But at that point Richie, who had used the policeman's focus on John to sidle ever closer, forcefully struck Swanson in the temple with the rock he had been concealing in his reversed hand, probably ever since he got up after the search of his prone person.

Swanson fell to his knees. Richie tore the pistol from him and was raising it surely to deliver the coup de grace, but John hurled himself forward and shouted.

"Don't do it! Christ sake, he's a cop!"

Richie shrugged, lowered the pistol, and kicked the officer in the face. Swanson feebly covered his eyes, and Richie slugged him in the back of the head with the gun butt. Perhaps the blow had been hard enough to kill him, but John could not have done much to stop it. At least he had blocked the shot; he had not simply stood there and let events take their course.

Richie took the keys from the fallen officer and freed John from the handcuffs. "Hell," he said, "it's good luck he came back!" He seized the officer's cap and popped it on John's head. "You look a lot like him. Take his coat."

"What?"

The pistol dancing in his hand, Richie said, "We've now got the way out I was looking for." He ran and fetched the shotgun from where Swanson had made him drop it, then returned to the fallen officer, squatted, and took extra cartridges from Swanson's belt. He proceeded roughly to strip the policeman of the jacket, Swanson's unconscious head lolling on a limp neck.

Richie handed the garment to John. "Get into this. We're getting out of here in this car."

John did not oppose the plan, for the simple reason that he was certain Richie would kill the officer if he did so. Also, fleeing from this place would remove the menace from Tim and Sharon.

He received explicit instructions. "Put the jacket on and straighten the cap. You drive. You'll look enough like him to get us through the roadblock."

As John took the driver's seat, the radio began to squawk. The dispatcher wanted more directions for the state troopers.

Richie had seated himself alongside, the shotgun between his knees. He seized the mike and addressed it in a garbled voice, covering and uncovering it in rapid succession with his palm. *"Can't copy,"* said the dispatcher. *"Got a loose connection, or what? Check it out."* Richie hung up and turned down the volume as the dispatcher kept asking.

John backed the police car out to the driveway and swung onto the road. He hoped that Sharon and Tim were watching from places of concealment and would come out when he had gone, tend to Swanson, and realize that what he, John, was doing was done only under duress.

He asked Richie, "You don't really think we can fool Swanson's partners at the roadblock?"

"The block we'll come to first is the state cops—they're the ones who don't know how to find the way up here!" Richie deftly elevated himself, turned, and slithered over the headrest into the rear, taking the shotgun with him. He spoke from the floor. "Goes to show you how dumb they are. Don't slow down when you get there. Step on the gas. Turn on the siren and flasher." He leaned over the seat and pointed. "There."

The siren began to wail, with a different note from that one heard outside and at a distance from a police car. Perhaps the difference was a matter of relative power, though by now John's own role had grown too complex to assess. With the current imposture it might have been farcical were not Richie quite capable of producing wholesale carnage: he now had two lethal weapons at his disposal.

"Drive faster, John!"

"Okay," John said, "but this hill winds a lot. You wouldn't want to go off the road."

"You're the only one worries about that."

He was right. That was what made Richie so difficult to deal with. By his own implication, he had nothing to lose. John was not a stunt driver who could presumably control a car crash so that, say, only the rear half of the vehicle would be smashed. He hoped he survived the day and could get home to explain to Joanie everything he had done or not done and so understand it all himself. This was ultimately more important to him than what the authorities might make of it.

He accelerated, and braked squealingly on the curves, but was sufficiently prudent to reach the bottom without even a close call. Woods lined the road on either side all the way down the hill, but on the level ground there was a development of high ranches that would have been within the price ranges in which he was wont to work. But not a living soul was in evidence, on this temperate afternoon, as he went speeding past with the siren and whirling red light. At such a distance he must look authentic, but it was unreasonable to believe the car could clear the roadblock with impunity. He wore a police jacket over his old work shirt, the collar of which protruded. Anyone glancing into the vehicle from close by could see Richie on the floor in back. It was likely that a gun battle would ensue, with Richie getting in the first shots and perhaps dropping more than one officer. John would be in the line of fire from the others.

"There it is," Richie said, peeping over the seat-back near John's shoulder. It took another few seconds for John to recognize that the vehicles up ahead were not blocking the road so much as constricting it to half a lane. He had expected a complete obstruction and therefore was relieved yet disheartened all the same.

"Floor it!" Richie cried gleefully, lowering himself again. He produced metallic sounds that signified he was readying his arsenal for war.

But what could he do if, just before reaching the road-block, John stood on the brakes, skidded wildly to a stop, hurled the door open, and rolled out? Unfortunately there was an all-too-reasonable answer: he was not skillful enough at the wheel to effect a maneuver of that kind, in a car he had not known for long. He might succeed only in killing himself. It was the habitual bad idea.

John accelerated. The police cars grew larger in his vision. Then, simultaneously, both vehicles pulled to the respective shoulders so that he would have no impediment! He felt he had no power to do otherwise than continue at high speed, and as he passed his supposed colleagues in law enforcement, he did not dare glance at them, let alone signal.

Richie eventually spoke from the rear. "We must have made it by now."

"Three-quarters of a mile back."

Richie rose to his knees. "Slow down and kill the siren and flasher as soon as we get past this next bend."

Going ninety-five with some pedal still left to go, John had become intoxicated by the speed at his command. The cruiser had a more powerful engine than any car he had ever owned, and it was ironically true that under current conditions he was not limited by traffic ordinance. He might have disregarded Richie's instructions—for what authority could a mere passenger have, even one armed with deadly weapons?—had he not been forced by a law of nature to diminish speed as he entered the bend, which was demanding enough to hurl them against a granite embankment if the tires lost adhesion.

"Where to now?"

"I'm thinking," said Richie. "Don't ever worry about that. My mind is always working. I know you have your doubts about me, but at least give me that much credit."

Now that he did not need both hands for the steering wheel, John used one to adjust the police cap. The sweatband felt clammy, reminding him of the cold water he had exuded while approaching and running the roadblock, though consciously he was more frightened now than he had been then.

He addressed Richie in the rearview mirror. "Why don't I just pull over and give you the car and say goodbye? I'll be on foot, so I can't do you any damage."

Richie shook his head. "You're *still* trying to dissociate yourself from me? After all we've been through? I don't want to rub your nose in it, but legally you're an accessory, you know. You're a fugitive."

John nodded. "And impersonating a police officer, wearing his stolen uniform and driving his stolen police car. So what?"

Richie sniffed. "They'll throw the book at you."

"Let me worry about that," said John. "Just let me go."

"When have I ever tried to hold you?" Richie asked. "The fact is, you might not want to think about it, high and mighty as you consider yourself, but we've got a lot in common, you and me, underneath it all. It just might be I'm more honest with myself than you are. I admit I wish I was more like you. I envy your way of life, wife and kids and home and all. But so do you envy me, if you would admit it. Else why did you continue to hang on with me all this while? You had plenty of chances to dispense with my company. Didn't I tell you to go on and leave if you wanted?"

John pulled the car onto a sandy shoulder. He really saw no purpose in trying to make a rational point with the man. "Be that as it may," he said, struggling out of Officer Swanson's jacket, "I'm accepting your kind offer here and now." He left the garment on the front seat and stepped out of the car. They were on a three-lane blacktop road, flanked on either side by undeveloped land. In the distance he could see what looked like a collection of structures, perhaps the beginning of a village. He had no idea where he was now, but judging from the sun, he assumed he faced east. Home was presumably in that direction.

Richie made a serpentine transfer of himself from back to front seat. He saluted John with two fingers to his hairline. "If that's your pleasure," he said. He clapped Swanson's hat onto his head. Why it seemed to fit was a mystery: his skull obviously could not match the circumference of the cop's or of John's own. "Okay, John," he said out the window as the vehicle started rolling. "I'll be waiting at your house." Then he violently kicked the accelerator, and the car sped away.

John felt terror as a physical effect. He was breathing not air but an inflammable gas: his head was afire. He wanted to pursue Richie, imploring him with cries and gestures, but the police car seemed almost instantly to be so far away that its blue and white had already become the gray monochrome of distance, and he was unable to move his brittle legs at a faster pace.

He tried to restrain his mind from attempting a rough calculation of how long it would take Richie to complete the trip compared with his own travel time in reaching the buildings ahead, among which would surely be a phone he could use to alert Joanie, but he was obsessed with the matter. Soon those elements of the state police that were searching for the farm would *have* to find it. A general alert would be sent out regarding the stolen police car. If Richie stayed in it, he would be apprehended long before he could drive all the way back to John's house.

Unless he ditched the car and stole a civilian vehicle.

With an intensity of effort he had hitherto exerted only in bad dreams, John managed to pick up the pace to a kind of hobble, and stimulated his morale with indignation against the public: for no apparent reason, all motorists were boy-

110

cotting this perfectly good road. Had one come along, he was ready to deploy his body so that the car would either have stopped or run him down. But nobody appeared during the endless march, the later phases of which were made even more unhappy by his eventual identification of the buildings as a pair of sheds in decay.

He stumbled onward in the conviction that outbuildings were not normally placed so far from any main structure. Reason did rule, though we might not always be able immediately to understand given examples of reality. But the fact was that these sheds stood by themselves, purposelessly, monuments to the prevailing nonsense of a world in which Richie roamed with impunity.

But then, plodding on, he saw that the road took a sweeping right-hand turn and a short descent, and that not a hundred yards distant was a gas station, and another on the opposite side, and a third within an eighth of a mile. Also two motels and an array of fast-food places. The rational was back in command. A six-lane limited-access motorway roared nearby. He was offered a choice of public telephones. But Richie had been presented with a means of high-speed travel.

John limped as rapidly as he could to the nearest gas station. He was no longer alone in the universe, for all the good that any of these people could do him, but there they were. In this full-service facility, every lane was occupied by a car, and two attendants were on the pumps or cleaning windshields. Inside the open garage a mechanic examined the underparts of a vehicle high on a lift, as its probable owner paced gravely behind him.

John found a phone in its outdoor clamshell and quickly did what was required for a collect call, but as quickly heard the busy signal.

"Operator," he said, "this is a serious emergency. Please break in!"

But that functionary, a male voice, had already left the line. John was forced to repeat the earlier procedure. Now the number rang again and again, until a new and female operator informed him needlessly that it was not being answered.

"How is that possible when a few seconds ago it was busy?"

"They went out," said the operator. "Or to the bathroom. Or it's a wrong number, or was when it was supposedly busy. Want me to try again?"

She was a decent person. "Please," said he.

She did it, and the line was busy once again.

"Please cut in," he said. "This is a terrible emergency. This is not a hoax. Lives are in danger. Get your supervisor, but hurry. Let me give you my name. . . . " He could not stop talking, terrified as he was by the possibility that this sensible woman might doubt his credentials—even while realizing that she had gone away.

After a moment she was back. "No one's speaking on that line, sir. The telephone seems to be off the hook."

For God's sake, Melanie was up to her newfound trick: picking up one of the extensions and dropping it elsewhere than in its cradle. He had begged Joan to be on the constant lookout for such behavior, but no one could be so attentive at all times—hence the childproof caps on medicaments and toxic cleaning materials, annoyances to those without small kids but godsends to the harried contemporary parent, and even so, not perfect: had not a toddler on the next block from the Feltons somehow worried off the fastener of one container and swallowed something or oth— Come on, John, you'll have to do better than babbling! He stared desperately

112

at the pumpside cars. Could he get one of the drivers to believe his story and rush him home? With a gun he might have commandeered a vehicle. There were situations in which force was not only justified but the only means to an end.

Of course he was ignoring the obvious: a call to the police. If it were only that simple! He was a wanted man, and the official mind, even when striving to be well-meaning, tended toward rigidity. Look at Swanson's performance at the farm. He had chosen John as the more dangerous of the fugitives, manacled him with the only set of handcuffs, and refused to let him speak. It was really this mistake that had led to the officer's downfall, maybe even his death, which then could be added to John's other supposed crimes, none of which had any basis in reality but all of which would no doubt be doggedly cherished by the cops until time could be spared for their enlightenment, in a place where his safety could be assured while he was so establishing the truth. At the moment—and who could blame them?—they were like sharks in bloody water.

Even at such an extremity he must call no further attention to himself by breaking the law. He hastened to the mechanic in the garage, who at the moment was lowering the car on the lift.

"Excuse me. This is an emergency. Can I rent a car from you?"

The mechanic's blue-gray pants and shirt looked impeccable, unmarked by grease, but his face was streaked. He failed to acknowledge John, simply continued to stare at the vehicle until its tires met the floor.

"It's an emergency. I've got to rent a car."

At last the mechanic glanced at him. "Look in the phone book if you want." He nodded in the direction of the office.

"No time for that!" But John's urgency had no effect on

the man, who turned coolly on his rubber-soled shoes and went to the rear of the garage, where he rubbed his hands on a blackened rag.

The owner of the automobile at hand had strolled away before John got there and had not come back. He was likely in the men's room. John opened the door, stepped into the car, started the engine, and rapidly backed out of the garage. He had no interest in whether he was being pursued and did not look back. At the ramp leading onto the motorway, he was far too exercised to read the signs and could only hope he chose the right way home. The traffic was too heavy to have allowed him prompt access in his normal state, but he cared nothing for personal safety now and less for that of any stranger, and he forced a savagely grimacing man in a red car to brake and let him enter the procession, which almost immediately thereafter, too late for him to back out, slowed to a bumper-to-bumper crawl.

He had made a bad choice of route. By now rush hour had arrived. Any local road would have been preferable. The only hope was that Richie, too, was frozen in traffic—if indeed he had been as stupid and taken the motorway. This was the worst situation John had been in throughout a day of misfortunes. He had been holding off, for he was mostly an unbeliever who would have considered it unethical to pray only when he was in trouble. But he felt so powerless now as to have returned to early childhood, when the Almighty could be implored with all honesty, and he asked God to give him help in his dire need, for he had exhausted all the measures at his own command. He told himself he could hardly expect to get a favorable response after all these years of neglect, but in fact he lied: he did look for immediate aid, and when it did not come, he was infused with resentment. It should not be possible to get up one morning and guiltlessly meet the day, only to have it claimed by evil so soon thereafter, by now threatening all that he held dear.

The traffic had at least been creeping along until now, but all at once, as if in perverse response to his prayers, it stopped altogether, and not only in his proximate segment but as far as the eye could see, a mile or more, for the roadway ahead went into a gentle incline.

John hurled the door open and leaped out. First he ran in the direction in which the cars in his lanes were pointing, between the files of static vehicles, with an intent eventually to reach a stymied Richie, but after a while he realized that the man had had too good a start on him to be overtaken soon in this fashion—if Richie had even taken the motorway, as to which there was no way of knowing—and cut horizontally through the ranks to the corrugated-steel guardrail, ran down a gritty embankment to a blacktopped local road, and hurled himself with agitated cruciformed arms into the route of the next vehicle that came along, which finally stopped, though until the last moment he believed it would not.

Only after a man in a wide-brimmed felt hat appeared behind an opened door on either side of the car, and each twin pointed a pistol at him, both shouting abusive commands, did he react to the automobile, the rooftop light-rack of which should long since have identified it as a police car.

If the appearance of the state troopers represented the prayed-for intervention in his affairs by the Deity, then quite clearly God despised him.

The troopers handcuffed and searched and arrested him. Again he was read his rights.

"Okay," he cried, "I'm not resisting. But will you just please send somebody to protect my wife and children? An insane criminal is on his way to get them." He shouted the address several times.

At close range the troopers were anything but twins. One was much taller than the other and had red-brown eyebrows that all but joined over his nose.

The other, thickset and swarthy, said, "Do yourself a favor and don't talk like that. You'll be lucky as it is if you're not lynched."

The taller trooper asked, "What'd you do with the weapons?"

"I didn't have any!" John said. "Will you please protect my family? I'll give you all my story, but get on your radio and send somebody to protect my wife and kids." He told them the address again. "I know this guy. He's capable of anything."

"What's your real name?" demanded the dark-complexioned trooper, whose own name, Brocket, was displayed on a tag over the upper-left pocket of his tunic.

"John Felton."

"You got no I.D."

"Everything's at home," said John. "Take me there. I've got to protect my family. I can prove who I am. I've got a wife and two kids, a job with a prestigious—"

"Jesus," said the taller officer, glowering under his sandy eyebrow, "it turns my stomach to hear you talk about yourself like you were a normal human being instead of some sick piece of shit who would try to kill some old lady invalid just for kicks, I guess, wasn't it? She didn't have anything to steal."

They seized John, one on either side of him, marched him to the car, and put him in the rear. Brocket climbed in after him, while the tall trooper, whose name tag he had been too distracted to read, took the driver's seat and immediately thereafter began to speak into the handpiece of the radio.

John continued to shout during this sequence.

116

"If you don't shut up," Brocket said calmly, "I'm going to shoot you."

John tried to impose control on himself. "Just listen. My wife and children are in terrible danger. Please check on them! I've never tried to kill anybody in my life. I've spent most of the day saving other people from being killed by this maniac, or anyway doing everything I could to keep it from happening. You just ask—" In his anxiety, he had forgotten her name. "You found her, didn't you? At the farm? With the young boy? *Save my family!*"

"Don't worry about it," Brocket said. "Now we got you, there won't be any more trouble in this part of the state."

"*I didn't kill anybody!* Or try to. Why would I? I'm not a criminal."

"Come on," Brocket said, as the trooper behind the wheel started the car. "We got you now, and you're not getting away. Might as well come clean. It'll make you feel good, believe me. You cut the throat of that girl who pumped gas this morning. She didn't make it. But the woman at the taxi company is still living. You botched that one, slashing from behind that way. She was able to give a good description. She's in Intensive. She'll live to nail you, buddy. Then there's that business with the tractor-trailer driver. We got witnesses who put you at the scene."

The car was traveling at high speed, and now the trooper in front hit the siren, the sound of which was like a screw penetrating John's cranium.

"None of that is true! All of it was Richie's doing. I didn't even—"

"I'm not talking about this Richie. He was just along for the ride, wasn't he?"

"*Sharon!*" John shouted. "That's her name. Haven't you

found her yet? She can vouch for my story. She was there the whole time."

"Spare me this crap," said Brocket.

"*My family's in danger.* He's heading for my house."

"Let's make a little deal," Brocket said in a seductive undertone. "You just own up to what you did, and on our side we'll call the local force to look in at this home of yours."

"I didn't do anything to own up *to*. You'll learn that if you catch this guy. He's a maniac. But he told Swanson up at the farm, the officer, that I had nothing to do—"

"The town cop whose head you smashed?" Brocket asked. "Yeah, I'm sure he will want to give you a clean bill of health."

The radio was quacking, but John could not understand a syllable. He returned to asking again about Sharon and the boy. "Didn't you find them?"

"How could I?" Brocket said. "We weren't at the farm. We were looking for you."

"You know that Swanson was hurt. By Richie, not me! Why don't you know about Sharon and Tim?"

"John," said Trooper Brocket, "we been trying to put the pieces of the story together. But we don't exactly yet understand just how it was you went on this rampage in the first place. Maybe you got some kind of reasons. It might help if you try to explain, get a head start now, before we take you back to formal interrogation, which I assure you will be an awful long session. Maybe we can cut down some on that, right here and now, just between you and me and, of course, my partner Franklin up there. But he won't bother us, will you, Franklin?"

At the steering wheel, Franklin shook his close-cropped skull and raised a finger but said nothing. He had removed his wide-brimmed hat, as had Brocket, who had dropped his into the front passenger's seat.

John was so relieved to hear that Brocket wanted the whole story that he almost wept. He began, "We were having breakfast—"

"You and Richie?"

Already it was going bad! "No! My wife and myself. Joan, my wife, and the children—actually the kids and I had already had ours. Joan was—"

Brocket interrupted again. "Okay, John, granted. But how do you get from there to killing the female gas-station attendant? Do you even know the poor thing's name? She was nineteen. Kelly Holt."

John lowered and shook his head. "God Almighty. But you see what he can do." He looked up. "I'm not going to say anything more unless you send somebody right now to my house."

Franklin was looking at him in the rearview mirror. "They been trying to call the number, but the line is busy."

"It's off the hook," John shouted. "My little daughter does that. Please *send a car there*."

"Settle down, John," said Brocket. "Let's get back to your story."

"I refuse to say anything more until I know my family is protected from this madman."

"If he's so crazy, John," the trooper asked, "then what did you see in him?"

"He knocked on my door and asked me to give his car a push."

Brocket nodded. "And you just left home and went off with him? He must have had something you wanted. Good-looking guy, is he?"

John decided not to react to these innuendos. "The car started going downhill. My shirt was caught in the door. I had to run and jump—no, wait a minute . . . " That did not make sense, but for an instant he could not remember the precise sequence of events.

"Well, what difference does it make?" asked Brocket, moving his heavy dark jaw as if chewing. "What matters is a witness puts you at the gas station at approximately nine twenty-five."

"Sure," said John. "Richie was out of gas, so I stayed with him in case he needed another push, but he made it to the station all right. I was going to leave and walk back home then, but I hurt my leg jumping into the car, and he insisted on giving me a lift back."

"You couldn't tear yourself away from him?"

"I told you, my leg hurt. Now listen, I'm not going to—"

"All right," Brocket said, "you already mentioned that. They're sending a car."

"Why couldn't you have told me that before?" John asked angrily, though he was relieved as well. "Why do you keep treating me like a criminal, after what I've been through today? I don't have anything against the police. I've always admired the job you people do. Christ Almighty, all day long I'm stuck with this guy, and I didn't even know, I swear to God, that he was committing these crimes you speak of. I mean, I knew he ran down the truckdriver, but he had some kind of excuse for that. I admit I made a mistake in going along with him on that even partially—I mean, I had nothing to do with driving into the guy, who by the way was coming after me with a tire iron for something I didn't do, and—"

"Calm down, John," Brocket said. "We'll get everything in eventually, and we'll be doing it all on video so there can't be any mistake, but right now just stick to the time frame if you can. . . ." He had brought a black notebook from the pocket of his tunic and was scratching in it with a push-button pen.

120

"Okay, but how could I know what he was doing to that girl at the gas station? They went inside the office. I didn't see them. I didn't try to watch them. Why should I? He mentioned later there was some problem with his credit card. I don't know. I wasn't anywhere near the office. I stayed out by the car."

"So when did you make the assault on the woman in the taxi office?"

"Oh, no!" John said. "I didn't touch her in any way. She refused to accept me as a passenger, probably because she didn't like my looks and she absolutely would not take my word that I lived in a perfectly nice part of town. . . . Oh, yeah, that's right: I didn't have any money with me. She wanted the fare in advance."

"So you knifed her in the course of this altercation?"

John tried to breathe deliberately. "I don't carry a knife. I didn't even say anything threatening to her. I was just sad that she wouldn't take my word."

Brocket himself assumed a sad expression. "Thing is, John, there are eyewitnesses to all of this, and the perpetrator's description—the guy at the gas station and later coming out of the taxi office—matches yours real close. And just about the same thing is true with all the other felonies. I should warn you about that, in case you're going to stick to this same story for everything that happened all day long."

"That's nuts! Richie does all these crimes and nobody *sees* him? Just find Sharon, I tell you. She was at the farm. Why hasn't anybody found her? And the young boy, Tim. He can—"

Brocket interrupted. "John, there wasn't any girl there."

"The cops have got to the farm? You've talked to them?"

"We been in touch."

"Sharon was behind the barn when Richie tried to set fire

to it. Maybe she got up the hill and into the woods. Are they at least looking for her?"

The trooper shrugged. "I don't know, John. I'm not there. If she really exists, then she ought to turn up on her own when she hears you been apprehended."

"She exists!" John said. "She'll confirm everything I said. She was another prisoner of Richie's."

"And also a prisoner of yours, isn't that what you mean?" Brocket put up a finger from the hand that held the pen. "Because if she wasn't, then why didn't you get him to let her go?"

"It's complicated," said John. "If you haven't believed anything else I've said, then you probably won't listen to this. Some of the time he was armed and we weren't. During the earlier phases we didn't take him seriously—or anyway *I* didn't. I can see now that she was leery of him from the first. I came to her defense a couple of times, but—"

"But what?" asked Brocket, interrupting again. "Maybe you two ganged up on her?"

"Then at least you believe there is such a person?"

"I didn't say that." Brocket sniffed disdainfully. "That's real dumb, John, to play word games at a time like this."

"But the boy? Tim? Surely the police found him. He was locked in the barn."

"Yeah." Brocket sighed. "They talked to Tim, all right." He sighed again, but in more exasperation than sympathy. "John, I wish I could figure out why you think he'd say anything good about you. It shows disrespect for my intelligence. Here's what Tim says: you appeared at the door armed with a shotgun. You tried first to get him to let you inside with some phony story, and then, when he refused, you tried to make forcible entry, then cut the outside phone line. Then you and the other members of your gang broke in through

122

the back door and attempted to set the house on fire. You held him prisoner, but he escaped and took refuge in the barn, which you were trying to burn down when the town cop showed up."

John wondered how in the world he could ever explain which parts of this account represented the facts, and in what degree. Was he in a position to admit anything at all at this time? He was aware that he had not been obliged to say anything whatever in the absence of a lawyer, but at the outset he had not wished even to consider that the situation would get so far out of hand that he would need an attorney. Having one would imply that his position needed defending. All along he had been telling himself he had done nothing criminal and would therefore have nothing to fear from the police once the truth was known, but speaking with this officer now, he saw he had committed certain acts which, though his motives had been of the highest, were technically breaches of the law that might cause him grief unless he could establish a clear distinction between them and Richie's terrible deeds. Perhaps he did need a lawyer.

He glanced out the window for the first time since entering the car. They were still traveling through country, on the motorway. "How long till we get there?"

"You got no reason to hurry," Brocket said. "If I were you, I'd use this time to get the whole business off my conscience, John."

"There's nothing on my conscience," John said. He became more aggressive than hitherto. "Doesn't it occur to you that a respectable person like myself just doesn't without warning turn into a vicious killer? Don't you people work largely on precedents?"

Brocket smiled, but coldly. "John, let's leave the theorizing to the professors of criminal law. They can afford it.

Franklin and me are on-the-job guys. My last partner stopped a nicely dressed, respectable-looking man for speeding; instead of handing over his license and registration, he pulled a three-fifty-seven magnum and shot Jim Conti through the heart, leaving a fine girl without a husband and two babies without a father. The felon served all of three years for that crime."

"That's awful," John said with sincere emotion. "*I* have never criticized cops, I assure you. I'm grateful for the job you do. What I meant was, you are wasting time with me, when Richie is still out there. If you'll just check with my firm, Tesmir Realty, you'll find out who I am." He gave the address and both phone numbers. "My neighbors, too, can tell you about me. My wife and I are fairly active in community affairs. My wife's uncle, Philip Dixon, ran quite a successful floor-tile business in Eddington until his retirement. He can certainly vouch for me, as for that matter can my other in-laws. Most of them are local, at least in the county. I don't have any nearby folks of my own. My father passed away, and my mother remarried and moved out West."

"Everybody's got a life story, John," said Brocket. "Let me just ask you why in your opinion several eyewitnesses would describe a guy who looked exactly like you as the probable and principal perpetrator of these felonies?"

"That really bothers me," said John. He bit his lip until it felt as though ready to bleed. "All I can come up with is this Richie is so inconspicuous. He's skinny and has a light complexion and wears nondescript clothes. I'm somewhat shorter but a lot heavier—easier to remember, I guess. If you see the two of us together, I suppose you'd remember me because there's more *of* me—especially if you're too far away to notice many individual characteristics. But the taxi-office woman would know! I talked to her, standing right there in front of her."

Brocket picked at his ear. "She can't speak yet, due to her cut throat. But she can write on a tablet, and what she writes is you jumped her from behind. She was talking to a driver on the radio: you came in, reached around, and slashed her throat."

"There you are! She's not an eyewitness, then. She didn't see her attacker."

"But another woman saw you come out of the office," said Brocket. "She voluntarily got in touch with the local force when she heard about the attack, says she saw a guy looking like you come out of that office carrying a knife—or rather, in the act of putting one away."

"That's crazy! I didn't have a knife. I didn't touch her. Wait a minute. Maybe the guy wasn't even Richie! Richie couldn't have been carrying a knife that was big enough. He was wearing a T-shirt and a pair of real tight jeans. Where could he have carried a knife?"

"I don't know about Richie," said Brocket. "But in both the attacks a very thin blade was used, like a razor blade or, more likely, on account of the depth of the wounds, one of those utility knives you can buy at a hardware store. Something like that would fit in a shoe or a sock, and in fact this woman says you bent down and did something with your leg—"

"I hurt my knee!" John cried. "I was probably feeling it, looking at it, you know. For Christ sake."

The car stopped at this point. John had been peripherally aware it had left the motorway, but he was startled now to arrive at a destination.

Brocket slowly put his notebook and pen away, and

reached over into the front seat and retrieved his felt hat. Franklin left the car and opened the door next to Brocket, and the latter slid out. Then he leaned back in and stared into John's face.

"God," John said plaintively. "Are you really taking me to jail?"

"John, John, John . . . ," said the trooper, extending a helpful hand.

RICHIE'S threat to visit John's home was, like a lot of the other stuff he told him, mostly a joke. John was the kind of guy it was fun to kid: he took everything so seriously and wanted so much to do the right thing. A man like that was also very vulnerable, the type that bad people tended to abuse. Richie felt protective toward him and had avenged him on that woman in the taxi office and saved his life from the truckdriver. He was sure that eventually John would come to understand those incidents for what they were, morally admirable, and appreciate that he had a code which was unaffected by the condemnation of others for whom he had only contempt. He did not easily make a friend, but when he did, it was all the way. John, balanced and decent as he was, would not take forever to understand that. Meanwhile, it was probably all to the good that John be given some time alone and suffer a limited amount of privation, be all by himself in a hostile world and recognize that he could not cope with it in the absence of his friend.

Therefore Richie drove only a mile or so farther along the

127

road on which John had left the car and, on reaching the area of motels and gas stations, took the underpass beneath the motorway to the next cross street and there attempted a sweeping U-turn at a sufficiently high speed to ruin the right front tire when it made forceful contact with the far curb. He banged his face on the steering wheel, but what hurt worse was his embarrassment at so poorly estimating the turning circle of the police car. Luckily for them, nobody seemed to be around to witness his accident, for he could not endure being shamed and would have had to deal with those in whose eyes he had been less than proficient, even though he could grant they bore no personal responsibility, but neither did those who perished in hurricanes or epidemics.

He simply abandoned the police car where it was, leaving the officer's cap behind as well as, with reluctance, the shotgun, which could hardly have been concealed on his person. The .38, for that matter, seemed also to pose a problem, but finally he took the folded cap from the right rear pocket of his jeans and, having replaced it with the pistol, snug against his buttock, he jammed the cap behind it so that the flopping bill came over and hid the butt of the weapon. This would do until he made better personal arrangements in general, which could not wait for long, for when he started walking he remembered what he had been distracted from for hours: he had not urinated all day, nor had he eaten anything since the doughnuts.

Among the motels and gas stations along the road near the motorway ramps were fast-food places offering the usual burgers, pizza, and deep-fried chicken, but Richie was not in the mood for any of that garbage. What he really would have liked was meatloaf, say, or thick beef stew, preferably a day old, vegetable soup with big golden-yellow dumplings. The woman at one of his foster homes had fed him well. For that

128

reason, though he stole from her purse, he never struck or cut her. One criticism he would make of current conditions was that it was almost impossible to find edible food in any public place, and a cellmate had once told him the same thing was largely true of Canada and, it went without saying, Mexico, but anybody who would go to the latter deserved anything he got. Richie himself had never been out of the Northeast. In fact, what with the juvenile-detention center, then one prison term soon succeeding the last, and then the eternity he had been at Barnes Psychiatric, he had not been at liberty long enough to travel far.

As to his physical well-being, however, he had led a charmed life: had never really been hurt in prison fights with homemade weapons; had been missed when shot at, sometimes point-blank, by a cop; and once even failed to get hit with double-O buckshot from ten or so feet away. God was preserving him for some purpose. He half believed that, which meant he also, by the same degree, did not believe it. He realized he was inconsistent about much. Sometimes he was not offended by what on another occasion would have made him go crazy. He would not use a blade on a man above the shoulders: he had no idea why not unless it was because male voices were richer. If you cut a woman's throat, you did not have to listen to her whine or screech. He had spared Sharon so long only as a courtesy to John, though all he had had in mind, so long as she remained quiet, was kicking her out of the car at the earliest opportunity. But then why had he not done so during the period when John went off by himself? Because he had *known* they would meet up again soon and did not want to offend him. It was their destiny to be brothers. Intuition was the faculty that most influenced what Richie did, though it might well seem to others that he acted altogether on sudden impulse. In reality he was much deeper.

John was one of the rare people who understood that, hence the addiction to him.

Now that he had lost his immediate transportation, he was in no hurry for a reunion. He was hungry and had to use the toilet. He knew John's home address and might very well go there, but only after meeting some human needs. There was plenty of time for everything: all was in circular flux, so that with patience you could encounter everything coming around again eternally. Because of this truth he never had either worries or regrets, nor could his spirit be broken, no matter how much they tried.

He entered the office of the first motel he came to and registered for a room, using a credit card he had taken from the wallet of the man from whom he had that morning stolen the car at knifepoint. As I.D. he displayed the same guy's driver's license, with the picture that bore very little resemblance to him even after he slicked his hair down, but the motel clerk was no more inclined to question it than the cop had been earlier in the day, in fact did not even look at the photograph as he laboriously copied out the lengthy number inscribed thereon. Such lazy, worthless people were everywhere you looked.

"Could you," Richie asked with his endearing smile, "tell me where I could get a real meal around here? I don't mean that instant junk next door, burger-in-the-box, bucket-of-grease, and so on, but roast beef, mashed potatoes 'n' gravy, chicken in the pot, you know what I mean, I hope. Buttered noodles, baked beans, macaroni 'n' cheese. . . ."

The clerk smiled back. He was a short man, small-eyed, and already balding though no older than Richie. "But you got to go into town to Mahoney's. It's a bar and grill, with the dining room out back." He gave directions.

Richie found his room, only after walking around most

of the motel, in the rearmost segment, which looked onto a narrow strip of parking blacktop and, beyond that, up to the motorway, which would surely roar all night. The TV had no remote, and the bathroom exhaust fan, which came on automatically with the overhead light, made a nerve-racking clatter. Charging what plus tax came to almost eighty dollars was criminal for such accommodations, and he was so indignant that he emptied his bladder not into the toilet but onto the bed. He had had the idea of washing up before going into town for the meal, but now this room was out of the question, and he anyway did not have a razor with which to deal with the stubble he felt on his cheeks.

He went outside. There was only one parked car in sight. At the moment, it was being unloaded by a stocky man in a dark suit. He took a valise from the trunk and brought it to the door of the room two down from Richie's. He had just inserted the key in the lock when Richie reached him.

"Excuse me," Richie said, showing his smile. "I'm very sorry to bother you, but my phone's not working. I was wondering if you'd call the desk for me?"

"Be glad to," said the man, who wore gold-rimmed glasses of a kind Richie thought elegant. "Just let me get inside." He turned the key and pushed the door open. He had picked up the suitcase and taken the first step inside the room when Richie struck him on the crown with the butt of the revolver. The body pitched forward, knees buckling, and fell full-length on the beige carpeting, parallel with the combination dressing table/luggage shelf. There was a soft moan and some writhing. Richie knelt and, after carefully removing the eyeglasses, kept hitting the head until it was an ugly red mess and there was no further movement of the body. He had not had time for tying and gagging, and there was no alternative.

He lifted the suitcase to the bed and opened it. He took

the leather toilet-article kit into the bathroom. The overhead fan here apparently did not work at all, which was a relief after the noise of the one in his own room but another outrageous example of the poor quality of the motel. If they thought he would take that lying down, they could not have been more wrong.

After showering the day's grime off himself, and the blood that had been splashed on him from the sloppy way he had disposed of the guy on the floor, owing to his inhibition against using a knife above the neck on a man (he never got a drop on him when using his box-cutter blade from behind), he shaved with the electric razor, combed his hair in more or less the style of the victim, and put on a pin-striped navy-blue suit, a white shirt, and a striped tie from the suitcase, all of which—except the tie, of course—fitted him loosely, for he was more slender than the man from whom the clothes had been acquired. The jacket was large enough to conceal the pistol in his waistband, as he ascertained in the mirror.

When he put on the gold-rimmed glasses, his face bore a slight resemblance to the photograph on the driver's license. Certainly it was a closer match than he had made with the previous license. Along with the wallet he had taken a set of car keys. He was about to leave when he had an idea. He stripped the body to its underwear, rolled it up in one of the bedspreads, and, having looked out the door and found nobody in sight, got his shoulder under it and, with one big effort, raised its leaden weight. He carried the body to his own, unlocked door. Inside the room, observing the niceties, he dropped it on the other bed than the one he had urinated on. From his pockets he took the twin flasks of aftershave lotion and men's cologne found in the toilet kit and sprinkled their fluids around the room, especially in and around the bed that held the body. He had brought along the matches from the farmhouse. He struck several of them now and started a series of little fires that quickly united into one. He watched the flames until they had taken hold, then left the room and, after dropping the empty bottles into a swing-top trash can in the nearby alcove that also contained a Coke machine, got into the car and drove to town, following the room clerk's directions.

The business section consisted of one block, with the bar & grill about halfway along. He parked at the curb almost directly outside, but when he entered the place he saw that it was full, which suggested that most customers lived near enough to walk. He liked this sort of village. At the end of the street was a war memorial in the middle of a little park inside a traffic loop, and the hardware store next to the bar had the waist-high show windows of yore, framed in dark-green much-painted wood.

A jukebox was playing in the front room of the bar, country music with words that could really move you if you listened. Richie went on into the back room, in which only one table was occupied. He chose a booth against the far wall. A fat girl wearing a gleamingly clean apron came to take his order. Her skin too was unblemished. That was important to Richie if he was going to eat.

He had not opened the menu. "I hope you got pork chops."

"We sure do," the fat waitress said with a simper that he did not much care for, but the prospect of the meal overshadowed all else. "I hope you bread them nice."

"Breaded? Why, I sure think we can. I'll tell him, anyhow. And what you want *with*? Limas, home fries—"

"Lima beans?" Richie asked with enthusiasm. "Absolutely. And mashed potatoes 'n' gravy." This place was living up to the room clerk's recommendation so far. Of course, you couldn't tell how it would taste, and whether the breading might not hide a lot of fat and gristle. He rejected lettuce-and-tomato with Thousand Island and a preprandial cup of coffee, ordering instead a blackberry cordial, which he downed before the waitress left the tableside. He told her to bring a refill.

"Well," she said simperingly, swooping up the empty glass, "that didn't last long."

Richie was annoyed by such comments on the part of people who served him in public, for they were necessarily insincere, but he kept himself under control by reflecting that they were in this case addressed not really to him but rather to the salesman or whatever he appeared to be in the borrowed clothes and eyeglasses. The latter distorted his vision slightly, and the strain caused him to wear a faint frown, but that was probably all to the good so far as his new image went.

The pork chops, when they came, were fine, the breading not too clammy, and he had no fault to find with the lima beans or the mashed potatoes, but the waitress had also brought him a little side dish of creamed corn, something he detested. If she had come back at this point and asked if everything was okay, as they did in some places the last time he had been released from Barnes, he might have pushed her fat face into the dish, and wrung her neck if she screamed, but as it happened she did not return until he had finished eating everything else, and even then did not mention the untouched corn.

He had continued to drink blackberry cordials throughout the meal. Richie never got drunk. If in motion, as earlier in the day when he swallowed the pint of vodka, he felt no effect whatever. But in a comfortable situation such as this one, with no purpose but to feed, alcohol brought out a natural warmth in him. If he settled in a town like this, he would eat here every night, and he would have a dog at home, to whom he could take leftovers from his meal. A nice big friendly sweet animal, golden retriever or setter, not some mean customer you'd have to shoot if he got his teeth in somebody and wouldn't let go. Richie didn't need a guard- or attack-dog: he could protect himself.

The waitress came back from taking the dirty dishes away. "What's your pleasure for dessert?"

"You got a dog?" Richie asked. "A pet, you know."

"Why, no, I don't. I used to have a cat, but that was when I was a lit—"

"I guess there'd be people around here with dogs, wouldn't there? I mean, they'd sell me one?"

"I bet we can find you somebody," the waitress said, bending slightly at the waist, creasing herself. She obviously ate too much of the fare she served; she had no discipline. "You came to town looking for a dog to buy, is that it?"

"Just passing through."

"I can ask Wally if you want. He's the boss. He'll be back in a little while."

"That's all right," Richie said. "You got tapioca pudding?"

"How about cup custard or rice pudding?"

Had the edge not been taken off him by the breaded pork chops and blackberry cordial, he would have been offended by this stupid suggestion that the desserts were inter- changeable.

"Forget it."

"How about coffee?"

He ordered another cordial instead. Caffeine taken after late afternoon would keep him up all night. The fat-assed waitress smiled when she brought him the replenished glass. He hoped she had not got the wrong idea from his question about the dog. He threw down the cordial with one gulp and wiped his lips on the napkin. He took the wallet out and looked through its contents. The driver's license and credit cards were in the name of Randolph J. Pryor. The cash was more than expected: six hundred dollars, most of it in hundred-dollar bills.

The waitress brought the check without asking. Richie liked that. What he did not care for was her comment: "Come back and see us real soon." He certainly did not look, but expected that she had accompanied this with a leer. He approved of efficiency but was repelled by familiarity on the part of strangers. Many had the warped idea that this was courtesy. It was not. He decided to pay in cash, having a supply of it, and he left a gratuity of 50 percent, his way being either to overtip or to leave nothing. When he gave too much, he exited before it was collected, so he did not have to endure the thanks of people so inferior they collected the garbage on the dirty plates of others. When he tipped nothing, however, he always stayed and faced the servitor down, so that he or she would not believe it was an oversight. He got few complaints; they could usually see he meant business. But sometimes—in the city, of course—he had had to retaliate for the negative reaction. People who acted properly had nothing to fear from him.

On the way out he went to the men's room and peed again. That was also his style, to go all day without urinating and then do it more than once within an hour or so. Leaving the toilet, he was bumped into by someone entering. The impact was so violent that it unseated the eyeglasses from his nose. Nevertheless, it was Richie who said, "Hey, sorry!" He would rather take responsibility than appear a victim of a chance occurrence.

The other, drunk, gruntingly accepted the apology and

staggered into the men's room. People who let themselves get into that condition were pathetic.

On reaching the street, he decided to walk down the block and look at the stores, all of which were closed now that the sun was setting. One was some kind of old-fashioned dry-goods shop catering to both sexes, women's nightclothes in one window and blue work shirts and thick socks in the other. Farther on was a plumber's office with a desk in a shallow room in front and then an open door through which could be seen shelves and bins full of pipes and fittings. An emergency number was painted on the plate-glass show window. Richie had taken a plumbing course as a teenager at a juvenile-detention center and on completing it was supposedly qualified to start work as an apprentice, but he remembered little of the trade by now, except what crude but effective weapons could be fashioned from the old metal pipes, now almost entirely replaced by plastic, which was pretty useless for anything except conveying water.

At the end of the block he came to a firehouse, its doors wide open. He remembered hearing, while eating his pork chops, a nearby wail or whine that he now suspected had been a siren. The firemen in a town like this would be volunteers, local householders, married guys, fathers, fine people, a far cry from the police. Cops were the scum of the earth. It turned his stomach to see one even at a distance. Much of his trouble came from the police, starting when he was quite young. A cop could look at a crowd of a thousand people and zero in immediately on *him*. If you thought about it, what kind of person became a policeman? Someone who wanted to deny something to others. Who else would get any reward from that kind of work? They got paid very little, took all kinds of risks, and were out all hours and seldom home with their families. And most of the people they rubbed elbows with were either other cops—the same kind of morally inferior men they themselves were—or criminals. Richie had a low opinion of criminals, and he had known a number of them. In a life like his you met all kinds, but that did not mean you had to approve of everybody.

He walked back to where the car was parked, in front of the bar & grill, and a couple of the barflies came out from inside and stared at the distant sky.

"I can't see nothing," said one of them, and he turned and addressed Richie. "Wife called and says out at Exit Eleven one of the motels is on fire. Know anything about that?"

"No," said Richie. "I just finished eating a meal here."

"Sure you did," said the man with the beer, hoisting it at Richie. "I saw you."

"Out of control, she says," said the first man, peering at the sky. "Heard it on the radio. Think you'd see some smoke if it's as big as they say. But you'll see it all if you're driving out that way."

"I'm not," Richie said. "I'm going in that direction." He pointed.

"West Picket," the man said smugly, nodding.

More people were now emerging from the front door. Richie got into the car and drove slowly along the main street and then into a residential neighborhood, where he increased speed slightly so as not to look as if he were casing the area. The day was in that transitional state from afternoon to evening. Some windows were lighted, some not. He prudently put on his headlights (after he had found the switch, which was located in a different place in every car he had ever driven: there ought to be a law). He did not want to get stopped by the police for such a trivial matter. That was where criminals made their mistake, and why they couldn't win for long: minor matters. In the city they would jump a subway turnstile and get busted for that and then be found to have a list of outstanding warrants on them for felonies. Or out here in the sticks, they'd shoplift a beer or run the only traffic light in town and get nailed by the local law, who'd find an automatic weapon under the seat and a kilo of drugs in the trunk. Richie had been called disturbed and put on lithium, but obviously the people with the real problems were out and roaming around the universe, being unbelievably stupid, causing trouble for good men like John.

Now that the joke about going to John's house was a distant memory, Richie thought about really going there. He had lost contact with John back before he had gone to the motel, he forgot exactly how, but could remember having no bad feeling. And he had not worried about losing touch with him completely, because he did know where he lived. Of course, he would not want to go to John's house at dinnertime and upset the wife, who might have a certain prejudice about him to begin with, the way that redheaded little whore with the car did: right away, on sight. A certain kind of female hated his guts after one look. Others, like the fat waitress, could get the hots for him with very little encouragement. Which was scarcely better. He detested immorality. He hoped he would be allowed to make that clear to John's wife when he met her, because as yet John seemed to have the wrong idea about him. Richie was willing to admit that some of this was his own fault: he probably pulled John's leg too much, but it was fun to kid him. You always got a reaction, and that was something Richie was always on the lookout for. So many people walked around half dead. For them life was a complete waste. If they were awakened from their stupor, they tended to be rude. John, on the other hand, stood for something, had something to defend, was a real man.

A bouncing red ball followed by a little dog suddenly appeared in the street. Had he been driving any faster, he would most assuredly have killed the animal. As it was, he stood on the brakes and just missed the dog, which continued on its heedless way to the opposite gutter, where it snatched up the ball with its teeth.

Richie saw a small girl on the nearby sidewalk. He beckoned to her to come to the passenger's window.

"You ought to watch for cars," he said. "Your pet could have gotten hurt, and you wouldn't like that, would you?"

Close up, her face was somewhat blurry when seen through his borrowed glasses. "No," said she. "I'm sorry." A few strands of dead grass clung to her dark hair. She was probably a tomboy and had been rolling around with the dog.

"You oughtn't be outside anyway, now it's getting dark," Richie told her. "Pick up your doggie and show him to me." She proceeded to bend down and do so. The animal, some kind of poodle mix, was still holding the ball in its mouth. Richie slid across the seat to where he could reach out the window and rub the dog's black nose. "Good boy," he said, and then to the girl, "You take him in now."

"I will." She turned and went toward a nice-looking house with a porch from the ceiling of which hung, on chains, an old-fashioned swing. Earlier in the year, in the heart of real summer, the people inside probably came out and sat in the swing in the evening, maybe with glasses of lemonade. Richie had had no personal experience of that, but knew it well from TV commercials: some kindly old gramps, accompanied by a freckle-faced kid like this one and a dog. Nicest kind of setup imaginable. He grew angry as he thought about the many things that had degenerated from the olden, golden times, and drove out of this neighborhood at a much faster speed than he had heretofore used, for now that he had saved the dog's life, he knew he had acquired immunity for a while against all troubles. That's how it worked. You paid your way or had to answer for it. John would agree with that.

The darkness was coming quickly now, and even with the headlights switched on he saw too little at night in the country and thus tended to fall into a state of dispiritedness. If it was bad now, think of what it would be in the middle of winter, say a late January evening, dark since late afternoon, the chill penetrating to the bowels, the cold air painful from nose to lungs, no people at large, all inside in warm, lighted houses from which you were excluded, you all by yourself, in permanent exile, uncared-for; they encircled, insulated by loved ones. Could he be blamed for being hurt by the flagrant injustice of it?

Now that the effects of his meal were diminishing, Richie began to have negative thoughts. While other people might take him for the most decisive of men, he was not always as confident as he seemed. He knew he was basically always right, but he was not without second thoughts as to the best means to the desired ends. He was often too soft; he realized that. He should not have allowed himself to be talked out of shooting the cop outside the barn. No good could come of it. In future he should not allow John to bully him morally and cause him to compromise on principles. It was impossible for a policeman to be other than an enemy, and there could be no sense in not mercilessly exploiting any advantage you had over someone who never missed an opportunity to do you dirty when fortune ran the opposite way.

As he drove through the night, on the dead-black back roads on which the only light came from his headlamps, Richie decided that with the first police car he subsequently encountered (which would probably not happen until he reached the next town, unless he got lucky), he would pretend to be lost and would ask for directions, and when the cop started to speak, would shoot him point-blank in the face. It was essential that the man see it coming, if only for a split second. *Blam!* In his last instant of life, he knows he has been suckered, has done a lousy job, couldn't even protect himself, dies in disgrace, not honor. Brave men should piss on his grave. It took no courage to bully people when you wore a gun and a club and handcuffs and were part of a big nationwide army, paid to interfere with anybody you decided to bother. What took bravery was Richie's way of life: standing alone against all comers, never giving an inch—except of course for friendship, and then being ready to go all out.

He was pleased when he at last came to an interesting road that held more promise of life. Looking down it, he could see, within half a mile, an area of light and movement. Having driven there, he pulled into the parking lot of a medium-sized shopping center with discount pharmacy, liquor store, supermarket, women's-wear, and others, all open but none crowded at this hour. Though he did not need money at the moment and had better things to do, he amused himself by quickly assessing some of these stores as to their vulnerability to robbery. Supermarkets had more and more people to maintain surveillance from high offices, either eyeballing or with monitor TVs, and some liquor-store managers kept guns beneath the registers. He would not have feared a toe-to-toe gunfight but hated the thought of being blindsided while he turned to another customer. The paint store might be easy to knock over, but who could say how good a day they had had, how much was in the till? The discount drugstore might offer better possibilities. There was sure to be a woman at the register. The prescription department was usually too far in the rear for the pharmacist, who was always busy anyway, to see clearly up front.

Richie looked hard for a police car, for cops always spent a lot of time around shopping centers, on the take, naturally, but before he could spot one he saw a lighted telephone booth at an outside corner of the supermarket, and he went there and asked Information (now called by another name by an annoyingly perky female voice) for the number of John Felton, giving the address he had maintained in his flawless memory.

He used the telephone credit card from Randolph J. Pryor's wallet. The first ring was answered by a woman with a voice in complete contrast to that of the operator. It was ladylike even when suggesting some anxiety.

"I hope I'm not bothering you at mealtime," he said, "but I have business with John."

"I'm sorry," said she. "I just don't know where he is. He's been out all day. I'm worried."

"Don't be!" said Richie. "He's fine. He spent the day with me. I just bought a real nice house from him. He stands to make a sizable commission."

"Oh, God. I was mad at first. Then when hours went by without hearing, I got worried. I was even going to watch the TV news to see if there had been a big accident, but wouldn't you know, our set chose that moment to stop working—and the batteries in the little radio were dead." She chuckled. "But this is great."

She had whined too much: Richie did not like that. Nevertheless, he laughed grandly. "Well, ma'am, he was in good hands with me. I'm a business executive, being transferred up here from down South."

"Oh, that's terrific." No doubt her excessive emotion was

due to the relief with which he was able to provide her. "I was really worried. He called a couple of times early on, and talked sort of crazy, which isn't like him, and it made me mad at first."

"I'm sure he was just joking," Richie said. "He wanted it to be a surprise, and I'm sorry now if I blew the whole thing. I just wasn't thinking." He cleared his throat for effect. "This is a pretty good-size sale. John was real excited."

"Must have been," said the woman. "He doesn't ordinarily joke very much. But he hasn't made a sale in a while. We can really use the money."

"Speaking of money," Richie cried, "that's just why I'm calling, uh, Mrs. Felton—you *are* Mrs. Felton?"

"Please call me Joan."

"Fact is, I guess John was so excited he forgot to take the deposit check. I discovered I still had it after leaving. I sure would like to get it to him so there's no possibility of somebody else buying the place behind my back. I called his office, but it's closed by now."

"Are you nearby?"

"Maybe halfway between there and Hillsdale."

"So he *was* out there," said Joan. "Funny, I never knew Tesmir to list properties so far out. . . . If you could give me an address where John can pick up the check—he should be home soon."

"I'm heading for the city."

"Well, would you mind dropping it off here? It's on the way. But I'm awfully sorry to put you to the trouble."

"No problem," said Richie. "I assure you." He pretended to need the address.

"John might beat you home. Who shall I say . . . ?"

"Pryor," said Richie. "Randolph J. Pryor."

"You turn at the second light on High. That's Bacon, and you—"

Richie politely interrupted. "Thank you, ma'am. I'll try to find it."

"Mr. Pryor," Joan said, "if you were trying to get this number earlier and it was busy, my three-year-old had the phone off the hook. She does that. I'm sorry if it happened."

"Think nothing of it," Richie said and hung up before he got too suspicious about why she was always apologizing. He liked women to be modest, but there was something wrong with demanding forgiveness for damages that had not been done, and he wanted to preserve the elation evoked by the new idea, which was so intense as to make him forget what the previous plan had been, recalling it only vaguely as, en route to the exit, he passed a parked police car, the driver of which was drinking from a cup and took no apparent notice of him.

THE nightmare, or at least the worst phases of it, had begun to come to an end, and much more quickly than it had developed. First there was a jurisdictional dispute among the various police forces, and though John was "booked" at the state-police substation, he was soon taken, still manacled, to his own town, actually a medium-sized city, for arraignment, and his pleasure in going home, or anyway closer than he had been to home all day, was, once he began to recognize landmarks outside the windows of the car, almost immediately soured by the humiliation of returning in handcuffs. Suppose someone he knew saw him? He had watched with scorn the captured criminals who hid their faces from television news cameras as they were herded toward jail, but now was grateful for their example.

"Could you please handcuff me in front?" he asked Brocket. "Or to yourself? I think I have a right to cover my face."

"I can see why you would be ashamed," Brocket said, ignoring the request.

But things suddenly began to go John's way when they reached city hall, one wing of which was occupied by police headquarters. Beneath the building was a parking garage for official cars. Trooper Franklin, still at the wheel, drove down the ramp and into a far corner of the underground enclosure. There was no need for John to hide his face: only some local officers were in attendance.

In the elevator, which traveled only one story but so slowly that the trip seemed eternal under the prevailing conditions, one of the local cops murmured something into Brocket's ear.

"Huh?" Brocket asked in apparent disbelief, shaking his large head, turning to glance back, raising his brow, at Franklin. He was clutching John's right elbow. John was still handcuffed at the small of his back.

Nothing further was said by anyone until the delegation, which attracted stares from a few corridor passersby (none of them reporters), went inside a large corner office and faced an incongruously frail-looking man wearing a gold-buttoned blue uniform and a white shirt the collar of which was slightly too large for his neck.

"Hi, John," said he, putting out his hand. "I'm Chief of Police Marcovici." He scowled at Brocket. "Take those cuffs off."

"Chief, he's our prisoner."

Marcovici's scowl grew darker. "That's going to quickly change, Officer! This man should not have been collared in the first place. He's been well vouched for. The lady came in who was a fellow captive. She not only cleared him of any possible suspicion, but she says he's a hero, for God's sake. The fugitive we want has been identified as Richard Harold Maranville. He was just released from Barnes Psychiatric, first thing this morning. He's got a sheet it takes all day to read."

148

Brocket was shaking his big head. "What about all the so-called eyeballs?"

"I don't know how long you been in law enforcement," said the chief, "but if it's half as long as me, you know how questionable all witnesses are, I'd say especially those people who claim to have seen the whole thing, whatever that might be, if only a fender-bender."

Brocket shrugged and admitted the truth of that sentiment. He unlocked John's cuffs. "What were we supposed to do?" he asked the chief. "We got the call."

The chief put his hand out again to John but spoke to Brocket. "I'm a good friend of your superintendent. We'll do this informally. I'm going to tell him you and your partner did a fine job."

"Appreciate it. I'm Brocket. My partner's Franklin."

"You owe me one," the chief said amiably, then to John, shaking his somewhat benumbed hand, "We're real sorry about this. The young lady's right down the hall, and they brought the boy in, too. He's settled down now and says you're okay. He got you wrong at first, he says. Also the fine ladies at your place of business gave you a report that should make you feel good; they think the world of you. Mrs. Marcovici, my wife, knows Tess Masterson from the businesswomen's association." He grasped John's shoulder. "We're all proud of you, John. You're one of our own. Now, if you don't mind going down the hall and giving my men all the information you can on this Maranville." He took his hand away. "You deserve a lot of credit for doing what you did with him. He's got one of the worst records I've ever seen. In and out of one penal facility or another since he was a teenager. Lately he's been working one of those fake deals at Barnes: 'antisocial behavior due to an explosive personality disorder.' They treat them with drugs for a while and let them out as cured. You see what happens. Maranville's a lot worse than when he went in. In the past he's assaulted a lot of people and pulled a lot of robberies, usually getting very little money but hurting as many people as he can, but he's never committed a homicide until today. Not for want of trying, though. He's cut people real bad, and once he beat a man with a baseball bat, so savagely the victim's brain-impaired. He's the kind who should be burned, but no: we'll go all through this again in a few years when they let him go still another time."

"Excuse me, Chief," said Trooper Brocket, "we're gonna need some paper on the transfer."

Marcovici said nothing but with a finger directed the trooper to one of the uniformed men who stood in wait.

Brocket spoke at John's side. "No hard feelings. It's the job."

John felt light-headed. He nodded at the trooper, whom he could see clearly in the physical sense but who seemed morally a blur.

"Now, if you don't mind going down the hall with this officer," Marcovici said, pointing at another man in uniform, "we can—"

"My family!" John said. "Richie was heading for my home. Have you checked on my family?"

"Let me just get the latest on that," said the chief, reaching for the phone on his desk and stabbing at one of the buttons on its panel.

"He was driving a Smithtown police car," John said.

Marcovici winced and waved, and spoke into the telephone. John had now emerged fully from his momentary stupor and was exercised once more.

The chief said rapidly, "Okay, okay, get going! The man

is justifiably concerned." He hung up. "Seems they've been trying to phone for quite a while, but the line's been busy, and—"

"Oh, for Christ's sake," John shouted, "what good are you people, anyway? You don't send a car there, when some maniac is roaming the streets?"

"Now, take it easy, John," Marcovici said, waving a pencil. "Let me set your mind at rest on one matter. The Smithtown car was found abandoned, just off the motorway at the Costerton exit. That's a good thirty miles from here, and there haven't been any reports of car thefts out that way." The chief smiled. "Anyway, one of our cars is probably at your home by now. You live right near DeForest Park, I understand. Nice area. Your people will be okay, I guarantee. How many children do you have?"

"Two," John said impatiently. "Look, can't I go right there first and see them, then come back here?"

"We really have to nail this thing down," Chief Marcovici said, coming to him and taking his elbow, though with a lighter touch than Brocket's. "If you don't mind, John. I know how bad your day has been, but—" With his free hand he was signaling to the remaining uniformed officers.

These men surrounded John as if he were still a prisoner and inexorably escorted him out the door and along a corridor to a roomful of shirt-sleeved men, some uniformed, some not. In a far corner was a partitioned enclosure, with a door paned in frosted glass. It was closed and bore no identification.

One of his escorts opened the door, and John saw Sharon and Tim for the first time since the episode at the barn. Sharon took him unaware with a cry of delight and a hug that was quite forceful for a woman of her size.

She thrust herself at arm's length, holding onto his arms. "It's so great to see you, John! God, it's great!" Then she hugged him again.

John lost some of the fear that had obsessed him. These two were also a family of his, and he was deeply moved by Sharon's obviously sincere affection.

"I'm glad to see you, Sharon. I feared the worst." He felt a sudden access of guilt. "I'm sorry I couldn't do better."

"What is *that* supposed to mean?" she asked with mock severity. "Isn't saving our lives enough for you?"

"I don't know." He shook his head regretfully. "I wish—" He continued to touch her but extended his free right hand to Tim, and the boy rose from his chair and diffidently shook it.

"We're all okay now!" Sharon said with a rush of feeling, and she began to sob. John took her in his arms again and kissed her forehead and her cheek just before the tears reached it.

"I wish I could say I was as brave as either one of you," he said. "I made too many mistakes."

"Mr. Felton," a male voice said impatiently, "I'm Detective Lang." He wore a brushy mustache and was seated at the table in the middle of the room. A gold shield hung on a tab from the upper pocket of his tweed sports jacket. A tape recorder sat near his forearm. "Would you like to sit down, so we can get the whole story of what happened today?" As John approached the table, Lang stood up and shook his hand.

"Look," said John, "I can tell you later. First I want to check on my wife and children. They've been home alone all day, and nobody's reached them yet." He had no intention of being further obstructed by the police, and started for the door.

152

But behind him Lang, still standing, said, "John, please! As soon as our car gets to your house and finds everything okay, they'll call in. Please, we *got* to get this bad guy, and you can really help."

This was the effective note to strike, all right. Now that Sharon was praising him for his nonexistent heroism, John believed more than ever that he had been disgustingly inadequate in dealing with Richie. He came back to the table and sat down in the chair that Sharon and Tim had left vacant between them. Sharon was dabbing at her eyes with a tissue.

He turned to the boy. "You realize now, I guess, that I wasn't Richie's willing partner. But it was dumb of me to break that phone line. I don't know why I did that. I wasn't thinking, and it was stupid. I want you to know I'll pay for the damage."

Tim consoled him. "You had a lot on your mind at the time. You were under a lot of pressure. Sharon told me what you guys had to go through all day."

John asked Sharon, "Are you all right? I never got a chance to talk to you alone after we drove out of town. You seemed out of it for a while, but then you really snapped back." Having said as much, he wondered whether he should have: Richie had claimed she was on drugs.

It turned out Richie had been right, for the wrong reasons. "I've got a condition I take medication for." She smiled brightly, through smeared eye makeup. "It's not life-threatening, just a pain in the neck, but it kicked up there."

"*You* knew from the first what he was," John said. "That's what gets me. I didn't have a clue. If I had, just think, maybe I could have saved that poor girl at the gas station."

Sharon clasped his hand on the table. "And maybe not, too, John. He had a knife, didn't he?"

John shook his lowered head. "I guess. I didn't see it. But

he never threatened me, never raised a hand against me all day. You saw that. He got this idea I was his friend. I probably could have done a lot more than I did, using that against him. But I didn't!"

"John," said Detective Lang. "Can we get this going in a more structured way? How did you meet this Maranville in the first place, and then try to remember as many details as you can about everything that happened afterwards." Lang nodded at Tim and then at Sharon. "And you two can jump in at the right point if you remember something on your own. I got your original statements, but John might mention something that will trigger your own memory, either one of you."

John turned his hand so that he was clasping Sharon's. "Christ, how could I know he would go into the taxi office and attack that woman!"

"How *could* you know?" Sharon asked. "Nobody's blaming you, John. So just stop this stuff! Think of what you did for Tim and me."

"John," said Lang.

"I think you two saved yourselves," John said, "in spite of me. That's what I think."

"John," asked the detective, dancing his fingers above the tape-recorder buttons. "If you would, please?" He spoke toward the machine, identifying himself, John, Sharon, and Tim. "Now, John, when did you first encounter Richard Harold Maranville today, and did you know him prior to today?"

John stirred in his chair, taking his hand from Sharon's. "There's been enough time now for your people to get to my house and report! Why don't I hear anything?"

Lang touched the side of the machine. "I'm sure we will any minute now. We're giving it priority. Maybe the officer was delayed getting there." He gazed blandly at John's stare

154

but in the next instant turned off the tape recorder and stood up. "Let me go check for you. I know you're concerned." He carefully closed the glass door on his departure.

"The least he can do," Sharon said indignantly. "You know, you can sue them for false arrest, and I guess he knows that."

"It was the state troopers who did it," John said. "They had no choice, I suppose. Hell, several people said it was *me* who committed the crimes." He immediately regretted having made the statement: Tim was probably one of those witnesses. He turned to the lad. "I don't mean you. You had good reason."

Tim had been looking bored, but he now displayed a grin. "Dumbest thing I did was not go out and grab the twelve-gauge when you left it on the porch. Then I coulda shot Richie when he showed up."

"I'll bet you would have done it, too." John was sincere. "Living out in the country, you probably know about guns." Beyond that, the boy had proved to be resolute.

"There's not a whole lot to know about them," said Tim. "You just point them at what you want to hit and blast away." He lost his grin and said soberly, "Well, there *is* something to learn. My dad taught me what I know. But when he left, he took all his guns with him."

"I was wondering," John asked, "If maybe I bought a gun and took it out there, you might give me lessons? I'd be willing to pay you."

Tim was enthusiastic. "You don't have to pay me. We could shoot skeet if you'd bring a trap and the clay pigeons. Bird season hasn't opened yet."

John remembered the boy's age. "If it's okay with your mother."

"Do you know," said Sharon, "he refused to say anything to the police unless they promised not to tell his mother until after she got out of class?"

Tim explained. "She's studying accounting at night school. It's tough enough as it is: she's pretty old to have to go back to school. I left a note if I don't get back by the time she comes home."

"That will only worry her more," Sharon chided. "Can't you see that?"

John played the father's mediating role. "Maybe he'll get back in time." He smiled at Tim. "If not—" But Lang returned at that moment.

The detective appeared to be smiling under his brushy mustache. "John, you'll be happy to know everybody's okay at your house. The patrolman went to the door and talked to your wife. She and the kids are just fine."

John expelled his breath and squeezed Sharon's hand.

"Furthermore," Lang added, briskly reclaiming his chair, "it might settle your mind to know we're keeping an unmarked car in the neighborhood until Maranville is apprehended. We don't think he'll head there, but in view of what he told you, we're taking no chances. Now, when we're finished here, we'll give you a lift home."

"All right," said John. "Let's get this over with as soon as possible. My wife's been alone all day. I haven't even been able to reach her by phone for hours."

"You'll be glad to hear somebody's with her there now," Lang said smugly. "A business associate."

"Oh, that's nice. Did you get the name?"

"Patrolman didn't pass that on," said Lang, manipulating his machine.

Could it be Tess, or Miriam? Nice of them. Until Chief Marcovici's reference to those "fine ladies," John had not

156

been aware of their alleged high opinion of him. He had not made a sale in several months, and Miriam, who handled the money, had recently not been eager to advance him more funds. She liked him better than Tess did. Tess was the married partner. Miriam had been divorced many years before. In his opinion she was more attractive in personality than Tess. John was the only man currently working with Tesmir. He had no special feeling about female as opposed to male bosses, unless it would be that he preferred the former. He had always got on better with his mother than with his father. His father had worked on straight salary for almost thirty years in the payroll department of Bickford Industries before dying suddenly of a heart attack. John had never come close to satisfying him. He had not made the football team in college, nor studied law or medicine, nor even finished school.

When he got out of this thing that had consumed his entire day and called into question, in the most basic way, what he was or was not, John determined to get hold of himself and take a hard look at which opportunities might be available to him. He was still young. It was not out of the question that he go back to school and get whatever credits separated him from a degree. Should not be too many; he had put in three years, more or less. Probably have to do it nights, which would take longer than full-time, but so what? Meanwhile, maybe the real-estate market would pick up again. He could sell houses if buyers were available; he had proved that. He was especially good with the wives. Women, married women anyway, still trusted male salespeople, at least in his experience. What they wanted was someone who would demonstrate an authoritative concern for their interests, which nowadays were not confined to kitchen, nursery, and home laundry. You could and in fact certainly should address them on electrical, heating, and plumbing matters. They would be flattered in any event, but in point of fact some were more knowledgeable in these areas than their husbands (Joanie was a better driver than he, knew more about automobiles), and all were much less likely to be competitive on such subjects with a male agent, even when, as sometimes happened, they were really better versed than John about heat pumps and bringing the circuits up to code.

He now told Detective Lang every detail he could remember of his day with and without Richie. Ironically, he recognized that he had himself performed better in Richie's presence than when he had gone off on his own. The episode at the farm, in which his role had been so sorry before Richie and Sharon appeared, might well not have happened at all had he stayed with the car, in leaving which, abandoning Sharon, he had surrendered to feelings of selfish impatience. He had simply walked away from a situation with which he was fed up. That had been wrong at the time and got no better in retrospect.

"I did some foolish things due to panic," he told Lang. "I thought that man was really going to shoot me. That's why I took his gun away from him."

"The shotgun's been recovered," Lang said. "Maranville left it behind when he abandoned the Smithtown cruiser."

Tim spoke up in his eager voice. "You lucked out. It had a custom stock. It looked like big bucks."

"Yeah," said the detective, winking at Tim. He switched the tape recorder off. "English. Owner valued it at eight grand, though between you and I"—he was speaking to John now—"people sometimes exaggerate for the insurance claim. *Eight* thousand?"

"Handmade!" said Tim. "They can go higher than that."

158

"Not with me they don't," said Lang, switching the machine on again.

"That's one relief, then," said John. "I don't have eight thousand dollars. I haven't got eight hundred." At another time he might have been embarrassed to make this confession into a tape recorder, but he had the wonderful warm feeling that he was among friends here. His emotions had gone into a very vulnerable state, no doubt as an aftereffect of his ordeal with Richie, which seemed more harrowing in retrospect than when in progress. Perhaps this was the routine interpretation, but he suspected that all clichés having to do with extreme situations are true and therefore remain eloquent to the participants.

"Yes," said Lang. "Haverford's not going to press charges. He'll get his gun back."

"That's his name?" John asked. "I didn't even know it. I probably couldn't even find his house again." He stared at the detective. "It's crazy. Nothing like this ever happened to me before."

Lang shut the machine off again and said, with understanding, "John, that's the way it goes with a lot of people we meet in our line of work. We get more solid citizens than bad guys, you know. And thank God, huh? You did just fine. Nobody expects you to be experienced in these things. Because how would you be unless you were one of the villains, right?" He added, with obvious pride, "Or an officer of the law."

Sharon spoke up. "John pulled us out of some tight corners. I already told you that, but I want to make it extra clear."

John said quickly, "Enough has been made of that. I just hope you can catch Richie soon, before he does any more damage to the human race."

"I'd like to see you kill him!" Sharon cried.

Lang was wry. "You can be assured we'll do everything we can to see his civil rights are protected, even if the lives of police officers are at risk. We'll wrap him in cotton wadding and take him in so he can be sent back to Barnes Psychiatric, to be treated at taxpayers' expense till they let him out again."

This kind of cynicism was familiar from television crime shows, and in the past John had become bored with it. Whether or not it was justified, chronic exasperation was simply tiresome, at least in John's existence. He might be changing now, but he did not want to dwell on the matter. He just wanted to go home.

"That's really all I can recall," he told Lang, nodding at the tape machine. "If I think of anything else, I can phone you, can't I?"

"Just a couple more things, if you don't mind, John." Lang proceeded to ask what turned out to be a whole series of further questions, some of which John believed he had already answered. Eventually he had had enough, and he stood up.

"That's it. I'm going home."

"John, you've been very helpful," said Lang. "I'll get a car to give you a ride back, and you, too, Sharon." He rose and smiled down at the boy. "Tim, Smithtown's sending an officer for you, and your mom will be with him."

"I just hope," Tim said disapprovingly, "you didn't drag her out of class."

Lang did not respond to this. He said to John, "This is a young fellow who's going to do all right in life, wouldn't you say?"

John still felt shy with Tim. "Maybe we could go into the city and see a ballgame sometime," he told the boy. "Or whatever you like to do for fun." He felt inept. He had been a boy himself, but at the moment could not remember what he had liked at that age. He was weary now, and it had been so long ago.

"Sure," Tim said, and then he asked if there was time for him to have a look at the radio-dispatching room before his mother arrived.

"Bye, Tim," Sharon said gaily as Lang led the boy out. "Keep in touch, huh?" She turned to John. "I don't want to get you in trouble at home, so I won't say the same to you." She had not had time to refresh the heavy makeup, which by now was the worse for wear, but she had naturally fine brown eyes.

"I misjudged you," John said. "I want you to know that."

Sharon showed a brief expression of chagrin. "Yeah," she said, "I came on to you after the car accident. I panicked. I can't get to work without driving, see, and I just had that learner's permit, which isn't legal without a licensed driver in the car. My old man went away, too, like Tim's father. I don't know how to do anything but cocktail-waitressing, which doesn't take any talent, at least where I work. Just legs and a butt that doesn't look too bad in the little outfit they give you to wear."

"You have any kids?"

"No, and that's good, the way things have gone so far."

John was suddenly in danger of being overcome with emotion. He already loved her as a loyal comrade in conditions of danger, as cops are said to love their partners, but at the moment this feeling had become a passion: he adored her, and all the more so for how she looked, with her unkempt red hair and her clothes so touchingly bedraggled. Now that he had received reassuring news about his wife and family, to whom he was connected by duty, he had an impulse to run away with Sharon. Part of this was not desire but rather a need to atone for what, despite her asseverations to the contrary, he stubbornly considered to be his failures as a man.

"I really want to keep in touch," he said. "Would you mind if I dropped in at the cocktail lounge . . . ?"

"You stay home, John," Sharon said, patting his arm maternally. "There's nothing better in all the world." She snorted. "I'm a real authority on that subject, because I haven't got one. . . . I didn't tell you the whole truth. My husband didn't run away. He's in federal prison. He tried to drive across the border with a spare tire full of cocaine."

In his current state, John was not as shocked by the information as he knew Sharon expected him to be. "That's your private business," he said. "You're a wonderful woman. I wasn't suggesting anything illicit. I'd just like to know from time to time how you're getting along." This was a necessary lie, for actually he was profoundly in love with her at this moment, in a way he suspected she would not find to her liking. Like Richie, what she approved of in him was the husband, the father, the householder, the drone, the nontaker of risks because he could not jeopardize those and that for which he was responsible. What a convenient moral armor enveloped him!

Sharon smiled slowly. "Naw, John. Better we shake hands and go our separate ways. I hope we don't even meet at the trial, because I'm hoping the cops kill that bastard this time."

John nodded, but he did not want to think about that subject right now. He and she had been comrades. Surely that meant as much to her, if she would admit it, as it did to him. Tim too was a part of it. They might all go together to some sporting event, as a team, which would neutralize any hint of impropriety.

At this point Lang returned, without Tim. "Okay, folks. The DA's people will want to talk to you both once Maranville is caught, I know. But let's get you both home safe and sound right now."

"Tim's mother get here?" John asked.

"On her way. Sounds like a nice lady on the phone. Good people out there. My wife and I have been thinking of moving out in that direction. Fresh air, and I believe prices are a lot lower."

John was brought back momentarily to professional normality. "They are, in fact. Home prices run a good fifteen-twenty percent under what they are in town here. I'm in local real estate."

Lang smiled down from his greater height. "Sure. Think you could find us something I could afford on a cop's income?"

"I could locate some agent for you in the Smithtown area. We all belong to associations."

"Anything around here would do even better, though," Lang said. "If the price is right. I'd *rather* be closer to work if I could, and my wife teaches at Midvale Avenue Elementary."

"I'll get onto it soon as I return to the office," said John. "You can never tell. Every so often a bargain comes along. Maybe a fixer-upper?"

"Worth considering," said Lang. "Appreciate it." He led them along a corridor and down a stairway and through a side door to a green-and-white police car waiting at the curb.

Sharon had the shorter distance to travel, so John climbed in first. Before closing the door, Detective Lang leaned in.

"John, don't you worry about Maranville. We'll keep that car in the neighborhood, not right in front of your house, because he might see it and take off, but it'll be close by."

For the first time John thought of the possibility that the same threat might apply to Sharon. He asked her, "Don't you want protection, too? Think he knows where you live?"

"Naw." She waved Lang off, and when he was gone, she whispered into John's ear, "I got a gun at home. I'm just praying he shows up!"

The uniformed officer at the wheel turned and spoke through the steel-mesh barrier between front and back seats, which distinguished this car from that of the state troopers. He introduced himself as Patrolman Cardone. "Sorry about the screen." He tapped it. "It's the only unit free right now. We have had a lot of crime already, and the night is just starting."

His use of the word, and not the darkness through which they walked from lighted city hall to lighted car, was what made John belatedly conscious that evening had come.

"What time is it, Officer?"

"Eight-twenty." The car moved away from the curb.

Incredulously, John repeated the time. "God, can it be?" He asked Sharon, "Did you get your car back?"

"Cops impounded it for evidence," she said. "But they said they'll see I get a lift to work tomorrow."

"You're going back to work right away?"

The passing streetlamps intermittently illuminated her face. "Sure. I'll bet you do, too. I need the money. Don't you?"

"I'm not on a real salary," said John. "I need to make a sale. It's been so tough lately, I'm thinking of moonlighting someplace. I guess they don't have cocktail *waiters?*" His question was not serious, but she took it as such.

164

"Not at this dump. Maybe a nice bar at some hotel. You wouldn't want to lower yourself, John."

"I think you've got a lot of natural wisdom," John said. He *was* being serious now and worried that he might sound patronizing, so he added, "I mean, I think you know a lot about basic things. I wish I always did."

"That's why I've been so damned successful in life so far," Sharon said. "That's why when it comes to men, I didn't pick just one loser but a whole string of them." She stared at him. "I don't have anything you could use, John. Take my word for it." Her attention was diverted by what she saw beyond his shoulder. "Here we are," she called to Cardone. "Right up there at the fireplug." She addressed John again, gently. "I'm real sorry I don't." She kissed him quickly on the cheek, opened the door, and hopped out.

Watching her through the rear window as the police car pulled away, John recognized the area: there was the dough-nut shop and, on the other side of the street, the taxi office, across the glass door of which stretched the yellow tape that the police post at the scene of a crime, and at the moment Cardone was driving through the intersection at which Sharon had sideswiped Richie's car, or rather the car that Richie had stolen. He wondered whether the cops knew about that phase of Richie's day: had the vehicle's owner, too, been murdered? Surely it was that person's license that Richie had displayed to the officer. In any event, Sharon had either just been start-ing out from home when the accident happened or coming back. She must live in an apartment over one of the neigh-borhood businesses. She now vanished as the car took a turn, so he could not see just where.

He supposed he might encounter her accidentally if he drove this way persistently over the weeks, but why would he do that? He was a married man and a father. He had everything he should want, and undoubtedly she was right about herself. Yet his heart seemed broken.

"Nice part of town up here," Officer Cardone said genially, as if he sensed that distraction was needed. "You must be right near DeForest." They were climbing the hill down which John had had the wild ride with Richie in the morning. "Nice up here for kids, I bet. You a family man?"

"Real nice. Primary school's only a few blocks away. But neither of mine is that old yet."

"I got two girls and a boy," said Cardone. "Oldest girl's graduating high school next spring. Wants to go in the Air Force. How about that?"

"There it is," John said. "The white Cape on the right."

The nearest streetlamp was just beyond the edge of John's property. It lighted the front yard up to the junipers that flanked the big multipaned front window, which was illuminated now, but as always after dark Joanie had closed the venetian-blind louvers, not wishing to be unwittingly observed from outside. That was a unique practice on this block: you could look right into the ground floor of most of the houses from the street. When she had first done this John was worried that the neighbors might take offense at the obvious implication. What people thought of him and his had always been of concern, but after the day he had put in, he had less regard for the social gauges of others, he who had not long before worn handcuffs as a suspected murderer. Even now he could not be sure whether he had permanently escaped all legal liability. He must call the only lawyer he knew, Carl Kilmartin, who handled real-estate matters for the agency and had acted as his and Joanie's attorney when they bought the house. Perhaps Carl could recommend a colleague versed in criminal law and also skilled in dealing with the civil actions that still seemed possible in the matters of the ill woman into whose house he and Richie had broken; the gentleman farmer Haverford, who might on consultation with his own lawyer renege on the easy promise to dismiss any claim once the shotgun had been returned; and finally even Tim, whose mother, needing money, might be less tolerant than her son if a lawsuit promised, even as a threat, to be a possible source of funds.

John's position was all too uncertain, even though he had come through his ordeal physically unscathed—the damage to his knee had apparently been largely mental—and was held in respect by Sharon and the police of his own town. His reputation had not been harmed. Perhaps it had been enhanced, though that remained to be seen. It was probably all to the good that the authorities had, so far as he knew, kept his name from the media. He would therefore have time to prepare himself, and Joanie and the kids, for the public attention that would inevitably come in the days ahead.

He was suddenly struck by the thought that the story of his day might well have financial value. Would it be sleazy to profit from the misery of others? But did he not deserve compensation for his own travail? This was a matter to be discussed with Joanie, whom he would shortly see for the first time since morning, after a moral and emotional eternity. He would in effect be coming home from the wars.

"Now, you take it easy," Officer Cardone told him as John stepped out onto the curbing in front of his home.

As Lang had warned him, he saw no nearby vehicle that could be an unmarked police surveillance unit—unless the silver-gray sedan pulled well into his own driveway could constitute such. Now who could own that car? Lang had said a "business associate" was with Joanie, but perhaps it was rather a friend of hers. There were several women who qualified for that role, two of them old school pals who lived in the area. And Joan's cousin's wife was really more than a relative. Any of them might own this car, which looked new. John hoped it was not Renee Wilcox, who quite obviously had always thought little of him. Renee had gone through two divorces before she reached the age of twenty-five, and her third marriage seemed to be on the rocks within days of the exchange of vows, but ostensibly persisted, if on terms of mutual enmity. She could not be seen as ever being a positive influence. But John never said a word against her. Joan would have been hurt.

Standing there before his own door, he felt scarcely less vulnerable than when he had been arrested by the state police. He had no key and would therefore have to ring the bell. He must look a sight. It was more than a mere matter of clothes. Had he worn this attire for a day's worth of chores at home, as he had planned, he would have belonged to an altogether different category of appearance. In his normal world it was honorable to be besmirched with the stains of honest household functions: baby food, semigloss latex enamel, machine oil. He especially dreaded being let in by Renee, who might volunteer for the job if Joan was occupied with the children. He disliked Renee but, if he could acknowledge the truth to himself, found her physically desirable, which attraction she probably could detect and exploit while obviously thinking even less of him.

He braced himself to meet her sneering amusement. But it was not Renee who opened the door. It was Richie, wearing a warm smile. It was he, all right, though he was dressed in suit and tie and wore glasses.

"We were just wondering when you'd finally show up," Richie said, ushering John inside. "Run into some snags?"

John rushed into the living room. Joan, leaning forward from her seat on the couch, was in the act of pouring coffee from the silver pot (the most valuable of their wedding presents, gift of Uncle Phil's, naturally) into one of the heirloom bone-china cups contributed by his mother. The polished silver tray that went with the service held a silver sugar bowl and cream pitcher. Every piece was gleaming, though he knew for a fact that all had been covered with a like coat of black tarnish time out of mind, there on the shelf in the cupboard. But a more remarkable transformation had taken place in Joan herself. Her glistening hair was pinned up in the elegant style she ordinarily used only for certain holidays and celebrations: New Year's Eve, for example, for which they went to whichever home Renee née Wilcox was occupying with whatever husband. And the burgundy-colored dress was special as well, along with the pieces of tasteful jewelry: small pearl earrings, the gold brooch from her mother. She was wearing her best shoes, for perhaps only the second time.

John believed himself to be out of control, but in fact some sort of inner mechanism must have taken hold of him, for though he wanted to shout the question, he heard it emerge quietly: "Where are the children?"

"Well, thanks for saying hi," Joan reprovingly replied, her dark eyebrows rising. But then she brightened. "Is this what prosperity does to you?" She lowered the pot. "The kids are in bed, as they should be at this hour." She stood up and extended her arms. "Come here." She looked past him, smiling, and said, "I'm sure Mr. Pryor won't mind."

Under the same internal, involuntary management, John went to her and was embraced and kissed.

"Congratulations, kiddo," Joan said when she released him, employing the old nickname each had used for the other since seeing, some years earlier, a vintage 1930s film with a heroine who wore limp satin and a chain-smoking hero in wide-brimmed fedora.

"Are the children okay?"

Joan frowned. "Yes! They're in bed! Why do you keep asking that?"

"I got to help tuck them in," Richie said, behind John's back. John whirled around. Richie wore a simper. "I envy you, John. One of each, and both a prize."

"In view of the great news, I'm defrosting the steak we've been saving. I trust it's still edible." In addition to all else, Joan was wearing a good deal of eye makeup. "I talked Mr. Pryor into staying for dinner. He's in town alone."

"Now, Joan," Richie said, "I'm going to have to leave if you don't stop being so formal with me. We're friends, aren't we? Friends call me Randy."

John could barely move his frozen lips to ask, "What good news?"

"Why, the sale, of course!" Joanie was showing an altogether false animation for the sake of her guest. All was synthetic, from the configuration of her mouth to the angle at which she held her upper body. She smirked at Richie. "It takes John a while." There was the hint of a glare in her eye when she looked back at her husband. "I'm sure Randy would like a drink. That's your department."

"Anything will be just fine," Richie said.

"Sale" was an utterly meaningless word in this context. Richie had become Randy Pryor and was now an intimate of Joan's. He wore a suit and a blue tie and a pair of metal-rimmed eyeglasses. No weapons were in evidence. He had apparently not harmed anybody on the premises, not the children or Joan.

"You seem dazed by your success," Joan said in her new

170

bubbly manner. "Get going, will you please, huh? Things will move fast once the meat is thawed. Randy showed me how to put it under running water. I take it there's some red wine left?"

John went to the cabinet under the window that gave onto the side yard. He brought out the three-liter jug, which was about a quarter full. It sloshed in his trembling grasp. When he glanced up, Joanie was gone.

Richie smiled at the wine. He had yet to give John a knowing look. "That'll be just swell," he said now.

Joan returned immediately. She carried two wineglasses.

Richie asked solicitously, "You're not joining us?"

"If I had some now I'd be too woozy to cook the steak. I can't hold much. I'll drink a glass with the meal."

"You're slender," Richie said. "That's why it affects you. It takes a heavier person to hold their liquor."

"I don't want to mention any names," said Joan, leering toward John and back, and then actually giggling.

"Come on," Richie said jovially, "ole John's not over-weight by much, are you, fella? I imagine you're just about right for your build."

John lowered the jug to the coffee table and accepted the glasses from his wife. He filled one and handed it to Richie without raising his eyes.

"Okay," Joan said, "I'll leave you guys to your business affairs. I calculate the meal will be on the table in fifteen-twenty minutes, if that'll give you enough time. If not, then you'll have to wait till after! It's late enough as is." John found the persistent lilt in her voice to be unbearable.

He did not speak until he heard the noise of the pots and pans from the kitchen. Then he asked dully, "What sale?"

Richie had taken an overstuffed chair. He was slumped in it, with his legs spread and extended, his shoes resting on the back edges of their heels. They were black leather and so new that the margins of the soles were still light tan.

"I'm buying one of your houses. I don't care which one. The one that costs most and is hardest to sell, maybe. Whatever would make you happy, John."

"You're going to settle down and live here?"

Richie grinned. "Why not?"

"You're going to jail." John was speaking clearly but at a sufficiently low volume so as not to be heard in the kitchen. He had decided that Joanie must not learn the truth about Richie until after he was disposed of conclusively, and of course the children could not be disturbed in any way.

Richie's gleeful spirits were not visibly affected. He continued to grin. "No, John, that won't happen."

"You killed at least one person today and wounded several more," said John and added, perhaps naively, "How could you do that?"

Richie lifted his hands in what probably was a kind of shrug. His body movements had changed with the donning of the suit, as his facial expressions had been altered by the glasses. "You've been listening to the cops."

"You *did* those things. Why would they lie?"

Richie gave him a long, pitying look. "*Why would cops lie?* Can you be serious?"

"You were just released from Barnes Psychiatric."

Richie swallowed the wine in one gulp. "They gave me a clean bill of health, and I walked out the door." He passed the empty glass back and forth between his hands. "There's nothing wrong with me, John. Don't ask me, and don't ask the cops, for God's sake. Ask the doctors. And let's face it: if *they* don't know after all the examinations and therapy, who would? With all respect, *you?*"

John refilled Richie's glass, but hardly in the automatic

execution of his duties as host. He had resumed his old game of playing for time, even though it had been anything but successful when last tried, at the farm. He could see no weapons on Richie but had learned his lesson in that regard at least: the man was always armed with something. Whereas except for that brief period during which he carried Haverford's shotgun, which he had wrested from the man only for his own protection, John had never, his life long, borne any arms whatever.

He returned the wine jug to the coffee table. "I don't claim to understand you in any particular."

Richie smacked his lips loudly after a taste of the second glassful. "It's a manly thing on your part to admit it." He pointed. "That's why I'm so sold on you: you're a man. You don't carry a gun and club and wear a uniform because you got some kind of doubt about yourself."

"Look," John said, "I'm willing to consider that you've had problems, a bad childhood or whatever, but—"

"Come on, John!" Richie said gleefully. "I don't want your pity." He drank some more wine and assumed a quizzical expression. With his glasses and clothing, he could have passed for someone who worked at a desk in a large office full of people all with the same values.

"Yeah, you're right," John admitted. "It *was* false. I don't have any sympathy for you at all. I don't care what troubles you've had. They're not my fault."

Richie laughed. "Good for you! I haven't got any troubles. Certain other people have claimed to have had troubles with me."

"Listen," said John. "I want you to think about this." He was still standing by the coffee table. "I'm going to call the police. They've got a car right in this neighborhood. They can get here immediately. Since coming to my house you appear to have acted like a civilized human being." John took a breath. "Why not just keep it that way? What you've done can't be undone, but at least don't make it worse! I imagine you'll just get sent back to Barnes."

Richie had begun to shake his head. "No, I can't consider anything of that sort."

"What are you going to do, then? I'm calling the police."

"I'll think of something," Richie said negligently.

Joan arrived. "Excuse us for a minute, Randy, please. Something's come up in the kitchen."

Richie was on his feet. "Can I help?"

"No, please, really. I just need John for a minute. If you can spare him."

In the kitchen Joanie said, "I *don't* want to overcook this steak. If I'd known just when you'd be getting home, I'd have started the charcoal outside, and you could have taken over from there. But it's too late now." She shook her head toward the stove. "I've been knocking myself out ever since Randy called. Even managed to get the coffee service polished and the kids cleaned up, not to mention myself. Even so—"

"Joanie," John said, quietly but with urgency, "I want you to call—"

"*You* decide," said she, grinning. "Then I can blame you if the steak is ruined. *You* can take it. *You* just made all that money. How much will the commission come to, by the way? Also, which house?" But then she immediately threw up her hands and wailed, "I've got to deal with this steak!"

"Joan," said John, trying to catch her by the forearm, but she darted to the sink to lift the dripping meat from the colander in which it was being thawed.

"Nice? It would be a crime to overcook it." She replaced the steak and wiped her hands on a kitchen towel. "Where's your barbecue apron? I don't want to ruin this dress, God!"

174

John found his apron in a cabinet drawer and unfolded it for her. It had been her gift to him and was a butcher-striped garment and not the jokey thing sometimes seen. The length was okay for her; her height was within an inch of his. Melanie, too, was taller than the average girl of her age. It was still too soon to tell about little Phil. John had to protect them. He could not risk having a gun battle on the premises. Richie would not simply surrender to the police.

"All right," Joan said now. "I'll decide. I just needed the moral support. Better get back to your guest and keep him happy till he writes the check, huh?" She came to John and kissed him. "You did real good, big fellow," imitating some cowboy-movie actor. Joan was gifted as a mimic and had amused him in that fashion over the years. There would be nothing to gain and much to lose by any further attempt to tell her about Richie.

"The wine's almost gone," he said instead. "I'll run down to Sherwood's and pick up a bottle or two."

Joan pushed him back, sniffing. "You could use a shower, kiddo! And a shave and a clean shirt and pants. Meanwhile, I'll call Sherwood's and have them deliver. A nice Burgundy, you think? What else? Scotch?" While asking these questions, she was pushing him toward the doorway. "I'll put the steak on hold and go keep Randy company. It would help if you could snap it up."

John returned to the living room. Richie was not there: he had gone for the children! But as John rushed toward the nursery, Richie emerged from the guest lavatory at the head of the hall, and they almost collided. John, absurdly, found himself apologizing.

Back in the living room, he asked, "What's this 'Randy Pryor' stuff you've handed my wife?"

"It's a name I sometimes use, a professional name, like a

corporation, you know. All I've been telling Joanie is that you and me are doing business, and that's true enough."

"Don't *ever* call her Joanie," John said.

"You're the boss, kiddo."

John bit his lip. He sat down on the couch in exactly the place he found Joan when he got home. She had neglected to take away the coffee pot and cups. He had never seen her so excited. True, had he actually had a commission coming, it would be the first in a long time, but perhaps she had forgotten what he owed Tesmir, which would have to be returned off the top. It was a cruel hoax.

John stood up. "Get out of here."

"Pardon?" Richie was back in the chair, feet out and splayed.

"You can't stay," John said. "You're wanted for a long string of terrible crimes. I'm not going to serve you dinner in my house."

Richie wore his most charming expression, or what he probably thought was it, his left eyebrow slightly elevated above a twinkling eye. "It wasn't *you* who invited me. Now, was it?"

"I can throw you out, though."

Richie bowed, as it were, while remaining seated. He asked, with heavy irony, "Why don't you consult with *Mrs. Felton* on the matter?"

"Do you think she'd want you here if she knew what you did?"

Richie's hands were extended. "Well, John, let's tell her everything you think you know about me."

He was calling John's bluff. What good could possibly happen if Joanie were suddenly told? Her terror would inevitably obstruct anything John might try against Richie. And once the polite, even friendly illusion had been destroyed for her, and Richie unmasked, would not she and the children be in greater danger?

John sat down again. "Would you be interested in a deal?"

"Then you *will* sell me a house?"

"I'm serious. What I'm talking about is something like this: you eat dinner, and then you leave. I don't lift a hand against you during that time, and I don't notify the police. You eat, and then you leave quietly."

"That's nice."

"You accept?"

Richie frowned speculatively. "I don't know why I'd object. I don't get many offers, you know. A lot of people are just basically against me. No reason. They take one look and what they see, they hate. It's hard to deal with prejudice like that."

It was too much to have to listen to that sort of thing. John said, "Some more liquor will be here shortly."

Richie lifted his glass, with its inch of red liquid that he had been nursing since the jug was emptied. "I hope you didn't order it for me. I'm no drinker."

"You drained that pint of vodka this afternoon like it was water."

Richie seemed surprised. "If you say so."

"You don't remember?"

"If I recalled every drink I had, I wouldn't be using my mind for anything else."

John suspected he might be on to something. "Do you remember *anything* you did earlier today?"

"I hate to disappoint you," Richie said, returning his glass to the coffee table, "but there's not much worth remembering from day to day in my life. You'd fall asleep if you had to listen to it."

Joan came into the living room. She smiled at Richie. "John

MEETING EVIL   177

just has to freshen up for a minute or two. I didn't know selling real estate was heavy labor!"

"I won't be a minute," John told Richie, meaningfully, and went rapidly to the bathroom, where he removed his shirt, splashed water in his armpits, and applied deodorant. He hastily stroked chin and cheeks with the electric razor. He went to the bedroom and got a clean shirt. With its tails stuck into the old work pants, the ensemble was incongruous and might annoy Joan. Therefore he had to take even more time to change trousers and to trade the ancient sneakers for decent leather shoes.

It occurred to him that despite the need for haste, he should at least look in on the children whom he was obsessed with protecting, but he heard the doorbell just as he reached the former guest bedroom they called the nursery.

He rushed to the front of the house, but Richie already had the door open and was accepting the bagful of clinking bottles from a short young man who John was disappointed to see was not Wally, the elder son of the family that owned the liquor store, but rather someone new.

"Is Wally sick?"

The deliveryman presented John with a limp bill. "Wally's on vacation." He rubbed his prominent nose with the back of his hand and looked past the men at Joan, nodding.

Seeing an opportunity to get a note to the police (in which he could explain the situation and rule out a SWAT-team assault), John said, "I'll get a pen and sign for it." He was only worried that the new man might be unaware that though state law forbade putting liquor on the tab, Sherwood's did it regularly for folks they knew, even if, like John, they were not frequent customers.

But it was Richie who frustrated the effort. He briskly

handed John the bag and drew a handful of loose banknotes from his pants pocket.

"Lemme see the check again," the deliveryman said, rudely snatching it back from John.

"There's plenty there," Richie said, reversing him and literally pushing him out the door. "Keep the extra."

"Hey!" the guy cried. It seemed the sound of delighted surprise, not complaint.

John put the paper bag onto the coffee table. Joan gave him a frown. "You shouldn't let Randy pay. He's our guest."

"I wouldn't take no for an answer," Richie said, rubbing his hands together as though warming them. "You didn't expect to have me for dinner. What's fair is fair."

Joan continued her polite protest, which depressed John. He noisily unpacked the booze so he would not have to listen. The bag yielded a quart of the most expensive bourbon, a bottle of red wine with a French name, and a white from Italy. He had not examined the bill, but it must have been for fifty dollars at least, a good deal more than he would have been prepared to pay even if the imaginary sale had been made, given their debts.

"Then I'll get going," Joan said, springing to her feet.

"Listen," said Richie, waving a mock-admonitory finger at her, "I don't want you to go to any trouble, now! What's important is friendship, not food." He seized the bourbon, thumbnailed off the material that sealed the cap, and poured himself a glassful.

Judging from the sound, Joanie was halfway to the kitchen when she shouted back, "Need ice?"

"No, thanks!" John did not bother to ask their guest.

"Joanie doesn't happen to have a sister?" Richie asked jovially, in the chair again, leaning back. He drank some whiskey. "John, I want to thank you for taking me in this way. Not many people would have done that."

"*I didn't take you in,*" John said. "*You've got to get out of here, do you understand?*"

Richie nodded and poured himself more whiskey. "We see eye to eye, and—"

"No, we don't. We're not friends and never were. I'm only putting up with you now because I'm concerned about my wife and children." He realized immediately that he should never have said such a foolish thing.

But Richie asked, as if disingenuously, "Is something wrong with them? You might try sharing your problems. That's what friends are for."

John made a strenuous effort to endure. "Tell me about yourself. Why do you think you're always in trouble?"

"My philosophy is, if you *think* there's something wrong with me, then the burden of proof is on *you,* not me. Now, there are those who can't take that." Richie raised his pale eyebrows above the frame of the glasses. "They've got nobody but themselves to blame when things go against them."

"I've seen you in action, remember?" John had not resumed his seat. "You ought to realize that bad things are going to happen when you're out in the world. You're better off in the hospital. You don't belong on the outside. You can't control yourself."

"Come on, John. You can't believe that stuff. Else why would I be a guest in your house right this minute? If I'm so awful, how come Joanie insisted I hold the baby? How come your little daughter climbed onto my lap and hugged me and wanted me to be the one who put her in bed? God Almighty, John, I never saw a dog that didn't come right to me and put his chin in my hand. At Barnes they got patients who won't speak a word to anybody but me, guys who look at the wall

180

all day and would wet their pants where they sit rather than leave their place. *They* do what I say! I tell 'em to go to the toilet, they do it."

"You're allowed to roam around there?"

"They don't chain you to the wall any more and whip you," Richie said, laughing. "Though I've seen some who that might help. They got some real nasty women there, with mouths like sewers. I can't stand a bitch who uses foul language."

"Is that what happened with the gas-station attendant this morning? She swore at you?" John wanted to know, while at the same time he found it unbelievable that he was politely questioning a murderer, who, as the criminal himself pointed out, was an invited guest. He could not bear to think of Richie's caressing the children, because if he did, he might hate Joanie, which would be wrong, for how could she have possibly known Richie on sight for what he was? He had appeared harmless to John when wearing the T-shirt and cap. In suit, tie, and eyeglasses, he looked not only respectable but the embodiment of all that made sense.

The telephone rang. Joanie did not like the idea of a phone in the living room but put up with it because John insisted that he had to be always within no more than two rings of an instrument if he were to make certain sales. Strange as it might seem to those with no professional experience, there were people whom the littlest things dissuaded from a course of action, especially when the projected expenditure was in six figures.

The phone was unobtrusively tucked behind the large ceramic lamp on the table at one end of the sofa, where in truth it proved at least as convenient for Joanie's long conversations with relatives and friends as it was for John, who often, when the matter concerned business, would ask the caller to hang on until he could reach the little home office he had set up, again to Joanie's complaint, in a corner of their bedroom.

Perhaps he should have welcomed a call now, but he dreaded it.

"John? Hi. This is Lang. The detective? How're ya doin'?"

"Sure."

"Just checking in. Our guy reports all's quiet in the neighborhood. In my opinion Maranville's a long way from here. In the wind, like we say. He might be demented, but these people usually have a lot of basic judgment. They don't always go where you expect them to when they're fugitives. They can be pretty sly. But it won't last. It won't take him long to do something stupid and get collared. So . . . ."

"Thanks," said John. He knew he should probably say something that might give Lang a clue, but his mind was too weary now for invention, and the last thing he wanted would be to incite an assault on the house.

"Keep your place buttoned up, windows and doors locked if they aren't already. Make you feel safer. But we're not gonna forget you. The chief wants you to know he considers this a personal concern of his."

"You bet." John put the phone away, behind the lamp. He had not looked toward Richie during his conversation with Lang, but he had a feeling that the man had not been much interested in it, that he could have said anything without putting himself in jeopardy. Nevertheless, he explained. "Business."

Richie nodded and drank from his glass. "Which hasn't been good lately."

"My wife told you that?" John was furious.

"*You* told me, this afternoon," said Richie. He looked benign. "What Joanie said was how terrific you are."

182

John stared at him.

"We all think a lot of you, man. You got a lot of support. You're a winner."

"The hell with you."

Richie was wounded. "What brought that on?"

"Just remember we got a deal. You eat dinner and then you leave."

John felt a great need to look in on the children, whom he had not seen since morning. This represented more concern for himself than for them. They were sleeping through it all, and, if he could pull it off, would stay ignorant until they were adults, whereas he could use an exposure to their innocence.

But Joan came in at that moment. "All right, gentlemen: dinner is served." She exchanged beaming expressions with Richie and led them to the dining room, where the table was set with the Feltons' best china, the plates rimmed in gold, and the reserved-for-guests linen tablecloth and napkins.

"While you're having your soup, I'll be doing the steak, if you'll excuse me." Joan addressed these remarks to the guest. "It's the only way I know to make sure it won't get overdone."

Richie was standing at a diffident distance.

"Please." Joan indicated a chair.

"Right in the middle!" Richie said, extending a hand toward each of the extremities of the table. "You're spoiling me rotten."

"Wait till you've tasted the food. You might change your tune. Please sit down and begin."

"You're not having soup?"

"Now, don't you worry about me!"

John felt like the outsider. As such, he took his seat while the guest was still standing. The soup steamed before him in its bowl. It was recognizably the canned chicken-noodle fa-vored by Melanie, whom he had shown how noisily to suck up the strands of pasta while crossing one's eyes. This had not won applause from her mother.

Joan appeared in the kitchen doorway. "The wine, John, the wine."

So he had to get up and go fetch the bottles from the living room and find the corkscrew under the clutter in the drawer of the sideboard. By the time he had opened the bot-tle of red wine, Joanie was back with a filled salad bowl. "We're starting with *white*," she reproachfully told him.

"My fault," Richie said, with a little contrite shrug. "I was drinking red earlier. I don't know anything about wine."

John looked bleakly at the two of them, the stars of this grotesquerie, then dutifully opened the white wine and poured a glassful for Richie. Joan went to the kitchen. Richie began to drink soup from a dainty spoon.

John had eaten nothing since breakfast cereal, but he cer-tainly had no appetite now. In the suit and tie and especially the glasses, Richie looked genteel enough, and his features might even be called patrician, insofar as John understood the term, which would seem to apply principally to the nose, longish but narrow and poreless, and eyes on the small side. Where had he gone to shave and acquire the clothing? And what of the automobile parked outside?

"I'm sure you stole the car," John said in a voice designed not to penetrate the kitchen doorway, beyond which Joan anyway was making a clatter. "You robbed somebody, took his car and his money, and bought the clothes, maybe? Or stole them, too? But the glasses, I can't figure them out."

"I like the way they feel." Richie jiggled them with a hand to either temple-piece. "I just wish I could see better through them. Driving here wasn't easy."

"They're not your prescription?" John told himself that nobody stole someone else's glasses. In this situation, he did not wish to serve as waiter, his normal spousely role when his wife did the cooking, but somebody had to do it, and he would not suffer Richie's volunteering.

But when he stood up, bowl in hand, Richie said, reaching, "If you're not going to eat that . . . " John let him exchange it for the empty bowl. Why not?

Joanie entered with a napkin-covered platter and a narrow dish containing a hard new stick of butter, as opposed to the easy-spread tub margarine that was routine. He had not known any was in the house; this must have been frozen.

Richie chided her affectionately. "Hot rolls? Joanie, you shouldn't have."

She lowered the dish and looked from John to the empty bowl before him. "Aren't you the hungry one? But you can't have seconds. You have to leave room for what's coming."

She was talking to him as if he were one of the children. At the same time, he was touched to realize that however valid her other reason for giving herself no soup, the fact was that the two servings would have exhausted the only can. Which meant that their criminal guest had got every drop of it.

Richie nibbled daintily at a roll until Joan returned to the kitchen, at which point he devoured the rest of it in one bite and reached for another. While attacking the butter, which was still so hard that it tended to fragment against the dull blade, he said, "I'm starved. I had quite a day."

"I know. I was there," John said softly, though he had a feeling that Joanie would not have heard him had he shouted. "Sharon and Tim and I were just telling the police about it."

Richie helped himself to more white wine. "This is better food than I've tasted for a long time. They feed you like a dog at Barnes." He gulped the remainder of the soup and packed it down with a third roll. He groaned in pleasure while reaching for a fourth. "Be around here for long, and I'd be as heavy as you, John."

"But you won't be here after this meal," said John.

"Almost forgot these!" It was Joanie, bringing the wooden-handled steak knives. "You might want to sharpen them, John. They are pretty dull by now."

"Joanie," Richie said, "I can't keep my hands off these rolls."

She looked genuinely pleased, but in point of fact Joan did not like to cook and ordinarily resented any special notice paid to a meal of her making, with the idea that she was thereby being identified as no more than a housewife.

It was therefore a kind of remonstrance when John said, "We had the children before Joan could go on for her master's. But she wants to go back to school as soon as the baby is a little older."

She made no acknowledgment. "Would you mind, John, bringing out the vegetables? I have to concentrate on the steak now."

He found the bowlful of peas-and-carrots on the counter next to the microwave, the bell of which rang as he approached. He opened the door and withdrew the hot potato puffs. But Joanie, returning, stopped him from carrying them out in the plastic container. She had a dish ready.

"Did you sharpen the steak knives?"

"How could I?" he asked sharply. "You just mentioned it, and then said get the vegetables."

"Is everything okay with you?" She peered narrowly at him.

His response was bluff: "Why, sure!"

"It just seems like you ought to be in a better mood."

"I *am* in a good mood," said he. "I've just had a long day."

"You've had a kind of nutty day, if you ask me." She said it with obvious affection, a hand at the small of his back. "You leave without saying goodbye, and those crazy phone calls—what were they all about? I didn't even understand the last one. I guess you were joking—?"

"Sorry about trying to clown around," John said. "I realize I don't have much talent in that direction. It was just—"

She pushed him toward the doorway. "Get that stuff out there before it's cold, willya please?"

In the dining room Richie asked, "So you're not the boss in the family."

John picked up a steak knife and tested its edge with the ball of his thumb: the dumb way, he was aware, and occasionally he cut himself, yet he continued to do it.

Richie took notice of what he was doing. "Here's the only test." He pressed his own knife against the tablecloth and cut a long slit in it.

In the next instant John realized that Richie had used the back of the blade and done no damage to the cloth, but while watching the episode he had convulsively cut his own thumb, and it was bleeding. Still smirking over his trick, Richie, it could be hoped, had not yet seen the wound. John turned quickly and returned to the kitchen, where Joanie was just sliding the steak, on the foil-covered pan, into the broiler compartment at the bottom of the stove.

"Just cut myself," he said self-pityingly to her bent back. "The knives are plenty sharp."

"There's Band-Aids in the drawer. I'll get one for you."

John did not need her nursing. He knew exactly where the tin was kept—they had several, each on hand at another place in the house where Melanie might suffer some slight damage in daily misadventures—and got one of the slenderer of the selection of bandages offered. Meanwhile, the profusion of blood from the slit in his thumb was, as always, remarkable. He saw his spotted trail on the floor. After cleaning the wound with a dampened paper towel, he went along, crouching, to wipe the vinyl tiles.

When he returned to the dining room, the white-wine bottle was empty and only one potato puff remained on the serving plate. The peas-and-carrots, however, looked untouched.

Richie put both hands flat on the table and drummed them for a moment. "It might not be my place to ask this, John, but what are you doing in this line of work, anyway? You haven't been making much money at it. Besides, it's mostly a woman's game nowadays, isn't it?"

Only by exerting the maximum in self-control did John manage not to blow up at the question, which had already been asked, though perhaps not so candidly, by some of his in-laws and, of course, by his own father not long before the man died.

Richie went on: "It's just that you could do so much better."

John could not help it. "At crime? Killing people, hurting people? Taking their property?"

"You could do a lot of good in the world and make a buck, too, so far as that goes. You're a born healer, John. You've done more for me in a couple of hours than all the quacks in all the years."

John could not have explained to himself why he made a sincere response. "My father wanted me to be a doctor. He never had the least idea of what my aptitudes were, if any. Just be a doctor, because that's impressive as well as profit-

188

able. Don't be what he was, working in the same office of the same company all your life. Well, the latter was easy enough to manage. But to be a doctor you have to begin with premed: I couldn't even get past the basic chemistry course."

Richie frowned. "I'm talking about an inner thing, not the lies they teach in medical school. You'd be wasting your time taking courses."

The comment served to remind John, once again, that it was surely a waste to speak sincerely about anything with a madman. He could now smell the meat under the broiler. It was nauseating.

Richie went on, leaning over his empty plate. "You serve the truth."

Against his better judgment John said, "Then why don't you listen to me? Give yourself up."

Richie seemed to be thinking this over. After a moment, however, he said, "One thing is certain: it's a waste of time for all concerned when I'm in Barnes."

"But when you're there, *people don't get hurt.*"

The corners of Richie's thin mouth rose, but whether or not it was in good humor John could not have said. "I wouldn't put it that way."

"For God's sake, you killed somebody *there?*"

"I had some trouble once," Richie said, staring at John. "It was self-defense."

"Yet they released you?"

Richie threw up his hands. "It was their idea, not mine. I have a very low opinion of them, if you want to know."

"The doctors?"

"If you think about it," said Richie, "we're all human. Where do some people get off setting themselves up as better?"

"Yeah," said John.

Joanie came in with the steak, which at another time would

have been John's idea of a spectacular feed (it came from Uncle Phil's private source of aged beef) but now was seen as disgustingly big and thick and oozing with pinkish fluid. It lay on a platter which she held at a distance from her body, for she had divested herself of the apron.

"Golly," Richie said as she deposited the dish on a silver trivet between him and John.

John could not bring himself to go find the proper carving knife. Before Joan could object, he sawed off a hunk of meat with his steak knife (which, though it had been sufficiently sharp to slice the skin of his thumb, was dull at this job) and dropped it on Richie's plate.

Joan brought the candlesticks from the sideboard, found matches in a drawer, and lighted both candles, which were virgin. Had they dined alone, she would have switched off the overhead fixture, a modest four-branched chandelier, but fortunately did not do so now. She sat down at the other end of the table, facing John. Richie was on his right and her left.

John wondered what she would say when she saw that only one potato puff remained, or that his plate was as clean as when it had been put down, his glass empty. But if she noticed any of these phenomena, she left it unmentioned. She reached for the bottle and gave herself some red wine.

Richie had politely waited till this moment. He began to cut his meat into small squares.

Joan lifted her glass. "Okay," she said. "A toast to the sale. I want to hear all about it."

John raised his glass and drank air. "How much should I cut you?" he then asked, steak knife and fork hovering over the meat.

Joanie shrugged. "It got so late by the time I heard from you, I had a snack when the kids ate. Then this excitement." She pinched her fingers at him. "*Real* thin."

Richie meanwhile was chewing each little cube by itself, making a quick, emphatic event of it.

Joan looked from one to the other with a big smile. John's sightline to her, unless he leaned to the left, was narrow, between the two candles. It was up to him to invent the story. "It's the Murchison place."

"I don't even think I know about that one," said she. "Has it been listed long?"

His knife had grown no sharper. It was impossible to cut a reasonably thin slice, so he stopped trying. He realized that Joanie did not really want any steak.

"A long, long time. Tess and Miriam had given up on it."

Joan waited for more, but not getting it, smiled at Richie. "I'm sure you've got your plans."

Maliciously John said, "I imagine you heard all about his plans when you had coffee."

Joan looked fondly at Richie. "Fact is, I think I did most of the talking. We never did get around to his business. He's the rare man who's interested in what someone else says, a woman no less."

So that was it: Richie as feminist.

"He's in pharmaceuticals," John told her.

"I'm impressed," said Joan. "Just the word, to begin with."

Richie seemed to brood for a moment, but then laughed cheerily.

"You haven't mentioned your family," said Joan. "You know your way around children!"

Richie took a while to answer. "I used to be married. But she didn't want kids."

"Some people are like that. That's their right. Now with us, it was a calculated decision to go ahead and have the family and postpone the rest." Joan shrugged. "Not that I don't sometimes regret it, but—"

Richie asked, "What I wonder is why John doesn't go into some field where the income is more certain."

John was utterly taken by surprise, but if Joanie was embarrassed by the rudeness of the comment, she did not show it.

"That's just lately, with the downturn. John's made good money and will again. He's a terrific salesman."

John was moved. He could not recall ever having heard her defend him in public before. When members of her family were snide, she avoided the issue, went to the bathroom or whatever.

"He's got tremendous potential he hasn't yet used," Richie said. He speared a cube of steak and masticated it rapidly, waving his fork. "I'm trying to get him to listen to some proposals of mine."

"Really?" Joan smiled at her husband.

"The risks would be all mine, I assure you," Richie went on. "But I happen to see great possibilities."

Joan asked John, "Do you want to tell me about it?"

John looked away.

"I can put him in the way of something big, Joanie," Richie said. He put his fork down and swiveled his head, surveying the room. "Do you want to live here forever?"

Once again Joan showed no evidence she was offended. "I've been after John just lately to look for something farther out, with more land between us and the neighbors, cleaner air." She glanced at John. "Weren't you out in the country someplace today?"

The phone was ringing. John went into the kitchen, where he answered on the wall-hung instrument.

"John. Lang again. There's reason to think Maranville checked into a Red Wing Motel this afternoon, just off the motorway at Exit Eleven, using a driver's license and credit card name of Charles F. Brookhiser. Earlier in the day, right here in town, Brookhiser reported he was robbed by a perpetrator answering Maranville's description. Got his car and wallet with everything in it. Motel's the nearest to where the Smithtown cruiser was abandoned."

"Thanks," John said when Lang paused for a breath.

"There's more. Short time later a big fire broke out at the Red Wing. Took hours to put out, and the motel was just about totaled. Management and the volunteer fire department out there suspect arson. A burned body was found in the room Maranville checked into. Desk clerk's the last person reported who saw him. They're getting dental records from Barnes Psychiatric."

"It's him, all right," John said. "That's exactly what he would do."

"Better hold off on the celebrations, though. Be on the safe side."

"I *know* it's him. Anybody else get hurt?"

"Early in the day, and business wasn't too great, luckily. That part of the unit was empty except for a man next door, who was out at the time. And not back yet. They will talk to him when he returns. But it looks good for our side."

"You said he would just have been sent back to Barnes."

"You got it absolutely," Lang said.

"He's finished now, though," said John. "I know that was him who got burned. You can call off the stakeout of my house."

"We'll wait for the confirmation, but meanwhile it's a bad night for law enforcement so far: felonies all over the place, all at once. If we get a call out your way, like a routine thing, disturbing the peace or something, they might give it to that car, but it wouldn't take him out of the neighborhood."

"Sure," said John. The situation would not change. If he

had apprised Lang, it could only have led to a hostage arrangement—which did not exist at present—and an assault team would arrive sooner or later. What that would mean in terms of psychic damage (not to mention the possibility of physical harm) to his babies and his wife could be imagined. He still respected the police, even after the manhandling by the state troopers, but he had convinced himself that he must not look for their help in his extremity. By now he felt selfish about it.

When he returned to the dining room, Joan excused herself and left the room, presumably heading for the lavatory. She seemed to be walking steadily. She had not drunk much wine.

As soon as she was gone, John stared at Richie. "Did you check into a motel after I left the car this afternoon?"

Richie removed the glasses and rubbed his closed eyelids. "I really don't know how people can wear these things all day, though maybe it's different if you've got your own prescription. Ever wear glasses, John?"

"You took those from the man you killed at the motel, didn't you? You took his clothes and car and glasses."

Richie opened his eyes, which were now slightly pink from the rubbing. "Have you got one complaint about what I've been doing since I arrived at your house? I've been knocking myself out to do the right thing, but you won't give me any credit at all." He shook his head and changed his tone from the purely plaintive. "You just remember that if . . . You just realize, nobody could have tried harder."

"Is that a threat of some kind, you dirty bastard?"

"You ought to know me better than that," Richie said loftily. "I'm just concerned about you and yours if the cops throw the lead around. I don't want you to blame *me*, because frankly I think you have a tendency to do that. You understand, I like and admire you a whole lot, but I can't ignore your tendency to evade personal responsibility for your problems. You don't use anything like your real potential. That's the fault of the economy! It's Joanie's fault you got married so young and have kids to support, so you can't afford a better way of life." Richie showed his wry expression. "Sorry, John, but I finally had to give you a dose of your own medicine, show you what it feels like to be criticized by your best friend."

"Which I am not," said John. "You're my worst enemy. I would like to know you were removed from the earth." In saying this he realized he had lost control, but he got satisfaction in so doing. He was an amateur at murderous emotion. Just expressing it seemed to put him at an advantage, even though he was rationally aware that it would probably be considered a weakness by professionals in the field, among whom Richie was surely preeminent.

Richie was not offended. "That's just an idea of yours, John. It might sound good at the moment, but it doesn't really mean anything, because obviously you can't press a button and make me disappear, and what you certainly don't mean is murdering me in cold blood, even if you had a motive, and how would you get one? I've always been nice to you and yours, and that's all you care about in all the world."

Could he be right? But now Joanie was back.

"How are the kids?" Richie asked.

"Out cold."

It had not occurred to John that that was what she had been doing during her absence. Now he found her choice of words disquieting. "They're okay?"

She sighed. "Why wouldn't they be? They drove me nuts all day. But *they* had a great time. Then Randy came and spoiled them rottener. Did I tell you he wanted to give Melanie a hundred-dollar bill?" Joan chided Richie. "I mean, *really*."

"Such great kids," Richie said, simpering at her.

"Hey," Joan jokingly proposed, "you wouldn't be interested in including them in the home deal? Take 'em for free! Have an instant houseful." She moued. "That's the way I feel after a day like this one."

John said anxiously, "It's the same every day. You've got one coming. I'll make it up to you. I'll stay home tomorrow."

"That reminds me," Joan said. "Tess called a couple of hours ago and said something about vouching for you with the *police*? What was that all about?"

"I don't know. Parking ticket, maybe."

She smiled at Richie. "Excuse the personal stuff. Do you drink regular coffee?"

John seized the salad bowl and went to the kitchen, where anxiety kept him moving purposelessly about until Joan appeared with more dishes, stacked neatly atop the steak platter.

"I'll just get the dessert," Joan said.

"Dessert?"

"Of course. What's wrong with you? Why are you so nervous? You didn't even eat much."

"I didn't eat anything."

"Aren't you feeling well?" But she had turned to the refrigerator before giving him a chance to answer.

He lowered his voice and spoke to the back of her head. "It's him. He's—"

She turned around and said, indulgently, "A little drunk, I know. I guess that's permissible, among friends."

She was about to revolve again, but John restrained her with a hand to her wrist. "He's not what he seems."

"Is that some song?"

"I'm serious, Joan. I wish you wouldn't encourage him to stay. I'll explain later."

The request irritated her. "Look, I'm the one who has been stuck at home all day. I can use the company, believe me!"

"He's not drunk," said John. "He's crazy."

"I've been talking to the man for hours now," Joan said. "There's nothing wrong with him. He wants to help us. Is that crazy? Are *you* drunk?" She peered closely at him for an instant. "Don't tell me you're jealous. Is that it? You think something was going on while we were here alone?" She was enjoying this.

"No," John said humorlessly. "Of course not. Please, Joanie, I'm not kidding. He's dangerous." He had not wanted to go that far, but she was laughing at him.

"This is another of these jokes you've started to pull today, right? That's what a sale does?" She spun around gleefully and opened the freezer compartment. "Enough ice cream left. What I forgot to do, though, was take it out earlier so it could soften some. Will you get those glass dishes for me?" She was acting as if he had not said a word.

Incredulous, he asked, "Do you think I'd just say something like that and let it go?"

Joan gestured with the gallon container of strawberry ice cream, which neither of them much liked, but Melanie would eat no other flavor. "Don't ask me to explain your recent behavior. It's all new to me. But if it continues to sell houses, I'm not criticizing."

John was about to speak when Richie appeared with all the rest of the dinner dishes, including that bearing the untouched peas-and-carrots. He deposited them on the nearest clear portion of the counter. "Can I take something out?"

"Now, Randy," Joan amiably reproached him. "You go and sit down and let yourself be served."

Richie looked around, beaming. "I love a kitchen. It's the heart of any home."

John found the glass dishes in a seldom-opened section of the cabinets and delivered them to Joan. Then, using his wider body, he in effect forced Richie to leave the kitchen without actually touching him or speaking. Back in the dining room, he told him quietly, "I want you out of here right after dessert."

He was surprised by Richie's quick and submissive agreement: "All right."

John decided not to press the advantage and ask whether the man really meant it. That would be a symptom of weakness, and he was suddenly strong. He had defended his home, employing only moral weapons. He had been sorely tried all day but had met the test. He sat down and briefly closed his eyes.

Richie said, "You haven't even seen the children since you got home. You keep asking about them, but you don't go in and even look at them."

The triumph was short-lived. It was preposterous that a man like this could put John on the defensive. "God damn you," he said. "I have to get rid of you first, don't I?"

Richie lowered his eyes. "You hate me more than you love them? That's unworthy of you, John. It really is." In the next moment, however, he was bright again, for Joan had carried in three little glass bowls of ice cream and a plateful of Melanie's favorite oatmeal-raisin cookies.

"Coffee in another couple of minutes," said she, and having served the men, she sat down at her end of the table.

Richie had been emitting murmurs of pleasure since his first sight of the ice cream, and when he identified it as strawberry, he said, "My favorite! How'd you know?"

"I told you, this is all potluck." She smiled. "But it

198

wouldn't have been much different with longer notice. John can tell you I'm not much of a cook. He's better! He cooks three or four times a week."

Richie's scowl came and went. "You do all right. Maybe you should be the one selling real estate."

"And let John stay home with the little demons. I could handle that!" She included John in her throaty laugh.

"Tell him whose idea it is that you stay home," John said, defensive again and despising himself for it.

"Pretty much yours, isn't it?" She laughed again.

"The main reason I sell real estate is that I can be near home," John said. "The alternative around here would be to commute to the city, a ten-hour day."

"If you make good money, you can afford good child care," Richie said solemnly, incising designs with the edges of his spoon in the smoothed but as yet untasted ice cream. He made his voice markedly sympathetic in addressing Joan. "I say 'good' because so many places can't be trusted nowadays."

Joan agreed, with energetic chin movements. "But it's not a thing of just money! We had one in town here where the kids got food poisoning from the sour milk used for cocoa, and that place was the most expensive in this part of the state."

"Too many of them are run by perverts," Richie said, gesturing with his implement. "But then, what isn't? That's certainly true in the city. I was hoping it might be different out here."

"Not on your life," Joan said cynically. But then she caught herself and asked John in a jokey way, "Oops! Have you got Randy's check yet? He might want to change his mind."

"He and I have concluded our deal," John said levelly. "It's too late to change it now."

MEETING EVIL   199

Richie chuckled at him but spoke to Joan. "He's quite the negotiator. He can talk the birds out of the trees."

"I told you he was a good salesman."

They were both beaming at John, teaming up on him again. He missed Sharon terribly. She had been Richie's enemy from the start. He needed a partner with that sort of mettle. He simply could not do single-handedly what must be done.

He heard a distant cry. He reacted more quickly than Joan, whom he heard saying, as he ran from the room, "Melanie's still the noisiest at night. Not the baby!"

This was true. Melanie had frequent nighttime alarms, whereas little Phil was unusually placid for an infant once the lights were out. Melanie was scared of the dark but could not sleep at all in the presence of the feeblest nightlight. Her father, himself an uncertain sleeper his life long, was the more sympathetic parent: Joanie had once slept through an early-morning seismic tremor that caused a bathroom tumbler to fall and break.

Whatever the state of the nursery door—wide-open, closed, or just ajar—Melanie soon enough demanded a change. At the moment it was two inches from full closure. John had to open it all the way, so that enough light came in from the hall fixture to see by. His daughter was sitting up in bed. He hugged her narrow body, with its fine groove of spine, her hair in his neck. This was as intimate as he had been with anybody all day, except for the repellent wrestling match with Richie.

After a moment he realized that though her eyes had been wide open, the child had probably been asleep from the first and was not aware of who he was. He lowered her head to the pillow and pulled up the blanket.

Phil's crib was in the darkest corner, where the angled door cut off most of the reflected light from the hall. John could hardly see him and so probed very gently. A baby was there, all right: he found a tiny hand and heard a faint sigh. If he turned on the light, someone might awaken. Besides, Joanie had just returned from making her own bed check. The children were perfectly okay. All he had to do was get rid of Richie, and everything everywhere in his world would come back to normal. Once Melanie was safely grown up, he could kid her about voluntarily climbing into a murderer's lap as a three-year-old.

But suddenly he felt superfluous at the bedsides of his own children. He had an urge to flee from them, from Joanie, from every responsibility. As he went into the living room, this perverted idea obsessed him so much that, to prove he was impervious to it, he quietly opened the door and slipped outside. The silver body of the car was conspicuous in the light of the streetlamp. John could see nothing else.

The car was unlocked, of course. Richie had no need for personal security: were someone else to drive the vehicle away, he would lose only that which had never belonged to him, and could simply steal another. If someone offended him, he killed the offender. His freedom of action was unconditional.

John climbed into the driver's seat but did not yet close the door. He sat there looking at the building that his wife and kids currently shared with a homicidal maniac, but in fact they had done so, with impunity, for at least an hour before the master of the house came home. Richie was harmless when on those premises. To keep him there was to protect the rest of the world.

Richie had left the key in the ignition. John turned it far enough to empower the preliminary electrical system— numbers became visible on a digital dashboard clock—but not so far as to start the engine. He touched the knob of the gear selector. But it was a manual five-speed system. He was licensed only for automatic. He did not properly know how to operate a real gearshift, could certainly not still remember his father's instruction when he was fourteen: you were supposed to do something with the left foot and the clutch. He could probably not have driven away had he wanted to. But then his only obligation was to look after his own family, and *they* were not in trouble. By means of a simulated thrust of pride, he rejected any feeling of relief as being unworthy of him. To be no hero was not shameful, but taking satisfaction in that state of affairs would be.

Should he subsequently change his mind, he put the ignition key in his pocket before stepping out of the car and noiselessly pressing the door shut.

When he reached the dining room, Joanie said, "Everything okay? We thought you left town." This was jocular.

But Richie asked, as if seriously, "How's the weather out there?"

So despite John's care with all doors, coming and going, *he* knew. "Just took a breath of fresh air. It's a nice night. You driving back to the city?"

"Oh," Joan cried in dismay, "if we just had a guest room. This little house—"

John saw this as a personal attack. "Weren't you the one who wanted this place originally?"

"I'm also the one who has wanted to move for at least a year!"

Richie grew agitated. "Please," he said, raising his hands. "It's an honest difference of opinion."

"Well, not quite honest," Joan said. "The idea, which I *thought* we agreed on, was that we were not supposed to stay here for the rest of our lives."

"God," said John, "it's only three years, more or less. You were pregnant with Melanie." Without thinking, he looked

202

at Richie as if for confirmation, as one does when arguing in the presence of a third person, then remembered and suppressed his next point. Richie was scowling into the bowl of melted ice cream before him.

"The idea was," Joan went on, "we couldn't lose. Values were going up and up. You were the authority on real estate." Now it was Joan who sought Richie's moral support, smirking at him. "He talked himself into it."

"The slump is only now," John said. "Only temporary. Everybody knows that. Property can only go up: that's a fact of human existence."

Richie violently shook his head. "This isn't right!"

"You bet!" said Joan. Was she drunk on so little wine? John noticed that her glass was now empty.

"Anyway," John said, "would this be the time to move? With a baby?"

"That's an excuse, anyway," said Joan.

John happened to notice that Richie was trembling, but it seemed more important to address his own needs. Nothing could be more unfair than Joanie's general implication, which she had never previously been so bold as to make, even in front of Renee, though perhaps she did it in private with that mean bitch, who had always despised him. But this was far worse, even if she had no way of knowing what Richie was. "You're wrong," he said, and then he descended to pathos. "I've done the best I could."

Richie slammed a fist against the table, just missing the glass bowl before him but causing it to jump and loose silverware to clatter everywhere. "How can this be?" He avoided looking at either of them.

"Good question," Joan said wryly.

John now belatedly realized that she had been mostly kidding, making her point but not being angry about it, which in fact was often her style with him. He would not have been so touchy had he had another kind of day. "All right," he said, "so I'll try harder."

She stood up, smoothing her dress at the hips, and said with vivacious irony, "I'm glad we got that settled! I'll go get the coffee." She went to the kitchen.

Richie's teeth were clenched. "This is not going to work, John. I've only been holding back because of my friendship with you, but it's not doing you any good. She's your enemy."

For an instant, preoccupied, John failed to understand the reference.

Richie elucidated. "This wife of yours."

John leaped up and threw a fist at Richie's face. At the last moment, with his animal reflexes, Richie evaded the blow. John had swung with such force that, missing his target, he was thrown off balance and would have fallen—had Richie not stabilized him with a quick hand.

"It's only the truth," Richie said calmly. "A guy like you could go anywhere and do anything. I know you better than you know yourself. You might think you want to be limited, but underneath it all, you can't accept it."

John stood there gasping for breath. He had said as much to himself from time to time but considered it an exercise of the imagination and thus permissible, like modest sexual fantasies—for example, thinking of Renee when making love with Joanie. But his attraction to Sharon was more a moral idea than a sexual urge and had to do with her standing up to Richie and, in a personal sense, defeating him, for she had escaped from his control. . . . But then she only had herself to save.

"You want the gun?" Richie asked. "You really ought to do it yourself. I'll tell you why: you'd only blame me the first time something went wrong."

"Then what?" John asked. The chill of it had frozen his emotions, and he was able to proceed as if serene.

Richie smiled. "I know things about freedom. They've been locking me up all my life."

"You and I will go off together?"

Richie frowned. "I'm not queer, John. You can have all the girls you want. I've had every kind of sex, myself, and I don't care much for any. I don't like anybody, man or woman, to get that kind of hold on me." He spoke ever more rapidly, as if excited, though still at low volume.

But Joanie would be back at any moment. John had to arrive at some kind of resolution now: time had finally run out. "And the children?"

"Foster homes are another thing on which I'm an authority," Richie said. "I wouldn't wish them on any kid. The thing nobody should ever be in this world is little and helpless: you're just asking for it."

"You're telling me to—"

Richie interrupted. "Don't say that, John! I'm not telling you anything. You'd just get mad at me. You blow up at everything I say. I've learned my lesson." He grinned warmly. "Yet here we are, still a team. We must have some connection."

John was now beyond anger, which had failed him all day. "You're right. I'm thinking." But whether his thoughts were useful was another matter. Sharon said she owned a gun and "prayed" that Richie would show up at her place. Having seen her in action, John knew this sentiment was not bravado. But how in the world could he justify afflicting her again with Richie?

Then there were the police, whom of course he could not bring to the house without disturbing Joan and the children: that had always been out of the question. But what about leaving in the car with Richie, insisting on serving as driver, and driving to police headquarters? Would Richie sit there passively while he ran in and got Lang? It would have to be Lang, because explaining the situation to a new officer would not be simple: he now had had experience with cops, who were much more complex than he had supposed, no doubt necessarily so, for theirs was a world of Richies and Sharon's drug-dealing husband, homicides and madmen, mutilators and molesters.

The coffee was taking too long. John was suddenly worried about Joanie's current well-being, and, regardless of Richie, left the room. This must be fake guilt, since he was supposedly, for Richie's benefit, thinking of killing her. If that was fake, then the guilt had to be as well. Nevertheless, he felt awful, and when he reached the kitchen and saw her standing intact at the counter, fiddling with the coffee maker, it was as if some great menace had been removed—an irrational feeling, for Richie was still alive.

"Is that thing acting up again?"

She tossed her head. "What *does* function around here?"

"You."

She turned around and said tenderly, "You do, too. I didn't mean that."

John wanted to embrace her but could not permit himself to do so at this point: he might not find the strength to let go. "It's probably a loose connection. I'll take a look later. He can't stay for coffee anyway."

"Randy? Really? Oh, too bad."

But her disappointment seemed tepid. Was she no longer enchanted by the man? Perhaps she was finally beginning to have her doubts.

She went on to prove otherwise. "But we'll be seeing a lot more of him when he moves out here. I guess we don't want to wear him out the first time." Before John could restrain her, she breezed out to the dining room, where, when he reached them, she was urging Richie to call on her for any help he might need with his forthcoming move.

Richie meanwhile was frowning ominously at John.

John said quickly, "I said you had to leave now." He turned to Joan. "What I didn't say, though, was that I've got to go, too. I made a mess of the Agreement to Buy and don't have another form here at home. We're going to stop by the office." To which he kept a key for just such after-hour uses, which were common enough. The story was plausible.

But Joanie was not quite finished with their guest even yet. "Not that I'm going to play matchmaker! But if you'd *like* to meet somebody—"

John too was dogged. "Leave everything till I get back. I'll clean up."

For the first time all day Richie, and not he, was the one off-balance, asking, "*Where* are we going?"

"I told you, " said John. "The office of Tesmir Realty. The bosses are surely gone by this hour, but if not, you must meet them. They are women, two nice women."

He led Richie to the door, Joan following. Before going out, John said only, "See you soon." There was not a moment to spare now, and nothing further to say that would not be distracting.

Joan persisted. "If you're taking Randy's car, then he can stop in for a nightcap on the way back."

She was persisting to the end in being the perfect mate. Had Richie been a legitimate buyer of property, her performance would have been flawless. The pity was that John had never had such a desirable client as Richie seemed. He had never brought another home. There was a lack of moral balance in his profession. Clients might live all their lives in a house he had sold them, and be succeeded by future generations of their own blood, but never see, or even know, where the agent lived. Or care. Why should they? They were not Richies.

Richie continued to be passive when they reached the car and John returned the ignition key to him. But once behind the wheel, he asked, "You mind telling me what this is all about?"

The interior of the car received some dim illumination from the little carriage lamp at the front door of the house (which Joanie had helpfully switched on) and, through the glass hatchback, from the streetlight at the curb, but before John's eyes were habituated, Richie remained a silhouette.

"I had to have some excuse for getting out of there."

Richie was shaking his head. "I'm sorry to have to say this, John, but you don't seem to have anything in order."

"That's true."

"You're boasting about it?"

"I'm admitting it. That's different."

"Where's your pride, man?"

"Start the car," John said. "Let's get going."

Richie complied reluctantly. As he backed out of the driveway, he said, "You're leaving loose ends."

"You mean I should kill them all?" John wondered at the ease with which he heard himself ask the question.

"It's not for me to say, is it?"

"Why are you so mealymouthed? If you're capable of doing something like that—and you are—why can't you talk about it?"

"Come on, John," Richie complained. "There isn't any connection." Using only one wrist, he swung the car effortlessly around when it reached the street and headed in the

208

direction opposite to that he had taken in the morning. "There are things you do and things you say, and they're not the same; everybody knows that. I'm surprised at you. I thought you were the one who always made sense."

"Not me," said John, and he was not being disingenuous. "I proved that today. You caught me off balance. I never knew what I was doing, and that's a nightmare for a guy like me. I'd rather die than go through that again. I lost all faith in myself for a while."

"And you blame *me?*"

Richie's question had little moral weight, but John responded as if it had. " 'Blame' may not be the right word. You might say you gave me an opportunity. What I did with it was up to me, in which case you deserve neither credit nor blame."

"I don't understand that at all," Richie said. "You seem to be bothering yourself about things that don't matter. I thought you really cared about your family and your home, but I guess you don't really. What you care about is yourself, how *you* feel at all times, whether you're living up to some idea of yourself, whether you're getting your own way. If that's really what kind of man you are, then you might not be any better than me, and I'm nothing."

Earlier on John would have been devastated to hear this, but he was not at all disconcerted now. "You're right, and you're also wrong. What you're right about is me. But maybe I can still make something of myself. You're wrong about yourself: it isn't true that you are nothing. You've brought great harm! You're no nonentity. You've proved you exist."

Richie whistled. "Is this what you got me out here for, John? I could have told you that. We don't need to bring God into it."

"God? Who mentioned God?"

"You know what I mean. When you talk that way, what you're really getting around to is religion, aren't you?"

"Do you believe in God?"

Richie snorted. "I sure as hell didn't make myself. That's basic. You can take it from there."

"You mean, you can't be held responsible for what you do." This was not a question. Neither was it a matter of concern.

They were approaching the streets of the DeForest Park area, where the affluent lived. Probably the cop in the unmarked car had been called off the stakeout: there was no sign of him. That was all to the good. An explanation would have taken too long to make. No more time was available.

Richie nodded at what he saw through the windshield. "Nice neighborhood. You bring me here to sell me one of these places?"

"Yeah," said John, relieved by a moment of irony. "How about that one?" He pointed at a stately white mansion to which the term "colonial," much abused by realtors (who used it for almost anything that could not be called "contemporary"), could legitimately be applied. As a professional, he knew who owned each of these houses, though when Tesmir sold a listing up here, one of the partners handled it and the six-figure commission. It had not taken John long to understand that if he was ever to make a big score, he must have his own agency. But that seemed less likely to happen as the months, and now years, went by. Yet neither was he ever prepared to take a job with a regular routine and a fixed salary. It had become almost enjoyable to tell himself he might be hopeless, like a man confessing he was too fat while smugly patting a potbelly. That had to change.

210

Richie pulled the car in against the curb and stopped. "What's something like that go for?"

"They'd probably try to get a million four, maybe five. That's five acres, and there's a three-bedroom guest cottage in back, big pool of course, gardens. Not exorbitant here, but in the present market maybe it would go for a mil two or even less. But that's theoretical, of course. It's not for sale. That's J. William Osgood's house. He's CEO of—"

"Think he's home?" Richie revved the engine and, before John could respond, added, "Now, that's the kind of house you should have, John."

"I'd settle for the commission on its sale."

"Why should *he* have it and you not?" Richie asked. "All you need is some kind of break, and you'd get back your faith in yourself. I can see that. You're all ready, just waiting for the opportunity to show your stuff."

"Sure," John said. "You've got that right. Maybe I'll even win the lottery."

Richie responded soberly. "Don't look for that to happen, because it won't. It's too impersonal; that's not your game."

John was suddenly nervous about sitting there at the curb. Not only did the municipal police furnish extra protection to the area, but the DeForest Park Association employed its own private security force. Anyone afoot on the pavement after dark or an unidentified parked car at any hour would soon encounter one patrol or another. Richie could be expected to fire without warning.

"Let's get going."

Richie chuckled. "Let's go in there and nail him."

John had no emotion left for such matters, horrifying as they would have been at an earlier time. "Do you think you can just walk in the door on somebody like that? Surveillance cameras, alarms, maybe a big dog, and the neighborhood even has its own private cops."

"Hell," Richie said, "we could try. All we need's an idea. I could cut my arm, see, and bloody up my shirt, ring the bell and ask them to call an ambulance, talking through the system, you know, not even trying to get inside. Then sit down on the steps, bleeding. Laying down would be too much. You want to hold back some to be believed. You should even decline at first if they ask you to come in."

"You'd have no time at all," John pointed out. "Ambulances come right away out here. It's not like the city."

This information embittered Richie further. "He's got the whole world where he wants it. But he doesn't impress me."

"J. W. Osgood? Do you know him?"

"No," Richie said. "But I'd like to meet him. Just once."

"Why?"

"I hate him. I hate his name. I hate his house. I hate this street. Let's get out of here." He kicked the accelerator, and they were jerked into motion. "Where now?"

Good question. Someplace where no innocent strangers were likely to be afflicted, but that might mean another planet. "Take a left there."

After a while Richie said, "We're leaving the good parts."

"You can settle down now."

Richie laughed. "I'm not worked up, John. You should see me when I'm upset."

"Like this afternoon?"

"When?"

"You've already forgotten, haven't you? Do you remember my family?"

"Are you kidding? We just left them." Richie cleared his throat. "Believe me, I don't want to hurt your feelings, but you could do better there, too."

212

"Don't say any more about them."

"You're right," Richie said. "I apologize. I'm out of order."

They were approaching a main thoroughfare. "Take a right here," said John, indicating the lesser street that came before. "What about the doctors at Barnes? I can't believe they're incompetent."

"John, you must understand what kind of person becomes a doctor. It's somebody who does so for one reason alone: to have power over people they say are sick." He nodded solemnly. "And they've got the right to call anybody sick they want to, like cops can arrest anybody at all. Just think of it. What they say they want to do is *help* you. But who asked them? They force it on you."

They were now traveling along the secondary road, more or less parallel with the highway but at a slightly lower elevation. It was a place of commercial garages and warehouses, now mostly dark. Here and there was a night security light, but streetlamps were rare. John's vision was used to the dark by now, and in the illumination from the dashboard Richie seemed as visible as if it were daytime.

"Doesn't the medication do any good?"

"Ha!" Richie cried. "It makes you impotent. That's all it is supposed to do." He squinted out the window. "Why are we driving along here? It's depressing."

"You're a wanted man. You might be recognized out there on the main road."

Richie spoke tenderly. "You're always looking out for me. You're the one person I know who doesn't try to get the hook in somebody. We're friends for life. I want you to know that."

"Yeah. I do."

"We argue sometimes, but brothers are like that."

"That's right," John said. "That's really more what we

are than just friends: brothers." He was not being entirely hypocritical. By now he and Richie did have a genuine connection. It could not be denied that they were close, like a jailer and his prisoner, though in this case it was difficult to say which was which, who was the greater criminal to the other. Perhaps each played both parts simultaneously, which would indeed be brotherly. John was aware that he could never settle with the man without an act of fratricide.

"I wouldn't have turned out this way if I had had a brother like you years ago," Richie said. "You would have looked after me."

"I would have kicked your ass," John said, not unkindly.

Richie chortled. "Damn right you would have!"

"I'm an only child," John said. "That's why I wanted another kid right after the first." He had just remembered that. "Joan was right in saying that all we've done has been *my* idea, and she's always gone along, postponing a career of her own. She came from quite a big family. I don't have anybody. My dad died four years ago, and my mother married again and moved out West. That hit me hard. I was closer to her than to my father. I never really got along with him. She's never yet seen either of my children." John was saying these things for his own sake, so as to try to feel human for a moment.

"You got no worries now, Brother," Richie said. "Your troubles are mine. Neither one of us is alone against the world any more."

"That's fine," said John. "But I'm the older brother, and I'll decide when I want you to help me. You get into too much trouble on your own." He put his hand out. "I want your gun. I'll return it when there's good reason."

They were still traveling along the road of warehouses, and the blacktop under them was suddenly full of potholes, the first of which gave the car such a jolt that Richie reduced the speed.

He asked John, "Can you give me your word?"

"On what?"

"That I won't regret it."

John snorted. "You like to do damage. You might see somebody you want to kill and regret not having the gun. Is that it?"

"Come on, you know what I mean."

"I'm willing to promise I won't turn you over to the police. I can't see that it would make any sense for you to go back to Barnes, or of course to any prison."

Richie laughed. "Amen, Brother! I'm finished with all of that. But that's exactly why I have to keep the gun. You can understand."

"Didn't I say I'd give it back when you really needed it to defend yourself?"

Richie stared through his window. "God, am I thirsty! Let's go over there and get a six-pack."

He was referring to a convenience store that could be seen, looking between a darkened commercial building and a parking lot full of school buses, out on the far side of the highway. It was all the brighter for being the only local source of illumination except for a self-service gas station, at the moment devoid of cars, an eighth of a mile to the west.

"Okay," said John. "But I'll be the one who goes in for the beer."

Richie whined. "I might see something else I want! I like to look around those places. You don't know what it is, being cooped up for a couple of years, not able to buy snacks except from a machine, and you couldn't always get out to the lounge area. You might be under restraint. Have a heart, Brother!"

He turned onto the next cross street, drove to the highway, and waited submissively at the traffic light there, even though it stayed red forever and during this time there was but one vehicle, a battered pickup truck, that passed on the main road. John himself would have been tempted, having determined that the coast was clear of police, finally to run the light or anyway make a right turn on the red, illegal in city limits, and then a quick, sneaky, equally illegal U-turn, but he was suffering from an anxiety in which everything crawled in slow motion. Whereas Richie seemed to have all the time in the world.

Eventually the light changed and Richie drove across to the parking lot alongside the convenience store. Only two other cars were there. At least one must belong to whoever was working in the place at this hour. Such businesses were notoriously attractive to criminals, open as they were at all hours, and often, as was true of this one, in an area that at night was remote from all humanity but those persons who might pause in transit to buy tomorrow's breakfast or a late-night snack. The clerks must worry about each new arrival. What a job. John instinctively viewed such matters from the perspective of an employee and not that of whoever made a profit from the franchise, still less the absentee licensing firm. He could too easily see himself behind the counter when some Richie entered. Richie was incapable of that sort of imagination. He answered only to his own urges. The initiative was always his. Everyone else in the world must wait for what *he* chose to do, and therefore, as long as he was alive, no one could be protected from him.

Richie parked the car at a significant distance from the other two vehicles and, without shutting off the engine, opened his door.

John reached over and turned the ignition key. The noise

of the engine had not been loud, but the utter silence was startling.

Richie stayed in his seat. "Why did you do that?"

"You're not going to make a quick getaway, if that's what you had in mind."

"I wasn't thinking of that," said Richie. "I wasn't thinking at all."

"That's what people do when they get out of a car: turn off the motor." John put out his hand. "Let's have the gun."

"John, I can't do it. I just can't. Don't ask me."

"Then you sit tight. I'll go in for the beer." John had formulated a new plan, the old one (to get the pistol away from Richie and kill him with it) having now been revealed as pitifully impracticable for a real-estate man, father of two young children, husband to a woman who was his superior in moral strength. With Richie alone in the car, in an almost deserted parking lot at this hour, there could be no objection to an all-out assault by the police. He would ask the store clerk to call them and, with him and whatever other customers were at hand, take refuge in a locked office or storeroom until they arrived. There was sure to be a gunfight, in which Richie might well be slain. Of course, if he was not killed outright, he would be patched up and eventually sent back to Barnes Psychiatric. But it was the best plan John could devise. He was not a professional at this sort of thing, and he was all alone with the problem.

"I can't stay out here," Richie said. "I'll go nuts. You come along, John. We ought to do things together, then we can stick up for one another if anybody tries to give us crap." He left the car.

John had no choice but to accompany him into the store. A husky black man in early middle age stood at the register, totting up the bill for several items assembled by a corpulent white fellow in his late twenties: packaged doughnuts and a carton of milk among them. The clerk glanced at the new arrivals, and John ritualistically nodded at him, looking quickly away lest his fear be visible.

Richie loped swiftly to the rear of the store, where tiers of six-packs and ranks of stout plastic bottles could be seen through the glass doors of the refrigerated showcase. John stopped halfway along the aisle. All he could hope for was that they got out of there without incident. Apprising the clerk obviously could not be done in the time available.

Richie came back with two packs of beer, one under each arm, so that both his hands remained free. "Go get whatever else we need, John. Nuts, corn chips, or whatever."

John looked around, as if seriously considering the request.

The fat customer went out the door. The clerk asked, in a strong enough voice to carry to them, "Something you're looking for, gentlemen?"

"Chips," John said quickly.

"Next aisle, right side."

"Do we really need any?" John asked Richie. "I'm not hungry. Let's just hit the road."

"You're the boss," Richie said with verve and strode past the clerk toward the door.

John stopped at the counter as if to pay the tab, though of course he could not have done so, having no money on him. The clerk wore a short-sleeved blue shirt and a neat bow tie. With his heavy graying head and self-possessed expression, he looked as if he might be one of the retired cops who sometimes took such employment.

John made the situation clear by calling to Richie, "You got all the money."

"Let's go," Richie said.

"No," said John. "We've got to pay."

Richie put his back against the door and pushed it open with his rump. "Hell with that. Did you see the prices these crooks are asking? They're highway robbers."

"Just bring the stuff back here," said the clerk, in a voice of calm authority. John had not been looking at him, but he did so now. The man brought a large handgun up from beneath the counter.

Richie stopped where he was and produced an exaggerated grin. "Well, if you're going to get nasty about it."

"That's right," the clerk said. "I *am* going to. It's happened once too often around here." He included John in the gestures he made with the barrel of the weapon.

Richie came back to the counter and carefully, working one side at a time, deposited the cartons of beer in front of the clerk. While the second six-pack, which had been under his left elbow, was descending to the counter, he swept his jacket back and from the right side of his waistband drew the revolver he had taken from Officer Swanson. He fired twice.

The big man's body jerked, as if from the blow of a fist, when each of the slugs hit him. He lost the support of his knees and went down.

"There you are, John," said Richie. "You saw what happened. It wasn't me who drew first."

John felt himself shudder so violently that he could hardly maintain his balance, though perhaps that was only an illusion brought on by terror, for he quite competently went behind the counter and crouched to attend to the victim.

The man was alive. He sat there as his shirtfront turned red. Though struggling for breath, he managed to raise his bloodshot eyes and lift his gun to point at John. But he proved too weak to fire it. John had to exert very little force to take the weapon away. It was an automatic—ready to fire, he hoped, for he had never held one except in the form of a plastic childhood toy and would not have known what to do other than simply pull the trigger.

He came up behind the counter. He was conscious of the Band-Aid on his thumb and the wound under it, which was stinging and had probably started to bleed again.

Richie smiled disarmingly, his own weapon at his side, muzzle pointing at the floor. "Now you got yourself a gun, John. What in the world are you going to do with it?"

John never again looked at Richie's face. He continued to pull the trigger after the pistol was empty; the shots were still echoing across the aisles of shelved food. When he was finished, he tried to return the weapon to the fallen clerk, whose property it was, but by now the man was unconscious, yet still alive. Without looking at Richie, John knew that he was dead: they had had a connection.

He located the phone and called 911 for an ambulance. Then he dragged himself back to sit alongside the wounded clerk. Killing Richie in what was really cold blood had not yet horrified or sickened him, but he assumed that both reactions, and worse, might come when his sense of self returned. Perhaps he would not survive.

But when he heard the approaching wail of the ambulance, he felt affirmative enough to climb to his feet and wait standing up.

About the Author

THOMAS BERGER is the author of twenty-two novels. His previous novels include *Regiment of Women, Neighbors,* and *The Feud,* which was nominated for a Pulitzer Prize. His *Little Big Man* is known throughout the world.